# Accidental
## LIES

## BOOKS BY DANA MASON

*Accidental Groom*

# Accidental LIES

## DANA MASON

Bookouture

Published by Bookouture in 2019

An imprint of StoryFire Ltd.

Carmelite House
50 Victoria Embankment
London EC4Y 0DZ

www.bookouture.com

ISBN: 978-1-78681-857-7
eBook ISBN: 978-1-78681-856-0

To my mom and all the other single parents
struggling to do what's right.

# CHAPTER ONE

## Emily

This wasn't exactly what I had in mind. To me, a getaway doesn't include hundreds of other people. I should never have let Mac plan this vacation for me. I wanted a private, exclusive cottage somewhere in the mountains. Not a five-star resort in Maui and a list of activities an arm long. I'm going to kill my brother when I get home.

I finally get to my room. No, correction, my *second* room. The first one was only thirty feet from a construction zone, and I wasn't willing to listen to jackhammering all day. I drop the room key on the small table, and lift my face to the breeze that drifts in from the open lanai door. There's a wall of windows on one side of the room and the curtains are open to a spectacular view of the Pacific, but before I even have time to step out and get a better look, someone knocks on the door. "Yes, I'm already feeling relaxed," I mumble with an eye-roll as I tug the door open.

It's a bellman carrying a large basket full of fresh fruit and snacks. "Delivery for you, ma'am." And how badly I want to poke his eye out for calling me "ma'am".

"It's Ms. Thomas, and thank you so much. Who sent this lovely surprise?" I ask as he brings the large basket inside and sets it down on the small dining table in my suite.

"I'm not sure, but there's a card included." He lingers a moment then gives a slight bow before retreating from my room. When the door clicks behind him, I realize what I missed. Dammit. I grab my wallet and follow him out.

"Excuse me," I call.

He stops and turns toward me. His polite smile is the epitome of courteousness.

"I'm sorry. You were too fast for me. Here, this is for you. Thank you so much."

"Thank you, ma—"

"Please!" I hold my hand up. "Please don't call me ma'am."

I hear a chuckle behind me, but I don't turn.

"Yes, Mrs. Thomas." He gives me another little bow then walks away.

I turn back and come face-to-face with the guy I heard laugh a moment ago. He shrugs. "I get it. I don't like being called 'ma'am' either."

I look him up and down, from his worn-out flip-flops to the battered San Francisco Giants ball cap covering locks of chocolate brown hair, shading what look like golden brown eyes. His deep tan screams local, but if that were the case, he wouldn't be staying in such an expensive suite in this resort. Maybe he's an employee. Probably some maintenance man or plumber.

"I image you don't," I say as I walk toward my room, trying to ignore how incredibly sexy his dimpled smile is. I'm sure *he* thinks he's cute too.

When I reach for the door handle, I realize I don't have my damn key. Even on vacation Mondays suck. I rest my forehead against the door, sighing, and wonder when the *fun* part of this trip starts.

"Uh oh, you don't have your key," the heckler says, stating the obvious.

I straighten and turn, trying with all my might to act cool. Thank God I have my wallet. When I hear the chuckle behind me again, I try to ignore him.

"Do you want to use the phone in my room? You can call your husband... or the bellman to come open the door for you."

The word "husband" makes my insides ache, but I ignore it and turn slightly to look at him. "You're a guest here?"

He lifts his hands, palms up. "Yeah, what'd ya think, I was the maintenance man or something?"

Am I that transparent? I tilt my head as I look him over again. For a beach bum, he's pretty built. It makes me wonder if his physique is the result of daily gym workouts or from actual work. "Thank you for the offer, but I don't go into strangers' rooms."

He holds his smile and drops his chin to his chest. I can't figure out why he keeps laughing at me. "Is that funny?" I ask.

He lifts his head again, and the grin fades a little. "No, sorry. It's actually incredibly smart. How about I go into my room and make the call for you? It'll be quicker than going back downstairs and trying to find someone to open it for you."

I watch him for a quick moment, and I know he's right. "It would be nice if you could ask the bellman to come back and open the door for me. Thank you."

He holds up a finger. "Be right back."

Near the elevator bank is a small seating area. I eye an armchair and lower myself into it. The setting is beautiful, with a huge picture window that looks out onto the bright, colorful garden, bursting with flowers and a neat green lawn. The heat radiating from the glass feels good against my skin and suddenly, the thought of resting my head and taking a nap sounds tempting. But no, even when presented with this much beauty, I have trouble relaxing. I'm tense and wishing I wasn't here. What kind of woman takes a vacation alone? Hum... the kind of woman who has a dead husband, I guess. This is my first vacation since his death almost four years ago and I only agreed to this trip because everyone in my life insisted I needed it, but being here makes me sad. It makes me regret.

This is the sort of thing I should have done with Tucker and God, I hate that I wasted our time together. I regret all those hours I put in at work for those assholes at my old law firm while I was neglecting my wonderful husband. Yes, I need a break, but being here isn't making me feel any better about my life. That's just not something you can explain to people who've never lost their soulmate.

When Mr. Heckler returns, that smirk is back on his face, and I try for cheerful. I wish he were just a little ugly, but no, I can't deny he's attractive in a rugged dirty-sex sort of way. The thought almost makes me blush. He drops down in the armchair next to mine. "They'll be right up to get the door for you."

I gesture toward the elevator. "You were going out, please don't let me keep you."

He holds out a hand to shake. "Drew Whitney."

I glance at his hand, and I'm wondering where on earth this man is from. He doesn't seem to get social cues at all. I reach out and give his hand a firm shake. "I'm Emily Thomas."

"Nice to meet you, Emily… and nice shake."

I smile and say, "Not my first time."

One side of his mouth raises in a crooked grin. "In a suit like that, I believe it." He looks me up and down. "Did you forget to check the weather report when you dressed this morning?"

"You know, I wasn't in Maui when I dressed this morning."

"Oh, gotcha. First day of vacation." He gives me a thoughtful look. "I bet you're wondering when the fun starts."

"Yes." I wave my hand to signal the space around me. "It's starting off splendidly."

"This is just a small hiccup. You'll be enjoying Mai Tais on the beach in no time."

I nod as I consider that. "I don't think I've ever had a Mai Tai. Is that the drink of choice here?"

"What?" He leans back, acting shocked. "Oh, damn, woman. You need a drink, stat."

I chuckle and say, "Don't worry, my time is coming." It feels good to laugh. I don't do it much these days.

"I hope so." When the elevator opens, and the bellman steps out, Drew and I both stand quickly.

"You need assistance, Mrs. Thomas?"

"Yes, I do. Thank you for coming back." I turn toward Drew. "Thanks so much for your help."

"Of course." He reaches to press the down button on the elevator. "It was nice meeting you, Emily."

When the elevator opens, he steps inside, and as the doors close behind him, I'm struck by a familiar wave of loneliness.

Once I'm securely inside the privacy of my room, I look over the basket the bellman delivered. There's a card inside so I pull it out and read the script.

*Emily,*

*We know you didn't want this vacation, but you need it. As much as we're going to miss you this week, we're glad you're taking a break to enjoy yourself. The resort concierge should have given you a list of activities I've signed you up for. Please don't hide in your room. Go out, meet people, have some fun. Get some fresh air and take in the sights. This basket of snacks is here just in case you decide to stay in and not take any of the tours, but I hope that's not what you do.*

*Life is short, sweetheart. Too short to stay cooped up in your office pretending to live.*

*We love you!*

*Mac and Kelley*

I pick up the list of activities the concierge gave me when I checked in. The first is a dinner concert in the courtyard garden of the resort. The pamphlet for the show boasts a tribute show Hawaiian-style, with Elvis, Michael Jackson, and Madonna performers, along with fire knife dancers and hula. I shrug as I consider whether or not it's worth the effort. Sounds like it could be fun, I guess. The dinner ticket also includes an open bar. I'm sold. Two of the best words in the English language: *open bar*. With a snicker, I unzip my suitcase and start to unpack.

The room is bright and airy, and I try to focus on the advantages of vacationing alone. I don't have to share the drawer space. I can help myself to endless servings of the breakfast buffet without judgment. I can sleep on whatever side of the bed I want. It's a king-size bed too. I stare down at the swirls of green and blue on the elaborate bedspread. The use of these two colors helps bring the outside in, and it works. The wall of windows displays the glittering Pacific Ocean in all its glory… and danger, I remember with a gulp.

The sliding door is open, the sun is streaming into the room and the sea breeze is blowing through, making the turquoise curtains flutter. Off in the distance is a small cloud bank and I see three rainbows sinking into the ocean. From here, the ocean seems so harmless and inviting, I think ruefully.

When my phone rings, I have to wonder if I'll ever get settled into my suite. I glance at the caller ID and hit the answer button. "Hello, Bec. I hope you're not already running into problems without me?"

"Oh, stop! We're fine without you, Emily. How's Hawaii?"

"I don't know. I haven't had the chance to enjoy it yet. So far I've switched rooms, been locked out, been made fun of by my neighbor, and received a guilt trip from my brother. All before I've had a chance to unpack."

Rebecca laughs. "Who dares to make fun of you? What a bully."

"Oh, it was all in good fun. I snapped at the bellman for calling me 'ma'am', so I guess I asked for it."

"Oh, I hate that. Was it some kid?"

"The bellman, or the neighbor who laughed at me?"

"Wait, neighbor? I asked the wrong question. Was he hot?"

I crinkle my brow in confusion. Rebecca is a fast talker. Conversations with her always keep me on my toes. "The bellman was older than me. The neighbor was indeed hot, but also a bit annoying. At least, until he came to my rescue."

"I don't know what you mean when you say you haven't had time to enjoy yourself yet. Sounds like your day has been full of adventure."

"That's for sure. When the bellman came to deliver the fruit basket from Mac, I ran out to tip him and got locked out of my room. Only, I didn't realize it until he was already back in the elevator. Enter the hot neighbor who called the guy back to let me into the room. Anyway, I'm now comfortably back inside. How are things in Sacramento? How are things at the firm?"

"Things are lovely. Don't even think about worrying. I just called to check on you. What's the plan for tonight?"

"Dinner and a show in the courtyard garden. Some tribute acts. It's the open bar that's drawing me in."

"Nice. I hope you run into that hot neighbor while you're there."

"Oh, please. I'm here to relax, not get myself tangled up with some strange man."

"Speaking of strange men, Grant Russell was asking about you. What should I tell him?"

"Oh hell, I don't know." I should have listened to my instincts when they warned me against agreeing to a dinner date with a business associate. I walk onto the balcony and drop into a deck chair, breathing in the sea air. My suite is oceanfront, and the view is spectacular. "Tell him I'm out of town, but don't tell him where I am. Say it's a business trip. I don't need him getting into my personal business."

I hear Rebecca sigh on the other end of the phone. "What's your plan, Em?"

"I don't have a plan. We talked to him about designing our new offices, that's all."

"But you went out with him," she says, expectantly.

"Yes, I went to dinner with him twice. That's it. I spent enough time with him to realize I don't really want to spend any more time with him."

"Emily…" I know what she wants to say. It's been nearly four years since Tucker's death, but that doesn't make it easier.

"I get it, okay. I know you think it's time and I don't necessarily disagree with you, but that doesn't mean I hop in the sack with Grant just because he's shown interest in me. He's not the one."

"Okay, I get it. He's not the one, but you need to tell him. Let him off the hook. He's acting like you're his girlfriend."

I snort out a laugh. "Definitely not! We've only been out twice! My, have guys changed since I dated last."

"Well, don't let Grant give you the wrong impression. Most guys aren't interested in having a girlfriend. They're just trying to get laid."

"I appreciate his efforts, but I'm just not feeling it with him."

"I get it," Rebecca says. "If you're not into it, feel free to give it up to the hot neighbor instead. A vacation fling is probably better for you right now anyway. That way you can get in a little practice before you come home and ease back into dating."

It takes me a minute to realize what she said, but when I do, I fall forward and guffaw. "Excuse me? Practice?"

"Yeah, well, it's been a while. You might as well dust the cobwebs off with someone you're never going to see again, rather than someone who has the potential to be a lasting relationship."

I'm still laughing when I say, "You're so crude."

"But I'm right."

"I think I'll just stick to myself this week. It's going to be hard enough without the complications. I don't need any more regrets at this point in my life."

"Yes, you do! Girl, you so do," she says, emphatically.

"Listen, Bec, I know you think I need a man in my life. *Everyone* thinks I need a man in my life, but, believe it or not, I'm fine."

"I know you're fine. I wouldn't have given up my position at Tate, Brown, and McKennon if I didn't think you were fine. I wouldn't have walked away from my high-paying job at that well-respected, eighty-year-old Sacramento law firm to be your partner if I didn't think you were on solid ground. I just think a girl needs to get her wheels greased every once in a while." She pauses, and it's just long enough for me to take in what she's trying to say. "Just promise me you'll keep an open mind if you meet someone special in Hawaii, okay?"

"Have I told you lately how happy I am you're my partner?"

"Only every day, but that's okay, I wouldn't have it any other way."

"Thank you, Bec. I promise to keep an open mind while I'm here. Then I'll come home feeling relaxed and rested so we can get to work."

"And with a glowing complexion after having screwed the hot neighbor," she shouts into the phone as I disconnect the call. I'm laughing as I lay my phone down in my lap and think about Drew. I can't help but compare him to Grant. Two completely different types of men... I laughed at her, but maybe Bec is right; maybe it wouldn't hurt to live a little and try to enjoy myself with someone who doesn't know me. Someone I don't have to worry about running into while grocery shopping or having lunch downtown.

# CHAPTER TWO

## Drew

When the elevator door closes, I'm overwhelmed by an odd sense of loneliness. I don't often feel lonely at this stage in my life, but that doesn't mean there aren't times I miss being married. I bob my head back and forth, realizing I'm not being honest with myself. The truth is, I miss being married every day. I miss being married to Kayla. I miss my best friend. Missing someone you love is very different to loneliness.

There's no point in going down that road though. It's not like I haven't had relationships since losing Kayla, but she died over six years ago. I've had time to adjust, and I can't walk around in this life in a constant state of mourning. It's not healthy, for me or the kids. They don't remember their mother, so it's even more unfair to mope when they don't understand why.

As I step out onto the beach path, my cell phone rings in my pocket. I pull it out and answer: "Hello?"

"Dad?"

"What's up, buddy?"

"Gramps is teaching me how to surf."

My heart jumps into my throat at the idea of my eight-year-old son swimming in the Pacific Ocean with my sixty-five-year-old father-in-law. "Surfing? Grandpa surfs?"

"Yeah, he said he learned last year so he could take us when we visit."

"We? Is Hannah surfing too?"

"No, she's shopping with Grandma, this is just a boys' trip. Uncle Milo is with us too and Gramps' surf coach Chad."

"Are you at the beach now? Is there a lifeguard on duty?"

"Yeah! There're big lifeguard towers that look like tree houses without the trees, but, Dad, are you worried?"

"Yes, I'm worried," I say, fighting to hold back my smile. Damn, I miss this kid. I turn to face the tropical, white-sand beach and realize that he's also on a beautiful beach, but thousands of miles away in Southern California. "Are you worried?"

"Nah, I'm not scared. Gramps said if I get tired, I just need to hug my board and I'll float."

I want to balk at this logic and mention how that won't save him from sharks, but I hold back so I don't scare him away from the adventure. I realize I'm paranoid, but as a widower and a single parent, it's my prerogative. "Listen, Kyle, I want you to be careful out there. Follow the rules, listen to the adults, and don't take any risky chances. Okay?"

"Okay," he moans.

"Hey, but have fun, okay?"

"See ya, Dad."

I'm about to say goodbye and tell him I love him when I realize he's already disconnected. *Okay, then...*

I spin, hoping to spot a bench where I can sit, watch the swimmers, and call Hannah. I walk another ten yards and have a seat. Resting back, I stare at the white caps as they roll in one after another. To my right is a cloud cluster of rain over the sparkling ocean and rainbows dropping into the water. It's so beautiful. If I could pull it off, I'd pack up the kids and move here. But they would hate living away from their Nanna and Aunt Jennie, not to mention their cousins.

I pull out my cell phone and call my mother-in-law. "Hey, Sofia, how are you?"

"Drew, we were just talking about you. Hannah wanted to call and say hello. Hold on."

I hear a rustle and then Hannah's happy voice. "Daddy!"

"Hey, honey. Are you having fun with Gram?"

"Yes. We're having a girls' day, and I got a manicade, and pedicade—"

"Do you mean manicure and pedicure?"

"Yep, and we had lunch with Gram's book club, and my nails and toes are purple."

"Wow, sweetie, it sounds like you're having a great day."

"Yeah," she says. But then the cheerfulness of her voice drops considerably. "Daddy, when are you picking us up? I miss you."

"I know, honey, I miss you too. I'll be there this weekend. But remember, you only have this last week to spend with Gram and Gramps, so try to have some fun, okay?"

"Yeah, okay. But can you buy me some of my own fingernail paint and teach me how to paint my nails?"

Ah, crap. "Um, yeah. I'm sure we can figure it out. How about after you're home and we get settled, then we'll learn how?"

"Okay, Daddy. I love you. See you this weekend."

There's nothing better than the love of a child. This little girl and her brother own my heart. "I love you too, Hannah. Be good for Gram." There's a shuffle as she passes the phone over.

"Hello, Drew, Sofia here. I'm driving so I need to be quick. Will we see you on Saturday?"

"Yeah, I fly in early, and I'll be at your house around noon."

"Oh, good. Just in time for lunch. We'll see you then. Enjoy your last week in paradise."

"Will do. Thank you, Sofia. For everything."

I disconnect the call, drop my phone into my pocket and watch the last dregs of sunlight drop behind the horizon, leaving streaks of gold reflecting off the few fluffy clouds, turning them bright orange. The scent of plumeria and hibiscus is heavy in the air, and as I sit here enjoying the peace, I'm wondering if my three weeks away is too long. Am I selfish for leaving the kids that long? And if I am, what should I do about Sofia and Frank?

We made a deal years ago that they'd get three weeks over the summer and one week during Christmas break. I don't think they'd appreciate me cutting their time short. And I definitely don't want to put up with them trying to file another custody suit against me. I've spent too many years fighting them. After all this time we're just now on solid ground, able to put the past behind us and be civil for the sake of the kids. Before losing Kayla, I never would have thought they'd treat me the way they have. I'm not sure why they don't have any faith in my ability to parent… maybe they're just worried I'll keep the kids from them, but I wouldn't do that. Not even after what they've put me through.

I get that they want more time with the kids, but if Kayla were still alive, things wouldn't be any different. We'd still live eight hours away and they'd still only see the kids a couple of times a year. They just need to come to grips with the fact that I didn't take their daughter from them. I'm not the guilty party. We all miss Kayla, but she's gone and my kids don't get to be their replacement for her.

I glance at my watch and then back up at the rainbow-filled sky. This morning the news said a storm was coming, but it's beautiful right now. A bit of a misty rain but not enough to keep the tourists inside. That pushes my thoughts toward Emily Thomas. What's her story? She seemed tense and even a little sad, and I never did figure out if she was traveling alone or with her husband.

After another ten minutes of watching the shore, I stand and head back to my room. I have tickets to the show in the courtyard tonight, and I could use a laugh. In a few days, I'll be back to the grindstone of life, and I'll be missing my Hawaiian summer home.

*

After cleaning up and checking in on the kids one more time to wish them goodnight, I head down to the garden for the show. Once outside, I follow the usher to my assigned seat, but before we reach my table, I stop a few feet from where Emily is sitting. She's dressed in an off-the-shoulder, little black dress that drops to just over her crossed knees. Her hair is light, not brown, but not quite blonde either. It's like the color of caramel or honey. It's pinned up, similar to how it was earlier, and she doesn't really look much more relaxed than she did then, despite being out of the suit. I stop in my tracks. I don't want to stare, but I can't help myself. Her features are delicate and soft, like her figure. She's slim, but fairly tall. I remember that from standing next to her earlier. From her profile, I can tell she's unsure about this entire experience. She's holding up her meal ticket and looking at it with a perplexed expression before her pretty, wide, blue eyes bounce around, taking in the rest of her surroundings. It's the most adorable thing I've ever seen.

I'm rooted to the spot as I watch her and I'm overcome with warmth. It's been a long time since a woman has been able to drive me to distraction. Standing on the spot, I grin as I stare at her—I just can't help myself.

# CHAPTER THREE

## Emily

I'm not sure what to expect. With my ticket in hand, I approach an usher who shows me to my table. The place is absolutely breathtaking, with the mini palms and bushes of colorful native flowers planted around the giant space. The stage sits straight ahead, nestled between groups of larger palm trees and is lit with a dozen or so torches. The plush lawn under my feet is soft and trimmed short. It's not the easiest to walk on with my spiked high heels and, looking around, I notice that almost everyone is wearing flip-flops. I guess I didn't get the memo.

The ticket includes dinner and drinks, but the dinner is preordered, which makes me curious about what my brother ordered for me. After being seated, the usher lays a small folded card in front of me. I lift it to read 'Kalua Pig'. Ah, that answers my question.

When the cocktail waitress stops for my order, I'm struck with uncertainty. What do people drink at these things? I'd normally have some sort of vodka-mixed drink, but I'm on vacation. I don't want to do normal.

As I'm staring at the waitress, who is waiting patiently, I hear a voice from behind me. "She'll have a Mai Tai."

I shift slightly to see Drew standing to my right. He's wearing a colorful aloha shirt and chino shorts. He's lost the ball cap, and his dark brown hair is flopped to the side in a messy sort of style.

It's his smile that grabs my attention. His entire face is lit and his eyes sparkle, the torch light showing little gold specks in their depths, and it seems so genuine. I can't help but return it.

He shrugs at my expression. "If you want to be an islander, you have to drink like one."

It's hard to argue with that, so I glance back at the waitress and nod in agreement. "I'll have a Mai Tai, thank you." Turning my eyes back to Drew, I say thanks to him too.

Winking at me, he says, "I hope your evening is better than your day was."

I have to laugh at that. "Me too."

He watches me for a second, and I wonder if I should invite him to sit with me. It's as if I can hear Rebecca's voice in my head, urging me to talk to him. Just as he's about to turn away, I say. "Ah... Drew... would you like to join me? That is, if you're alone as well."

His eyes narrow as he takes me in. "You're alone?" He glances down at my table. "No Mr. Thomas?"

It takes me a moment to realize what he's talking about. Then I remember the exchange in the hall outside my room with the bellman. "Oh, no. There's no Mr. Thomas," I mumble. Saying those words out loud is physically painful, but I've become an expert at hiding the pain.

He watches me, as if unsure, and I wonder whether it's because he senses my discomfort about inviting him to join me, or my reaction to being asked about my husband.

"I would love to join you. Let me grab my meal card, I'll be right back."

As Drew steps away, the waitress sets my drink down. I move aside the little umbrella and the spear of pineapple before lifting it to my mouth for a sip. It's sweet, and a bit tangy but delicious, and it seems to go down awfully easy. I can see why people like it. I turn toward Drew in time to see him grab a meal card.

Both of our tables were set for two, and suddenly I'm worried about how they sell the tickets. Are the seats assigned? Will someone else have a ticket for the other seat at my table?

When Drew sits, I ask, "This doesn't break any rules, does it?"

"Hum… let's see." He looks around and gets the waitress' attention. "Excuse me, but I've moved my seat." He points to his table and flashes her a dazzling smile. "That table is now free for a couple. I hope that's okay?"

"Yes, perfectly fine." She simpers at him, and I get the sense that his sexy, magnetic smile often gets him what he wants. "I'll have the table set for someone else. Thanks for letting me know." She gives his arm a squeeze before walking away.

He glances over at me. "Problem solved."

"Thank you. That's one less thing we need to worry about."

"Emily," he says with his hands spread, "this is a vacation. There shouldn't be any worries."

I take a deep breath, knowing he's right. "Old habits die hard."

He lifts his cocktail. "Drink up. It's the best way to break those habits."

I do what he says and make an effort to smile. Since losing Tucker, I've turned inward and stopped showing emotions. I know it makes me come across as cold but hiding how I feel is a survival mechanism and a bad pattern I'm trying to change when in social situations. "You seem to be an expert at this vacation thing."

He chortles. "It's true. I love it here. I spend three weeks at this resort every summer."

"Whoa, three weeks. That's expert level!"

He nods and lifts his drink as if in a toast. "Yes, I know."

"I haven't had a vacation in years. I guess it shows, huh?"

He bobs his head as he looks closer at me. "I wouldn't say you look like someone who hasn't vacationed. You've more of the look of someone who works hard and takes that work seriously."

"Well, yeah, that too." Maybe sometimes a little too seriously, unfortunately, but I am surprised by his accurate portrayal of me. He's pretty perceptive.

I give him the same assessing look, which he responds to by saying, "I know, I know, I look like the maintenance man."

"No," I blurt with an open-mouthed laugh. "You look comfortable. What do you do?" I wave my hand and say, "For a living, I mean. You know, when you're not vacationing."

"Oh, ah." He narrows his twinkling eyes conspiratorially. "Let's not do that."

I tilt my head, confused. "Do what?"

"Talk about our jobs. This is Maui. Let's enjoy it and not burden each other with real life."

I lift my brows and nod. "That sounds lovely."

"No rules, save one. We don't talk about life outside of Maui."

I stare at him for a long time, and I have to wonder if there's another reason behind his rule. "Wait. I need one question answered before we continue with this…" I brush my hand between us, not really sure what *this* is, "…dinner."

"Okay, shoot."

"Are you married?"

He lifts a hand to his chest with a surprised expression on his face. "Me? No, Emily, I'm not married."

"Any significant other at all?"

"I do not have a life partner. Does that answer your question completely?"

"Yes, thank you. I also do not have a life partner of any kind… at least, not a personal life partner. I do have a business partner—"

"Wait! Stop right there. You're already breaking the rules, no talking about work."

I place a hand over my mouth and mumble, "Right. Sorry."

We both laugh, and I realize that my drink is already empty. I lift the glass to look at it. "That went fast."

"No worries. There's more where that came from." He stops the nearest waitress and orders two more Mai Tais.

As the waitress disappears, the lights dim and the stage brightens. Drew and I both shift our chairs to get a better look, which brings us closer together. I'm trying to act natural, but I'm simply not used to being with men like this. People I work with, yes. My brother, yes. But it's been a long time since I've spent time with a man in a romantic way. Is that what this is? Romantic? Or am I getting ahead of myself?

I went on two dates with Grant and that even felt more like business than romance. This feels different, and I need to remind myself to relax.

"I don't bite, I promise," Drew murmurs moments before the spotlight shines on a large Hawaiian man in an aloha shirt. I listen to the introduction and laugh harder than I have in ages. He's truly funny. I've never been one to watch stand-up comedy, and now I'm wondering why. Something else I've missed out on, I guess.

The cocktail waitress sets down our drinks and then our appetizers arrive. They place a small plate of what looks like crab cakes in front of me. They smell so amazing, I could kiss Mac. "Oh, nice choice, Mac!"

I look over to see that Drew has the same on his plate.

"Name's Drew. How many of those drinks have you had?"

I laugh. "Mac is my brother. He planned this entire trip for me. Including choosing this meal."

"That sounds oddly overbearing for a brother."

"Doesn't it though?" I chortle and say, "I told you I haven't vacationed in a long time. This is his way of forcing it on me."

"I see... Well, good for him and good for you. These crab cakes are the best I've had, so he chose well."

I glance over at Drew and seeing his alluring gaze, I wonder what else this week has in store for me.

# CHAPTER FOUR

### Drew

I watch as Emily devours her dinner. After a drink or two, she's finally lightening up. Earlier today, she seemed to have trouble smiling. Now she can't seem to stop. Her pale, bare shoulders are screaming to be touched, and I'm having a hard time watching the show because I don't want to take my eyes off her. At this point, I'd give just about anything to see the layers of honey and caramel hair down… maybe draped over her porcelain shoulders.

As she sips her fourth, maybe fifth drink, I wonder how hard they're going to hit her. I think it's safe to assume they're all going straight to her head. Just as this thought crosses my mind, she orders another. So, what the hell, I also have another. She lifts her glass to salute, and I do the same. She's glassy-eyed and smiling, her perfect teeth are bright white, and her blue eyes dance in amusement.

"Are you having a good time?" I ask.

"Yes, so much fun! This show is great. They're so talented, don't you think?" She gives me the side-eye as if I've done something wrong. "Wait, you've seen this show before, haven't you?"

"Yes, but they change it every year."

She places her hand on my forearm. "How many times have you seen it?"

"Maybe five or six." I know exactly how many but I don't want to remember the first time right now, so I fight to keep my mind from venturing there.

"It must be nice to have a job where you can take three weeks off for Hawaii every single year."

I wag a finger at her. "Don't go there, Emily. That's breaking the rules."

Her eyes widen, and her mouth shapes into a perfect O. "Oh, sorry. I forgot." I notice that her words are slightly slurred.

"Are you feeling okay?" I ask.

"Oh, my God, I feel great. This is great. I haven't felt this relaxed in years."

Watching her makes me happy. I have the impression that she's either coming out of a bad breakup or she's somehow been hurt. Her eyes often reflect a sadness that's hard to miss. Which makes her current smile stand out that much more.

She's so beautiful. Her hair is starting to break free from its tight bun and the tension around her eyes is gone as well. Her brother must be right; she needed this. When the performers take their final bow, Emily stands and claps with the rest of the audience, but then she tilts and has to balance herself against the table. I had a feeling that was going to happen. Those Mai Tais can sneak up on people.

She laughs it off and sits back down, but I can see the spinning in her eyes as she looks over at me. "Can I help you to your room?" I ask.

She shrugs. "I guess it's okay since you're in the room across the hall."

I hold back my laugh at her nonchalance. "Might as well keep each other company since we're both alone, right?"

She points at me and slurs, "That's right."

Taking her elbow, I follow the crowd as it disperses through the open doors, then I veer her to the right, following the crowd toward the elevators. She's chatting away when it's our turn to enter and I'm glad she's not feeling sick. Her skin is bright, not pale at all, which reassures me she's still feeling fine.

When we're inside, she digs around in her handbag and pulls out her key card. Then she stumbles a bit before resting against me. The elevator stops several times as guests slowly exit onto their floors. After several stops, we're alone, and Emily is very quiet. I glance up at the mirror so I can see her face as she's leaning against my arm. Her eyes are closed, and if I didn't know it was impossible, I'd think she was sleeping.

"Emily, you okay?"

She nods slightly against my arm and murmurs, "Muhum."

Just then, the elevator dings and the doors open to our floor. I grab her arm and take a step forward, but she doesn't move. "We're here," I say in a sing-song voice but she only nods again.

I wrap one arm around her waist and grab her hand with the other to lead her out. She stumbles but finally moves along with my steps. When we reach her room, I take her key from her slack grip and open the door.

Carefully, I lead her into the room without letting her slide to the floor. She stumbles, but I grab her before she goes down and let the door close softly behind us. The stumbling must have brought her out of the stupor because she looks up at me with a hazy yet relaxed expression. Her eyes lock on mine and then she reaches up and expertly tugs three pins out of her hair, letting it drop down her back and drape over her delicate shoulders.

Fuck me. I'm a goner. Christ, she's beautiful. She comes closer, and before I can step back, she locks her lips to mine. My dick instantly twitches in my pants, but my brain knows I need to get out of here.

I pull away gently, and her hooded eyes dull slightly. "I'm sorry. I shouldn't have done that."

"It's not that I don't want to kiss you… It's *really* not that, but I'd rather wait until you're sober."

"Right! You're right." She spins around, and I hover in case she loses her balance. "I have a great room, look at that view," she says stumbling toward the lanai.

I grab her before she can reach the door. "No, you don't. Careful now. It's a long drop to the ground, and you've had too much to drink."

She sways a little. "I think you're right... I should probably go to bed."

"Good idea." I turn her, and she drifts toward the bed before sinking down. Fully clothed, she snuggles into the pillow, and I watch her for a minute, wondering if she'll be okay on her own.

Taking a step toward the bed, I gently remove her shoes then brush the hair off her face. The soft, thick waves are spread across the pillow, and I wish I could run my fingers through them. I trace my finger over her cheekbone, and she doesn't stir. She's certainly relaxed now. This thought makes me chuckle, and the sound of my own laughter reminds me of where I am. I shouldn't be here while she's sleeping, I know this for sure, but I can't help feeling a little concerned she'll need help in the middle of the night. So, I need to make sure she has everything she needs...

Once I get her completely set up for a morning hangover, gathering together Gatorade, and aspirin from my room and a glass of water, I watch her sleep for another minute. It's rough, not knowing anything about her, but I know she's shrouded in sadness, which was obvious from the second I first laid eyes on her. How I recognize it, I'm not sure, but it probably has something to do with losing the love of my life.

Do I still walk around looking like that? I know it took a long time for me to stop thinking about Kayla every waking moment, but that doesn't mean she's not on my mind a lot of the time. I try to remember the good things instead of thinking about her being gone, and I hope that shines through. I don't want to be the guy people feel sorry for. I don't want to be the bummer in the room.

Not that Emily was a bummer. She was actually a lot of fun once she allowed herself to relax, but even then I could see the cloud behind her eyes. Some asshole must have really done a number on her.

And I want to help her. Make sure she has a good time. Forget all the crap that comes along with real life and push her to live in paradise for the week she's here.

I sit at her small table and take a minute to scribble a short note on the hotel notepad. Once I'm happy with it, I lay it down next to her room key and leave her sleeping. If she's lucky, she'll wake up feeling fine, and we can hang out. If not, I'll catch up with her later. Whatever happens, happens. At least, that's my motto while in paradise.

And if I never see her again, I'll know she had one hell of a great night while she was here.

# CHAPTER FIVE

### Emily

I wake up to darkness... but not total darkness. There's enough light for me to see that I don't know where I am. I turn slightly, but it's hard because I'm tangled in the blankets. The bathroom door is ajar, and a sliver of light is shining through the crack. Why did I leave the... oh, right, vacation, hotel room, Maui.

I look down and realize I'm not tangled in blankets, I'm tangled in my dress. It's ridden up and is bunching around my waist and neck. I sit up and yank the zipper down before shimmying out of it and tossing it on the floor. My head is spinning circles... or the room is spinning... I'm not sure which and I think I might be sick. Closing my eyes, I try to settle myself. Once the spinning has slowed some, I glance around and notice a glass of water on the nightstand. So glad I thought of that before I fell asleep. I don't remember it, but I must have. That makes me think about the show and the Mai Tais. So many Mai Tais... How did I get to my room? I don't actually remember.

I lift my phone and check the time: it's just after four in the morning. Reaching over, I turn the lamp on and see an array of stuff on the nightstand. A packet of aspirin, the glass of water, my phone, room key, and a very large Gatorade. How the hell did I get that?

That's when I see a small note written on the hotel notepad.

*Good morning, Emily.*

*I hope you're feeling all right. I've left you some necessities in the hope it counteracts the inevitable headache. Drink lots of water, but sip it, don't guzzle. When you're sure you can keep the water down, then move on to the Gatorade, but drink it slowly too. Take the aspirin first, which should help too. If you need me, I'm just across the hall. Feel free to call my room.*

*If you happen to wake up feeling fine and looking for a great way to spend the day, give me a ring, I can show you the sights.*

*Yours truly,*

*Drew, Room 820*

I snort at his assumption that I'll be hungover. He obviously has no idea that I come from a long line of sturdy Scots who don't get hangovers. Of course, I instantly regret this thought when the room starts spinning again. Oh, my goodness. I rest back against the pillows and think about what he wrote in his note.

The man put me to bed... with instructions. I'm not sure whether to be embarrassed or impressed. Any other man would have... *Jesus, Emily*! I drop my palm down on my forehead.

What the hell was I thinking, getting drunk like that with a stranger? He could have taken complete advantage of the situation. My stomach turns at the thought. I close my eyes, hoping it'll pass. If there were a manual on how to find a decent guy, this would be in it. It would read, *get sloppy drunk and if he puts you to bed with hangover provisions, he's a keeper.* I'm such an idiot, but at least I'm a lucky idiot.

Those Mai Tais are sneaky. I didn't even realize I was getting drunk and I have no idea what happened after the Elvis impersonator. How many drinks did I have? Ugh. The two most dangerous words in the English language: *open bar.* I roll over and throw the blanket over me. I need more sleep, and after that, I'll come up with a decent way to thank Drew for taking care of me.

The next time I look over at the clock, it's nearly nine am. What is that in California time? Oh, who cares? I roll my eyes and sit up slowly, confused. I'm sleeping without any clothes, and I can see my dress bundled up on the floor. This makes me raise my brows and wonder... *I did sleep alone, right?* But then I glance around the room and my eyes land on the note from last night, from Drew. Right. The Mai Tais.

I remember now.

Getting out of bed, I find the resort-supplied robe hanging in the closet. It's plush and soft, and the feel of it relaxes me instantly. I hug myself and look around the room. The door to my lanai is shut tight, and this instantly makes me feel like I'm closed in. I need fresh air. I'm a windows-open kind of person. Drew must have closed it last night before he left. I walk over and try to slide it, but it won't budge. I stare at the glass, checking the locks and then trying to open it again. It will not move.

After a moment, my eyes catch on the little turning screw lock at the bottom, left-hand side of the door. He must have locked it so I wouldn't stumble outside last night. The man's thoughtfulness is endless, so much so that I'm *almost* annoyed. Did he think I wanted to take a leap off my balcony? Was I that much of a drag last night?

After getting the door unlocked, and sliding it open all the way, I grab my phone, and step out to sit in one of the deck chairs. The sky is cloudless and bright blue, with the sun shining brilliantly. No rainbows this morning, which makes me a little sad. Living in Northern California, I don't see much weather. I wouldn't mind a storm at least once this week. We get so little rain at home, I almost forget what it looks like.

This thought makes me wonder where Drew lives. He doesn't seem Midwestern, and he's way too relaxed to be from the New England area. Maybe he's a Southerner. No, not likely since he doesn't have an accent. Then I remember what Rebecca said about a vacation fling and realize that she's right: I should keep it simple and just enjoy it without getting too attached. Is that possible?

I'm sure it's easy for him—he probably has flings every time he's in Hawaii.

And now I feel like that's unfair since he was so kind to me last night. So, he's a guy who has flings but only with sober women who can give consent. Nothing wrong with that. I laugh at the thought.

I pull my cell phone from the pocket of my robe and dial Bec.

"Good morning, Sunshine," she says, answering on the first ring.

"Good morning. You sound mighty chipper for the early hour."

She laughs at that. "Early? It's a beautiful Tuesday *afternoon* in California. Sounds like someone slept in this morning."

"Well… I am on vacation."

"My, do you sound like you had some fun last night."

"Last night I discovered Mai Tais, courtesy of my neighbor."

"And how *was* the hot neighbor?" I can hear the innuendo in her voice, and I can't help rolling my eyes in response.

"He's quite polite. He put my drunk ass to bed and left me instructions on how to ward off a hangover."

"Oh, yeah, left you in bed, huh?"

"Do not misunderstand, darling. He *put me to bed*. He didn't stay."

"What?"

"That's right. He put me to bed, left aspirin, and a glass of water with a note."

The line is silent but then she says, "Wow. I don't know what to say."

"Right? I'm feeling pretty speechless too."

"I'm almost afraid to ask what state you were in that he had to put you to bed."

"I don't remember it, not really. Does that answer your question?" I chuckle. "I vaguely remember exiting the elevator with him and then entering my room... Oh crap." I place a hand over my heated face and roll my eyes. "I kind of remember trying to kiss him."

"Trying?"

"Yeah, the next thing I remember is waking up, fully dressed, with a note next to the aspirin and glass of water he left me. He also secured the slider to the lanai so I wouldn't have an accident."

"Emily, that is incredibly endearing. Any other guy would have taken advantage."

"I know. Too bad he's only going to be a vacation fling."

"You don't have to limit yourself. Get to know him, what have you got to lose?"

"And what if he, oh, lives in Dallas, or, oh, doesn't want anything to do with my drunk ass?" I'm bobbing my head as I'm speaking. "Anyway, it doesn't matter. You're—we're getting way ahead of ourselves. I'm not having a vacation fling. We haven't even kissed."

"It sounds like he's worth getting to know."

"I'm so embarrassed. I was stupid last night. I acted like some teenage girl who'd never had a drink before."

"Um, excuse me, but you needed that. You haven't done anything fun in years, Emily. Not months, but years! Don't forget who you're talking to."

"I can have fun without getting shitfaced, I can also have fun without the companionship of a man."

"I agree. You can have fun without a man, but you'll have a hell of a lot more fun *with* one."

The tone in her voice makes me laugh. "You're such a harlot!"

"I know, and I'm trying really hard to be a bad influence on you."

"You certainly are." I laugh when I say it because it's true, but I like it. I like that she speaks frankly. Everyone needs that one friend who's not afraid to tell you how it really is.

"So, what's on Mac's list for you today?" she asks.

"I don't know. I'm afraid to look. What's going on there? Anything I need to worry about?"

"Of course not. Grant came by this morning to recommend a contractor for the office remodel. We're supposed to meet with them when you're back. I had Eddie add it to your calendar. But don't worry about it. As a matter of fact, I'm hanging up now. Don't give this place another thought for the rest of the week."

"Okay, darling. I'll talk to you later. Thank you."

"Buh-bye."

As I set my phone down, it rings again. Maybe Bec forgot to tell me something. I lift it to see Grant's number on the display. I met him last year when I was representing his architecture firm in contract negotiations with a large commercial developer. When the negotiations ended, he tried getting me to go out with him. I was frank with him and made it clear I wasn't ready to date, but he never fully took no for an answer, as if I'm incapable of making that decision on my own. He acted as if I just needed convincing. Last week, I finally gave in and agreed to dinner—twice.

Boy, was that a mistake. Spending two evenings with him only proved my first impression was correct, and I can't help but wonder if it was that second date that gave him the impression that I wanted more.

I'm not sure why I agreed to the second date, I guess I didn't trust my own judgment the first time so I tried again to see if he'd be different the next time around. He wasn't and he didn't listen to anything I said on the second date either. That was a huge turn-off. It's as if he has selective hearing. Or selective understanding. He only retains the information he wants to retain. I consider ignoring the call but then decide to answer. Maybe if I talk to him, he'll stop trying so hard to reach me.

"Hello, Grant."

"Emily, so good to hear your voice. I was getting worried."

*Worried.* It's not like we've ever even stayed in constant contact. I fight to hide my aggravation and say, "Sorry, I don't have good service here."

"Oh, that's right, Rebecca mentioned you were out of town on business."

"Yes." I lift my eyes skyward and decide to be honest... or at least, semihonest. "I'm actually meeting with a client in Maui."

"Oh, well, business trips don't get much better than that. You should have told me. I have a condo there, I could've joined you and kept you company while you're working." That's exactly *why* I didn't tell him.

"Well, I'm not sure we're ready for taking trips together. Actually—"

"Well, we'll never reach that point if we don't start somewhere."

"Let me rephrase. *I'm* not ready for that, Grant." I pause but then say, "I'm not sure dating is in the cards for me right now. It's been lovely getting to know you but I'm just still not ready."

"Let's talk about it over dinner when you return."

*Ugh.* It's like I'm talking to myself.

"Bec told me we were meeting with a contractor when I return, is that true?"

"Yes, I have the perfect guy for you. He's the best builder I know and he's capable of doing the designs as well. You'll get the design and construction for the price of one."

"Thank you for setting that up for us."

"You're welcome. I'll see you then. Try to have some fun while you're on the island. Let me know if you need restaurant recommendations."

"Thanks again. I'll give you a call if I need any island advice."

I end the call and groan. At least he hears me when I talk about work, it's the personal stuff he seems to glaze over.

I quickly call Drew's room and I'm a little relieved when he doesn't answer. I leave a voice message thanking him for last night. After disconnecting, I hold my phone out to send a quick hungover selfie to Mac then stand, thinking about a good hearty breakfast to help me clear my head—and help me forget what a fool I was last night…

*

Hungover hiking… it's the order of the day. I know, it's stupid, but I can't help it. I need some fresh air and some good clean exercise. I park the rental car at the trailhead, and I'm thoroughly shocked at the lack of other hikers. I guess everyone else prefers the beach… I look up and see a few heavy clouds, marring what was a perfect sky earlier. I'm happy to see my wish is coming true even if it means I have to get wet.

I throw my pack on and head out. The Hawaiian air is thick, and I've already started to sweat in the humidity, but for the first time, I don't mind. I'm happy… The height gives me a clear view of the ocean, and the wilderness is such a refreshing change from living in the middle of flat-land Sacramento. Not to mention the lack of people.

So far, the trail is pretty easy, and I'm stopping every few yards to snap pictures for Mac. The abundant ferns and greenery flow over the lifts and hills in waves of different shades of green with the occasional rock face jutting out from the vegetation. Little pops of color show themselves in the form of native wildflowers. Some I recognize, but others I couldn't name to save my life. I wish I'd picked up a book about the island before I left home.

After walking for a while, I come to a clearing, and I'm stunned by the view. I can see for miles and miles. The luscious hills of Maui slowly roll over until they spill into the endless ocean. So different from the low, golden hills surrounding Sacramento. I take a panoramic photo before moving on.

Within an hour of following the trail, the sky turns dark, and I'm starting to get nervous. I was expecting a little rain, but these look like full-on storm clouds. I pull out my cell phone, praying I can use the weather app, but no, there's no signal at all. I continue to climb, hoping the darkness is just due to the fog. When I enter a thicket of trees, and climb further, I'm wishing I brought a flashlight. I keep going carefully, knowing there's a waterfall coming up soon. When the trees part, I continue through the ferns and realize I'm following a cliff-side trail. I carefully lean to look over the edge. Rock cliffs jut out from the mountain side – besides these, it's a straight drop of at least a hundred feet. It's frightening enough to keep me on the left side of the path. I'm not afraid of heights but the dirt is a bit slippery, and I definitely don't need to die on vacation.

When the trail turns from dirt to rocks, and I hear the rushing of water, hope blooms. Another ten yards and I see the falls. "Wow," I mutter to myself. The water freefalls from a cliff about thirty feet up with a four-foot ripple into a basin between walls of steep peaks. The pool under the falls is a dreamy green and I'm almost tempted to go swimming.

With my phone in hand, I step forward to get a better view for a photo. But my foot slips and twists. "Ouch! Son of a bitch!" I shout, thankful that nobody is around to hear me.

I sit on another large rock and gently slide my foot out from where it's wedged. Blood is oozing from a gash above my ankle, so I quickly slap my hand over it and apply pressure. But it's slippery, and I can't get a good grasp. Sliding my backpack off my shoulder, I tug the zipper before grabbing the extra pair of socks I brought. Folding one in thirds, I place it over the cut, then wrap the other around my leg and tie it tight.

I take a moment to collect myself, breathing deeply, and then turn my ankle to make sure it's not sprained. It's tender but not so bad that I can't walk on it. Relieved, I stand and carefully walk over to a sturdier rock and have a seat. I take out my water bottle and get a good guzzle, and as I screw the cap back on, the loudest bang of thunder sounds over my head and causes me to cry out.

"Holy shit!" A second later, the sky is alive with lightning. Before I can react, heavy rain starts dropping rapidly around me. Within seconds, I'm soaked.

I quickly get up, crawling into a little cove under the ledge of a huge rock. Now I just have to hope the rain stops before dark.

# CHAPTER SIX

## Drew

When I return to my room after breakfast, the first thing I notice is the red, blinking message light on my phone. I grab it and check the voicemail.

"Hi Drew, this is Emily Thomas. I can't thank you enough for taking such good care of me last night. I feel fine, and I've actually decided to go for a hike. I'm craving fresh air and wilderness. Maybe even a waterfall. Thanks again and I hope we can get together again before you leave."

*Hiking!* Hasn't she seen the weather reports? *Jesus, woman, are you trying to kill yourself?*

I disconnect and call the concierge.

"Concierge desk. How may I help you?"

"Gerry, Drew Whitney, Room 820. I need a favor."

"Anything you need, Mr. Whitney."

"Ms. Thomas from Room 819 left me a message to say she was hiking today. I'm a little worried about the weather. Did she ask you about hiking trails, by chance?"

"Ah, yes, Ms. Thomas stopped by my desk yesterday to pick up her itinerary for the week and she did ask about hiking locations. I suggested two trails. She didn't mention she was going today, otherwise I would have suggested against it with the incoming storm."

"I'm going to look for her, I don't think she knew the storm was coming. If I stop by on my way out, will you point me toward the trails?"

"Of course! Is there anything else I can do to help? Should I call the park rangers?"

"Um, that might be overkill. Save it for now. If we're not back by dinner, you can go ahead and call them for us both. She's a pretty smart lady, I'm sure she went prepared. I would just hate for her to get stuck in the weather alone."

Twenty minutes later, I leave the resort packed for a hike, and hoping I'm not overreacting. I'm guessing on the trail she chose. Since she mentioned a waterfall, I pick the one I know for sure has one. It's also the less dangerous of the two trails, I'm relieved to find out.

When I arrive at the trailhead, there're three cars in the lot, and one has a family getting ready to leave. I ask them if they've seen a woman matching Emily's description.

They have, and fortunately, they passed her less than an hour ago. I look up at the darkening sky. I might just be able to find her before the storm starts. What can I do but take a chance?

I head out in a rush. Luckily, I've hiked this trail several times, and I'm familiar with it. As I make my way toward the falls, the sky grows darker. I'm hoping she took her time as she walked. That'll make it easier to catch up with her. If she's smart, she's heading back this way already.

I'm an hour into my hike when thunder and lightning crack above my head. Jesus! It's loud, which means it's close. I'm about ten to fifteen yards from the falls, so I follow the rocky path until I see the water. There's nobody around, so I call out, hoping Emily has sheltered under the cliffs.

"Emily!" I shout. I don't hear anything at first, but then I see her head pop out from behind a large sheer rock face.

"Hello?" Her eyes focus on me, and I see the confusion before the recognition.

"Emily? You okay?"

"Drew?" Her brows scrunch together. "What are you doing here?"

I teeter down to her. "I'm looking for you. Are you okay?" As I say this, I try to wipe the water from my face.

"I'm fine." She drops her fists on her hips and asks, "Why are you looking for me?"

I fight not to laugh. Apparently, she doesn't realize what's coming. "Emily, there's a huge tropical storm coming. Didn't you know?"

She gestures toward the sky. "I figured it out when the sky turned black, but it's not like I can't handle a little weather."

That makes me feel a bit stupid. I have no idea where she's from and just because I'm not used to the weather, doesn't mean she's not. "I, um, well, it's more than a little weather. I didn't want you to get stuck in a washout or flood." Her face falls a little, and that makes me feel better about my decision. "These mountains can get ten to fifteen inches of rain in hours."

She looks around as the water runs past us in rivulets to the pool under the falls. "I was planning to turn back when it calmed down a bit."

"It's not going to calm down, at least not today. It's best to head back now." I look down at her ankle and see a makeshift bandage. "Are you okay?"

"Of course." She looks down, and points to the injury. "It's nothing. Just a small gash. I'm fine."

"I brought a first aid kit. Should I wrap that up a little better?"

She sits and takes out a small plastic bag from her backpack, wrapping it around the wound. "This will keep it dry enough. Don't worry, it's just a scratch, I'm fine." After she secures the plastic around her ankle, she turns and looks out at the falls.

"I'm sorry you have to shorten your hike," I say.

Her gaze cuts to me and I finally see her features relax. "Thanks for coming to fetch me, but I think I would have been fine."

"I didn't mean to imply you couldn't take care of yourself. I just know how quickly things can change up here."

"I found shelter, though. I would have been fine here for a while."

I try not to laugh when she says this. "Actually, you wouldn't be fine *here*." I glance around and point toward the falls and the basin pool. "You're sitting inside the basin. With this much rain, this spot will be underwater very soon."

Her eyes travel around then lift toward the sky, her cheeks flushing. "I didn't think of that."

"The sooner we get out of here, the better."

"All right." She lifts into a crouching position and is about to step out from under the rock when I grab her arm.

"I am really sorry, Emily."

"You don't have to apologize for wanting to help me. Really." She shakes her head and grimaces. "I'm sorry. This is the second time in twenty-four hours you've had to rescue me."

This surprises me. I never once thought I was rescuing her... just looking out for her. "I wouldn't say I'm rescuing you. You're not a damsel in distress. I'm just trying to help."

A pained look mars her face. "It's just a little embarrassing."

"In what way?"

She gives me an incredulous look. "*In what way?* Jesus, Drew. I..." She stops abruptly and closes her eyes. Then she inhales deeply. "How dumb of me not to check the weather before I left."

"Any other time, you would have been fine. July is the middle of hurricane season on the islands. They get lots of storms this time of year. They come in fast, like today."

"I should have checked. Thank you for finding me."

I grin at her, glad she's not pissed at me. I feel bad for not having more faith in her ability, but I'm also relieved. God knows how much worse this is going to get. "If you're up for the walk, we should get back to our cars."

I pull two plastic ponchos out of my backpack and give her one. "Use this."

She takes it and tosses it over her head. "Thank you."

I then hand her a waterproof flashlight. "Do you mind if I go ahead of you? I'd like to watch for trail washout."

She gestures toward the rocky path back to the trail. "I don't mind."

"Shout out if you need to stop or if your ankle starts hurting. We can take a break whenever you need it."

"I'm completely fine. Please, go ahead."

When she says this, I realize I'm pushing it. She doesn't need to be taken care of. With this thought, I hit the trail.

Over the next two hours, we make our way down the trail, and Emily has zero trouble keeping up with my pace. I try not to seem surprised. She's obviously in great shape, and this is far from her first hiking experience. I'm simultaneously impressed and a little intimidated. It's not that I don't know any strong women. Hell, I was raised by a strong, independent, single mother who takes crap from no one. It's just that I've not experienced a woman who can manage a hike like this, in the rain, after a night of drinking like Emily had.

When we reach the peak of the next incline, I stop to examine the trail ahead. It's hard to see with the pouring rain and the darkness from the storm clouds. I step forward gingerly and lose my footing. My right foot slips out from under me, and the forward momentum takes me down the hill sideways. After sliding about ten feet, I somehow stop. Digging my left boot in for traction, I look back to see Emily grasping my backpack with both hands, holding me from slipping further.

When I'm vertical again, I lean forward to catch my breath. Then I nod at her.

"Thank you!"

"You okay?"

"Yeah, I think so. Besides my heart pounding out of my chest."

She squats to see the blood trickling down my leg then leads me toward the shelter of two banyan trees.

"Sit down and let me take a look."

"I think it's fine," I say, looking down at myself. I lift the leg of my cargo shorts to see the trail rash. It's angry red with embedded dirt and rocks from the slide, but due to the adrenaline rush, I barely feel it.

She drops her backpack and squats to examine my outer thigh. "How high does it go?"

"Ms. Thomas, are you asking me to take my pants off?"

"We need to get it cleaned." She's dead serious, so I straighten my expression and stop trying to be funny.

I tug on the shorts to lift them above the trail rash on my outer thigh and she sits on a lifted root near the base of the tree. "Lean over a bit, please, so I can have a look."

"Okay, okay…" I ease over as she pulls out her water bottle. Before I realize what's happening, she's pouring water on my leg and gently brushing at the dirt. I instinctively pull away. A jolt of heat shoots through me, causing an internal shiver so strong it nearly takes my breath away.

"Oh, sorry. Does it hurt?"

"No, it's fine. The water just surprised me."

She glances up at me through her long, wet lashes. "It's not too bad," she observes as I pass her a pad of gauze.

"It'll be fine until we get back to the resort. Thank you though."

She lifts to her feet, and as I turn to do the same, we're nearly nose to nose. I want to touch her, but I resist the urge.

I can see the frustration dancing in her eyes, but I'm not sure why until she reaches out and smacks my chest. "Dammit. Don't scare me like that again."

This surprises me. I can't resist grabbing her wrist and pulling her closer. "Scared you, huh?"

Her breathing hitches slightly and damn, I want to taste her. Her eyes drift to my mouth, and I can't hold back any longer. I pull her the last couple of inches toward me, into a deep kiss. I'm worried she's going to pull away, but she doesn't. She leans in for more, and I'm a little dizzy from the rush.

She tastes so good. The moment lasts longer than I expect and surprisingly, the storm around us seems louder than it did seconds ago. It's like a soundtrack to our first kiss. We're both soaked through, but I don't care. I've wanted to kiss this woman since laying eyes on her in that uptight business suit. I wrap a hand around her to tug her closer. We're against the tree, and I'm grateful for the support since I'm a little light-headed, not to mention that all the blood is rushing to my cock.

Emily reluctantly withdraws and opens her eyes. She doesn't say anything, and I'm afraid to speak—I don't want to ruin the moment.

The sultry expression on her face is the hottest thing I've ever seen, and I fight not to kiss her again. Then she smiles and I take the time to thank her properly. "Thank you for keeping me from dying. You have a good grip. If it wasn't for you, I might have slid over the edge."

She chuckles. "Nah, you would have been fine, just more trail embedded in your ass."

I'm still holding her tightly, but when she tries to pull away, I release my grip.

"It's amazing how strong a person can be when they need to be."

I stare at her because I'm not sure what to say. She is amazing—downright courageous—and it's been a long time since someone has surprised me.

I'm about to suggest that we keep moving when the sky is lit with a bright flash of lightning and the ground shakes with the force of the thunder booming. We both instinctively duck.

"Holy shit!" she shrieks.

"Yeah, we'd better get the hell out of here before it gets any worse."

We head back to the trail, and by the time we reach the parking lot, I'm feeling relieved. I turn toward Emily, and she's smiling ear to ear. Her head is tilted toward the sky, and her mouth is open. She's covered in mud from her bare knees to the tips of her hiking boots and I have to laugh at her.

"Are you laughing at me again?"

"Most people would be dashing to their car."

"I love the rain!" she gushes with a child-like smile. That's something we have in common, and I look up at the sky. It seldom rains where I live, so I treasure the downpours when I get the chance.

She spins in a circle, and I can't help but think of my daughter Hannah. That's exactly what she'd do in a rainstorm like this.

After a long moment, Emily sighs and heads toward her car. I pop my trunk and throw my poncho and backpack inside before glancing over at her.

"Feel like lunch?"

She turns and squints at me. "What did you have in mind?"

"I know a great little café with a covered patio. We can eat and enjoy the rain at the same time." The corner of her mouth lifts up again, and the look on her face makes my stomach flip. Even soaking wet and exhausted from the hike, she's stunning. And she has the best smile—too bad she doesn't show it more often.

# CHAPTER SEVEN

## Emily

When Drew and I enter the resort, we're both a fright to look at but cheerful after our fun in the rain. I feel a bit out of sorts after our kiss and the taste of him still lingers on my lips. It's been a long time since I've kissed a man and I was actually afraid I'd forgotten how. Thankfully, Drew seemed to know what he was doing.

The concierge looks over at us and nods to Drew. I tilt my head and narrow my eyes questioningly.

Drew shrugs. "He showed me the list of trails he gave you yesterday to help me find you."

My pulse kicks up when I hear this. "Seriously?" I ask.

"When you left a message to say you were going hiking, I got worried. I wasn't trying to invade your privacy, but you see the storm blasting outside. Do you really think it was wrong for me to be concerned?" He punches the button to call the elevator. "How was I going to find you without asking Gerry?"

"But it's not your place to worry about me—much less conspire with the hotel staff to find me." As soon as the words leave my mouth, I feel horrible for saying them. He's been so kind, I'm just not sure how to take that. I've been on my own for so long, I'm not used to someone watching out for me. It's not like Grant, who was only worried about me because I wasn't paying him any attention.

Before I can apologize, he says, "Then whose place is it? Because that guy isn't here."

Heat shoots through me when I hear this. After we enter the elevator, I turn toward him with my hands on my hips, blood pounding in my ears, my guilt instantly flipping into anger. Does he really think I need *a guy* to look out for me? It was one thing for him to feel like he needed to worry, but I'm a grown-ass woman, I don't *need* a man to take care of me.

"Who do you think you are?"

He steps toward me, cornering me, nose to nose. My breathing hitches at the closeness. I can feel the weight of his wet clothes and the heat of his skin. His brown eyes darken and turn stony as he watches me, his perfect, full lips closed and nearly puckered.

I can't help myself. Why does he have to look so hot when he's mad? His hard, angry eyes are too sexy to resist. I lift to my toes and plant my mouth on his, sucking on one of those luscious lips. Before I can react, I'm against the wall of the elevator with his hands running through my wet hair. He's taken over the kiss and with every dip and swipe of his tongue, I become more and more turned on. It's been so long since I've wanted someone. And damn, I want Drew.

When I feel his erection press against me, I fight not to moan aloud. My arms are tight around his waist, and I'm fisting his wet t-shirt. I want to rip it off him, but I haven't forgotten we're in an elevator.

I hear a ding, and vaguely consider pulling away, but Drew doesn't. I'm not sure if that was our floor or if someone's getting into the elevator with us. Hopefully, Drew's paying attention, because I can't. I only know what I'm feeling right now, and that's a pulsing pleasure. A need. And a hunger that will not rest until it's fed.

The elevator dings again. When Drew lifts me off my feet, I'm surprised but I wrap my legs around his waist. He carries me out of the elevator as if I weigh nothing. Then he gently puts me down and tows me by the hand to his room. I grip him tightly as my heart races. Every inch of my body tingles from his touch, stirring things inside me I thought were dead. But no, every cell is alive and humming with the electricity between us.

It takes him seconds to get the door open. When he does, we both drop our packs and lunge at each other again.

I grab the hem of his shirt and tug it off, tossing it aside. Then my shirt is being ripped over my head. Seconds later, he's palming my breasts, and I'm unbuttoning and pushing forcefully on his wet cargo shorts.

I have to pull away from his lips to look down at the button. I take a deep breath, and before I get the chance, he says, "I got it." He unbuttons and drops his shorts before I have time to respond. With that obstacle out of the way, I tug off my wet sports bra. My bare breasts bounce free and Drew cups them. His eyes are focused, and his expression is pure delight. I almost want to laugh, but I'm too enamored.

As he's admiring my breasts, I glance down to see that he's completely naked. I don't even know how or when he managed to get his shoes and socks off, but they're gone. This actually makes me laugh—I can't help it.

Drew pauses and his eyes lift to mine. "This is funny to you?"

I'm laughing so hard, I can't talk. I'm not sure what's wrong, but it's probably just nerves. It's been a long time since I've... This thought cools my giggles. "I'm sorry, but how did you manage to get your shoes and socks off so fast?"

He glances down and chuckles. "The question is, why are you still wearing yours?"

My arm rests across my chest to shield my exposed breasts. I just can't let them hang out while I'm standing here laughing at him. He tugs my other hand until we're further into the room, then he sits me on the bed. He kneels in front of me, and his eyes travel up to mine as he tugs on the laces of my boots.

He slowly removes my shoes and socks while staring into my eyes. I fight not to look away but I finally close my eyes and say, "It's been a long time since I've done this."

"That's okay. It's like riding a bike."

"I hope you're right."

When my feet are bare, Drew leans forward and plants his lips on mine. Then he pulls back slightly. "I don't care how long it's been. Do you?"

"No," I whisper. "I only care about now."

His lips tilt up at the corners. "Me too."

Then he lowers his mouth to my nipple, and one touch of his tongue is all it takes for goosebumps to pop out on my skin. His hot mouth feels incredible against my cool skin. He lifts his hand to caress my other breast, and I drop my head back, enjoying the feel of him.

The storm is raging outside. The pounding rain and the crashing, angry ocean seem to echo our passion. Between the sun setting and the thick, murky clouds, the room is becoming darker by the minute. I turn slightly to see the water rivulets slipping down the window, but when I feel Drew grip my shorts and panties, I lift myself so that he can pull them off easily.

Once I'm naked, I push back into the middle of the bed. A second later, Drew's over me, his hair falling forward and his warm eyes lingering on me. "I take it you've gotten over your anger?"

"Shut up," I groan as he slides his hand down between my legs. I'm watching him as he does this, but as soon as his finger presses my clit, I close my eyes at the sensation. He's good. Just the perfect amount of pressure and movement. My entire focus shoots to my core, and before I can stop myself, I'm grinding with the movement of his hand.

"Oh God, Drew."

"Is that good?"

"Yes, yes, really good."

He moves his hand but before I have time to protest, his tongue is there, and with every lick, I lose more and more control. I'm moaning, and it's ridiculous, but I can't stop myself. It's been so long since I've been touched by a man. So long since I've felt this. My entire body stiffens, and a shiver breaks from my core, travels through my limbs, and fuck… it feels good.

"Please don't stop," I manage to say as I shudder through my orgasm, and Drew carries on licking.

When the intensity is winding down, he reaches over me and opens the drawer to the nightstand. I hear a wrapper open, and then he's hovering over me again. A shaft of light from outside is slanting across his face, highlighting the stubble on his chin and the firm lock of his jaw. He looks intense and hot as hell and after a moment of intense anticipation, he's pushing inside me. That's when his expression changes. The look on his face—eyes closed, mouth slightly parted, pure satisfaction—that look describes exactly how I feel.

Drew moves slowly and my God, it's torturous. Slightly painful at first, but it's a good kind of pain. Like a good stretch after a workout. He must understand because he's gentle, moving easily until we're locked together.

His eyes pop open, and his breathing picks up. I think it's because he's trying hard to go slow when he really wants to pound me. I can see the restraint in his eyes, so I lift to him. I lift high and hard. I want all of him and all of this. I don't need gentle, I need him to show me what he's made of—what *I'm* made of.

He takes my hint, and before I realize what's happening, he flips, and I'm on top. Holy shit! His hands grasp my breasts, then they travel all over before landing on my hips. This feels good. I lift to my knees, drop my hands to his chest, and find my groove, but damn, I'm not sure how long I can maintain this pace. I'm not sure how long I can last. My body reacts instantly, coiling like a spring. He lifts to meet my thrusts and I have my lip clamped between my teeth to keep from crying out, but I can't stop it.

Drew's not exactly quiet either and the sound of his grunting, his low, gravelly voice, pushes me forward. I tighten around him. I can't stop, and seconds before my release, crying with pleasure, I'm on my back again. Drew's got my wrists pinned to the bed, and I can't touch him. "Oh, God, Drew. I can't wait."

"Don't wait." And as he says this, he thrusts forward one more time. I can feel the tightness and the rigid pulsing inside me... and I let go.

# CHAPTER EIGHT

### Drew

I did not see this happening today. My face is resting between Emily's breasts, and I'm fighting to catch my breath. I inhale and get a whiff of jasmine. How can she possibly smell this good after spending hours in the pouring rain, and after the sweaty sex we just had?

Emily runs her hand through my wet hair and her chest rises in a deep breath at the same time. I can't believe how good this feels. How natural it is to be with her and how genuine our connection seems. I lift my head to see her face but her eyes are closed and she's frowning. That's not fair. How can I be completely satisfied just to find her disappointed? There's no possible way she didn't enjoy that. I can't be that bad a judge of great sex. *Really great sex.* I can't be the only person feeling so captivated.

I lift up and hover over her, placing my hands around her face. "What's wrong?"

She shakes her head, her eyes still squeezed shut.

"Emily, did I do something wrong? Something to hurt you?"

"No," she whispers. "It was amazing."

"Gee, for some reason, I don't believe you."

She inhales deeply, letting the breath back out slowly, and as she does, I feel the muscles in her shoulders relax. Her eyes open and focus on mine and finally give way to a smile. "Thank you."

That's a first. I feel like I should be thanking her. "Oh, no, thank *you*." I watch her for another moment, then ask, "Really, are you okay?"

She nods, but the sadness is back. Instead of pressing, I let it be. I have a feeling whatever is happening with her has nothing to do with me, and I don't want to risk upsetting her further.

She curls into my side, and for the first time since we walked into the hotel, my eyes look around at something other than Emily. It's dark. When did that happen? I glance toward the window to see the rain hitting the glass hard. "It's really coming down out there," I mumble as I plant a kiss on the top of Emily's head. I pull her closer, and I like the way she fits so comfortably next to me, her warm skin melding with mine.

"I'm starving." Emily yawns and I think I hear a faint tummy rumble behind her attempt to cover up the sound.

"Right, sorry. We never made it to lunch." I glance at the clock. "And now it's closer to dinnertime."

She sits up with the sheet clutched to her chest. "I think I'm going to head over to my room and get cleaned up."

I reach over and click the bedside lamp on. When I do, I see the mud all over the bed. "Oh, crap. I guess we should have cleaned up before…"

"Wow," she says, looking down at the filthy sheets. "We were a little distracted when we came in." She starts laughing, and I can't hold back mine either. It feels good to laugh with her… it's just plain good to see her happy.

She turns toward me, and I'm struck by how incredibly beautiful she is. Even after the long day in the rain and mud, even after our rush to get undressed and fall into bed. Her grin fades, and I reach out to draw her in for a long, lingering kiss. "Will you have dinner with me?" I mumble into her lips.

"Can I have a solid hour to clean up?"

"Of course." I turn and gesture toward the closet. "Feel free to take my spare robe for your jaunt across the hall."

"Thank you."

When the door clicks behind her, I pull my phone out of my backpack. I have a voicemail and several text messages from the kids.

Hannah: *Hi Daddy. We're at Disneyland today.*

She's sent a photo of herself with Minnie Mouse and all of the Disney princesses, including her favorite, Merida. Hannah's fiery red hair is nearly a perfect match to Merida's and it makes me happy to see that bright smile on her face.

Hannah: *I love you.*

Hannah: *How's Hawaii today, Daddy?*

Hannah: *Are you having a good day?*

Hannah: *I miss you!*

I start replying.

Me: *I love and miss you too, Hannah. It looks like you guys had fun at Disneyland. I'm sorry I missed it. I went hiking in a storm. Not as much fun as you had.*

Kyle: *Dad, check this out! We rode the Matterhorn! I got soaked!*

He's sent a photo of himself with his grandpa, and they're both pretty wet. I'm sorry I missed it. Not that I didn't enjoy myself today, but I miss them so much.

Kyle: *Dad, Gramps was talking about buying me a go-kart, would that be okay?*

Of course he's trying to buy my son expensive gifts like that. They'll do just about anything to buy my kids' affection. I'm sure it's done with the hope that the kids will one day choose to live with them instead of me.

Kyle: *You could teach me how to drive it. I'd let you drive it too.*

Kyle: *What do you think Dad?*

That was the last message, and it was sent an hour ago.
I tap out my reply.

Me: *We can talk about it when I get to LA. Did you have fun at Disneyland too?*

Once I've read all of the messages, and caught up on my responses, I'm feeling slightly overwhelmed at the bombardment of feelings. After two full weeks of relaxation, being away from them and living at an island pace makes me wonder how I manage to keep this family together on a daily basis. Even when they're thousands of miles away, they're still mine. I glance at my phone to see the time. It's a little after seven in the evening in Hawaii, so it's after ten in LA. They're probably getting ready for bed so I go ahead and call them.

"Daddy!" I hear the phone clunk around, and then I hear Hannah at full volume. "Daddy?"

"Hi, love. How are you?"

"I'm fine. I'm tired. We walked all day today." Her voice drops an octave and I fight not to snicker at how quickly her tone changed from the cheery greeting I got when she answered. This kid can go from a hundred to zero in seconds.

"I had a long day too, but I'm happy to hear your voice."

"Me too. Goodnight, Daddy."

"Goodnight, Hannah. Let me say goodnight to your brother."

More clunking and then I hear Kyle say, "Goodnight, Dad."

"Goodnight, Kyle. I love you."

"Love you too."

And then they are gone. Just like that. I sigh and drop my phone on the nightstand. I love the peace and quiet of Maui, but damn, I miss them when I'm away. I drop back on my pillow and my mind drifts to Kayla. I wish she could see how great they are. She and I made awesome little humans but she's been cheated out of experiencing them and they've been cheated out of having a mother. And what a wonderful, loving mother she was too. I often wonder what Hannah would be like with a mom. She has zero memories of Kayla, and even though I'm relieved she doesn't grieve for her, I mourn for the relationship she's missed out on.

I sit back up and look around at my messy bed and chuckle. Who knew we were carrying around that much mud from our hike? It's not like we got in bed with our shoes on.

I grab the receiver of the hotel phone and dial Housekeeping. I'll need my bed made up again before the end of the night and I'd rather not have to face them when they see the mud. I'm sure they'll figure out what we've been up to...

# CHAPTER NINE

## Emily

As soon as my room door closes behind me, I drop onto my bed and cry. I'm not sure what I was expecting. Did I think I could be with another man and not feel the emotions that go along with it? That's impossible. I know that. I just need to work through it. I just need to keep moving forward. It's hard though. Especially when I can't really talk about it with Drew, not after we made a deal not to share personal information.

I close my eyes and pick up my phone. I hate to be such a baby, but I need to speak to someone and I know Rebecca will talk me off the cliff I shouldn't be dangling from.

"Well hello there, Islander. How's Maui treating you?" she answers.

I'm on the verge of a sob, so I hold my breath, fighting hard not to let it out.

"Emily, what's wrong?" The tone of her voice changes, and I can tell I've scared her.

I slowly release my breath and say, "I'm fine."

"No, you're not. Are you hurt? Has something happened?"

"No. I'm fine."

She's silent for a minute, and I know she's trying to size me up. "Did you sleep with the hot neighbor?"

That didn't take long. I'm fighting tears again, so I don't speak.

"I know you're feeling super guilty right now, but you need to stop. You haven't done anything wrong." She sighs heavily into the phone. "You knew this would be hard and it's okay that you're having trouble dealing. Especially since it's the first time since Tucker, but after a good cry, you need to let it go. There's nothing to feel bad about, I promise. Okay?"

She's right. I know that, and I guess that's why I called. I needed the reassurance. I need someone to tell me it's okay. I'm not sure why. Normally I'm a take-charge kind of person, but when it comes to my personal life, I hesitate. And since I lost Tuck, I question myself even more.

My breathing evens out, and I try to talk again. "I'm trying."

"I know you are. I also know how damn hard this is for you. I'm glad you called. I'm so damn thrilled to be the person you call when you need to cry. But more than anything, I know you need to hear me say to knock it off."

I chuckle and nod. "It's true."

"Okay." I hear her shift the phone and her voice grows a bit louder. "Emily Thomas Tucker, get up off your ass, brush yourself off, and take a step forward."

Instinctively, I stand up and walk toward the balcony. The slider is open a bit, so the air flows through my suite but not enough to let in the rain. I stare out at the darkness and take a cleansing breath. I wipe the tears from my cheeks. "Thank you."

"Now that we have the preliminaries out of the way—look at you, doing it in the middle of the afternoon! Give me some dirty details. Tell me."

"He's incredible."

"Details."

"I went hiking, and just as I reached the spot I wanted, this beautiful waterfall, rain started falling. I stupidly went hiking without checking the weather first."

"Oh, right, I heard a news report about a tropical storm. It's a downgraded hurricane."

"Well, just like when I locked myself out of the room yesterday, and when I got too drunk last night, Drew came to the rescue."

"No way!"

"Yes way. He showed up at that mountain waterfall to get me the hell out of there." I grin widely, I can't help it. "I was super pissed at first but the heavier it rained, the more thankful I was."

"Don't stop there."

"When we got back to the resort, we sort of pounced on each other. I'm not sure if it was the adrenaline from the storm or just pure exhaustion—"

"Um, or pure attraction," Bec says, interrupting me.

I throw my hand in the air in agreement. "Or pure attraction. That wouldn't be a lie. He's amazing."

"So, tell me about him."

"I don't know anything about him, except that he comes to Maui every year for three weeks and he's self-employed." I lower myself back into a chair and say, "We made a deal to avoid talking about anything outside of Maui."

"Wow! That falls right in line with your plan to have a vacation fling."

"Huh! You mean *your* plan for me to have a vacation fling."

"Yes, and I still think it's a good idea, but that doesn't mean you can't continue this relationship after your vacation. I just thought it would keep things light and, well, help you get past the nasty guilt you're feeling about Tuck."

My smile fades as I'm reminded of him. I close my eyes and wonder what he would do if roles were reversed. What if I died?

"Guilt is stupid, Emily, even if it's inevitable. Tucker would already be with someone else."

I laugh a little because I know she's right. He wasn't good alone, he liked companionship. Well, hell, so do I. I just want to skip the guilt part.

"It's been long enough, Em. You're allowed to have a life."

"I know that, but I still can't help thinking about him and about how this feels so much like cheating."

"Like I said, inevitable. Work through it. You have to because you need to move forward. You're much too young and vibrant to avoid living a full life."

My grin slides back into place as I say, "It was good though. Drew was more than I could have wished for. Too bad I can't keep him."

"Maybe you can, but even if you can't, he's great practice."

"You're right. I should just try to enjoy myself while I'm here. Use this chance to work through my issues about Tucker and learn to let him go."

*Let him go…*

As if that's so easy.

"Time makes everything easier. You just need to try having normal experiences. Eventually it will get easier, I promise."

"I know this transition is going to be hard. There's no point in dragging this poor man into my black hole of grief. It's better that I don't see him again after I return home."

"Maybe… but maybe not. You feel bad about it now, and you're fighting with guilt, but in a week or two, you might be a little more indifferent. Maybe after a couple more rounds with this guy, you won't feel any guilt or grief."

*If only…* I look down at my empty ring finger and wonder how different my life would be today if I hadn't lost him. I'd probably be a mother. We'd have a child… at least, that was part of our plan. Now I don't know if I'll ever have kids. I'm not sure I'll get the opportunity. The clock is ticking, and at thirty-three years old, I'm running out of time.

"You have years and years to worry about shit. Let this week be fun without the stress."

"You're right. Thank you so much for being there for me. I don't know what I'd do without you."

"You're welcome. I love you—go have some fun. Dance in the rain or something."

\*

When Drew knocks, my heart flutters in my chest. I don't know where we're having dinner, so I wasn't sure how to dress. Hopefully, my beige, sleeveless, sheath dress and wedge sandals are okay for where we're going.

I open the door to his smiling face. He's clean-shaven, and his hair is neatly in place. If my body wasn't reacting when he knocked, it certainly is now. I almost lose my breath when he swoops in and kisses me. My body sings with tingles from my scalp to my toes. Damn, he's sexy. I inhale deeply… and he smells sexy too. Like nutmeg and musky cologne.

I was afraid of awkwardness after our under-the-sheets encounter, but I much prefer we jump right to familiar. His lips dip to my neck, and I feel the nibble as he works his way down. I fight not to squirm, but I can't help it, I'm super ticklish. When I wiggle a little, he snickers and cups my face.

"I'm sorry, I forgot to say hello."

A little giddy from the look in his eyes, I mutter, "Hello."

"How are you?" His eyes dance between mine as if he's examining me. "You look happy, but your eyes are a little red. You haven't been crying, have you?"

My stomach bottoms out. This guy is good. Am I that transparent?

"Why would I be crying?" I scoff, trying to throw him off. "I'm perfectly happy."

His gaze softens. "Good."

"Where are we having dinner?" I ask, hoping to change the subject.

"I thought, if it's okay with you, that we could eat in the resort. There's a great little place over in the east wing, with lots of windows and a patio where we can enjoy the rain without getting wet."

"Sounds perfect." I reach my hand out for his, and the warmth of his hold is comforting, almost familiar.

We walk over to the east wing, and I take the opportunity to admire his assets. He's very well put together, but without trying too hard. He looks relaxed, but then he always does. I envy him that because I seldom do. But it's been a long time since I've felt this good. I sigh at the thought and know that Mac was right. I needed a break… or maybe Rebecca was right, and I just needed to get laid.

I realize now that when I mistook Drew for a maintenance man, I was being irritable and judgmental. He's just at ease and confident in his own way. His long, muscular, tanned legs hint at the great shape he's in and even in the cargo shorts he's wearing, I can see the curve of his perfectly formed ass. As I watch him walk, I fight the blush that creeps into my cheeks.

When Drew catches me looking, I quickly ask, "How's the leg?"

"It's fine, I washed all the dirt out in the shower and rubbed ointment on it. I'm sure it looks worse than it is." As we approach the restaurant, he asks, "How about your ankle?"

I turn my leg to show him the small bandage. "It's fine, just a small gash."

Following the waitress to our table, I'm struck by the simple elegance of the place. At first glance, it doesn't look fancy, but once inside and seated, the delicate touches are obvious. Crisp white table linens and fine-bone china. We're surrounded by windows and stained glass and the room glows in subtle candlelight. It's still pouring with rain outside but the wind seems to have slowed some. The table we're seated at gives us a great view of the pool, with shadows of the trees blowing through the rain. The resort has removed all the loungers and the place looks a little deserted—I sort of like it this way.

After serving us ice water and giving us menus, the waitress leaves us alone. I glance across the table at Drew, and he's staring at me. He looks serious, which is quite a change from his usual playful expression. I glance down at myself, feeling self-conscious.

My dress isn't showing too much cleavage, my teeth have been brushed, and my hair is neatly pinned into a bun on the back of my head. When I look back up at him, I ask, "Is something wrong?"

"I owe you an apology."

"You do?"

"I'm sorry about conspiring with Gerry to find out where you were earlier. I'm sorry if that came across as overbearing."

"Oh, huh." I lower the menu to the table so I can see him fully. "No, you did nothing wrong. I'm sorry for being so sensitive. I just…" I tilt my head down and push at the hair at the back of my neck, not sure what to say. "I guess I'm just not used to people being concerned for my wellbeing."

"How can that be? Your brother obviously cares about you."

"Yes, oh sure, I have plenty of people who love and care about me. I mean…" I roll my eyes. I'm stalling, and I need to stop beating around the bush. "I mean, a man… specifically."

"Oh, I see."

I build up the nerve to look up at him again, and when I do, he's still staring at me. "Why is that, Emily?" He reaches out and takes my hand. "You're smart, funny, beautiful. Why has it been so long since a man has made you feel like you deserve more?"

Shaking my head, I reply, "You're breaking the rule. Remember?"

"Fuck the rule."

My eyes widen at his response, and I feel tension through the hand he's holding. "We can't just make rules and then break them."

"Now see, statements like that make me think you're a lawyer."

I laugh at that. How much more spot on can he be? Why bother hiding who I am when I'm so easily figured out?

"But I know you're not a lawyer. You're much too nice for that."

"Lawyers aren't nice?"

"No, they're sharks."

I stifle a smile at that. "Oh, so you're divorced."

"Actually—"

I throw my hand up. "No, don't tell me. Stick to the rule."

"Listen, Emily, when I said I didn't want to talk about anything outside of Maui, it was because I wanted you to feel relaxed. I sensed you needed that. It wasn't because I didn't want to get to know you."

"But, Drew, you can't deny telling each other more would complicate this. What if we live thousands of miles from each other? What if we have kids, ex-wives, different political parties? It could be disastrous."

Drew removes his hand from mine, and I sense I touched a nerve. "To be honest," he says, "I don't really care if you have an ex-wife."

I laugh hard. Too hard. With my hand on my belly, I realize other people in the restaurant are looking at me, but it feels good. For once I'm not worried about how I look. When I finally stop, my smile lingers on my lips. "I like you, I really do, but I'm not in the position to..." Tucker comes to mind, and with his memory, my smile fades completely. I can't help it. Between sitting with this man, who I'm surprised to find I really like, and laughing so hard it hurts, I'm reminded that Tuck isn't here, and he can't laugh. I'm reminded that I need to move on, but that moving on will probably be very messy and I'm not sure I want to put Drew through that. "Because I like you, I feel like I need to spare you from what may be a terrible and confusing time for me."

"So, you're going through a divorce? Is that right?" He leans back in his chair. "When I first met you, I sensed you'd been hurt. I see the sadness in your eyes."

I don't say anything. I don't need his sympathy. I need his understanding.

"Do you have children?" His eyes narrow and he shoots me another question. "New York?"

I don't respond, which pushes him to keep going.

"Can't be New York though, can it? I mean, you look like it fits. Buttoned up, the way you are. That take-no-shit stance and not wanting to be rescued... especially by a man. New York fits, but it's still wrong, isn't it?"

Curiosity pushes me to ask, "Why?"

"For one, you try like hell to come across as cold, but you're not." From the twinkle in his eyes, I know he's referring to earlier.

"People do often accuse me of being cold or unemotional." Since losing Tucker, I don't like pity so I fight to hide my grief.

He watches me, and I'm a little scared of what he's going to say next. So far, he's been pretty spot on. "You're not cold though. Not from what I've seen. Just reserved."

"Hum, you said *for one*. What's the second reason I can't be from New York?"

He shrugs. "That's easy, because it rains in New York. It rains a lot. You're from a place that's suffering from a drought."

I feel the heat in my face. What can I say? The guy's observant.

"But not Los Angeles either. Right?" He lifts his water glass to his lips, and when he sets it back down, he says, "You're not conceited enough or tra-la-la enough for LA."

"Tra-la-la?" I repeat with a raised brow.

His eyes close, then he shakes his head. "It doesn't matter. You're not from LA, are you?"

"No, I'm not."

When the waitress approaches to take our orders, Drew's eyebrows lift conspiratorially and he asks, "Mai Tai?"

I can't help the laugh that bursts from me. "No, absolutely not." And as I order, I'm thankful for the interruption. Drew's questions are intense, and I'm not sure how much longer I can refrain from telling him everything.

# CHAPTER TEN

## Drew

Dinner was quiet and full of small talk after she refused to answer any of my questions. I feel bad for putting her on the spot, but I'm not so sure I'm willing to walk away from her without some answers. What was I thinking when I made up that stupid rule? If I'd realized how much I'd want to get to know her, I never would have said that. Now I have less than three days to change her mind.

At least, that's what I want to do... But my mind drifts to when she said, *what if one of us has children*? After hearing that, I can't pretend she wouldn't care that I'm a father. Most women don't want to date single dads. I've been on many first dates. Second dates, not so much. Once they hear about my family, they don't stick around.

Maybe she's right. Maybe we should stick to our rule. Maybe this is just meant to be a vacation tryst. It wouldn't be my first.

When she slides her keycard through the lock and enters her room, I stand back. I'm not sure she wants me to stay, and I don't want to assume. She glances over her shoulder at me and her mouth tips into a grin. "Join me?"

I purse my lips and nod as I follow her inside. The door shuts hard, and the room is still dark. Emily doesn't turn any lights on, and all I can see is her silhouette. She drops her bag on the table and slips out of her shoes. Her hair is still tightly bound in the bun, and all I want is to pull the pins out and watch her thick, caramel locks drop to her shoulders.

When she turns toward me, I tug her closer. I'm taller by a few inches, so I have to look down to see her face. Lifting my hands to her shoulders, I caress her neck before running my fingers up to the bun on her head. I find the end of a pin and tug it free, then another two. When the last pin is free, her hair drops halfway down her back with a sexy sway. As it falls, the scent of her shampoo fills my nostrils. Coconut and vanilla. I run my hands through her hair and revel in the silk, then lift a handful to my nose and inhale.

"Why do you keep all these luscious locks all tied up?"

"Hmmm," she hums against my chest. "I don't know, I guess because it's tidy."

"Well, stop it." I drop my hands to her face and tilt it up so I can kiss her. There's a hint of light shining through from outside, and it's just enough to highlight one side of her face. Her porcelain skin is warm to the touch, and I can't stop staring at her. I can't even stop long enough to take her lips with mine. Our eyes lock, and I so badly want to know what's going on inside that head of hers—I want to know her.

"What's your favorite color?" It's a question but not personal enough to be against the rules.

"Favorite color?" she asks, and her brows draw together. "Blue, but red is a close second. Why?"

"Red?" I pluck at the strap of her beige dress. "I'd never guess."

"I know... I only have boring business clothes."

"Okay, moving on. Coffee or tea?"

She chuckles, and I feel it shake her body. "Coffee. Definitely coffee."

"Cake or ice cream?"

Her head tilts a fraction of an inch. "It's cruel to ask me to choose between cake and ice cream. They go together, like peanut butter and jelly."

I beam at her answer, and now I have to kiss her. There's nothing like peanut butter and jelly to bring two strangers together. When our lips meet, hers are warm and soft, slightly wet, and she tastes like the full-bodied Malbec wine she drank with dinner. I want to devour her. I want to ride her... Hell, I want her to ride me. I back her against the wall and slide my hands down her arms until I link my fingers with hers. I add pressure until she's flush against the wall.

"Do you trust me?"

Her blue eyes widen, and one side of her mouth lifts up. "If you were going to do something terrible, it would have been last night when I was stinking drunk."

"That doesn't answer my question."

"Yes."

The steady and sure sound of her answer sends a surge right through me. I push against her hands until they're pinned to the wall as well. My instincts kick in from there.

My dick is rock-hard as I grind against her. She pushes back, and a sharp cry breaks from her lips when I hit the perfect spot between her legs. That sound is sexy as hell and drives me forward, teasing her, and enticing her higher. I can feel the tension in her body as I trail my tongue and lips all the way down her throat.

She tries to break free, so I loosen my grip and release her, but before she can touch me, I spin her around, pressing her front against the wall. Again, I trap her hands as my erection presses against her firm ass.

She pants in surprise and all I can think about is that tight little bun coming loose... just like her tight little body is coming loose right now, in my arms. It's true, there's nothing cold about Emily. The way she comes alive when touched is proof of that. She just needs to be touched properly. Treated like the treasure she is. No, she's not cold… not in the least.

My weight pins her to the wall, my knees are bent, and my dick is rubbing insanely hard against her ass. No matter how hard I press against her, she's pushing back. She's on her toes with her ass in the air, begging for more. I lower my hand and wedge it between her and the wall, sliding it down between her legs.

Now that she's free, Emily reaches down and tugs her skirt up, freeing her legs and granting me access. I slide my hand under her panties and then inside her. She's soaking wet, and when my finger grazes her clit, she jerks hard.

"You're so ready, sweetness."

Her ass lifts against me, and as it does, she hikes her skirt higher, spreading her legs farther for me. I slid my knee between them, and she starts grinding against it.

"Fuck me, I want you, Emily." I release her other wrist and grip the zipper on the back of her dress, jamming it down as quickly as I can. I push the shoulder straps until they're falling, and faster than I expect, Emily shimmies her arms out and lets the dress drop to the floor. She's smoking hot in her white lace bra and thong, and her pale skin looks delicious. I have to taste her.

Without hesitation, my teeth sink into her bare shoulder, and at the same time, Emily's hand clamps down on my hip. I grab it and lift it high above her head, pressing it against the wall. Then I slowly withdraw my finger from her slick clit. When I do, she protests with a loud moan. I lift her other hand to join the first. "Don't move."

"Drew, oh, God." With these cries, I press my erection against her again.

"Don't move, sweetness." When she's still, I quickly pop the button on my shorts and shed my clothes, somehow never losing contact with her.

I can tell she wants to turn around. She's itching to touch something, but I've got her where I want her. I consider it my duty to make sure she walks away unable to forget my touch. Unable to forget how fucking hot we are together.

With one hand back between her legs, and the other tangled in those long, silky locks of hair, I pull her from the wall and turn her toward the low-back, blue velvet armchair. Then I slowly push her over the back of the chair. She leans forward and grasps the arms, lifting her ass to me.

My cock slides between her legs, rubbing up and down her wetness, and Emily's moving with the motion. I can tell she's close already. Her body is taut but completely reactive, and dammit, I want her. But I don't have a condom on yet.

I drop to my knees and nip at Emily's hip as I slowly lower her thong down her thighs. At the same time, I pull my wallet out of the pocket of my shorts and remove the condom stashed there.

Thank fucking Christ, because I'm not sure how much more I can take. I free the condom from the packet and slide it on.

"Drew…" Her sultry voice sounds tense, and I know she's losing her patience.

"No worries, sweetness, we're done playing."

I rub my cock between her legs again until she's grinding against me, and then I slide into her. Gentle at first, moving all the way in. When I'm deep inside her, I hear a sexy little gasp and when I feel the tightness around my dick, I can't hold back. I grab her hips and lift her slightly before plunging in again and again. It's not long at all until I feel her tighten around me even more. She's crying out as she comes, and as her back straightens and lifts toward me, I quickly unsnap the back of her bra and free her breasts. Within seconds, my hands are clamped onto them, holding firmly. They're amazing and I can feel the sway of their weight as I thrust inside her. As I'm holding on, the motion sends me spiraling.

I fight not to collapse on top of her, but it's hard to maintain my balance. We're both panting, and there's sweat dripping down my face. Jesus.

Once I catch my breath, I lift Emily off her feet. She weighs barely anything, and as I hold her against me, she's motionless. I lay her on the bed without bothering to turn the blankets down. Even with the rain, it's warm as hell. Emily curls against me and rests her head on my shoulder. She's quiet but so am I—it's as if we want to preserve the moment.

We're both exhausted from today, but I'm wide awake. Relaxed, even though my mind won't shut down. When Emily shifts, I realize she's not sleeping either. She lifts up to look at me. "Are you sleepy?" She's tousled and absolutely adorable with waves of thick hair draped down around her shoulders.

"No, not at all. How about you?"

"Wide awake. I don't think I've acclimated to the time change yet." This makes me wonder how off she is from her regular time. If she's from California, the time difference is three hours, but if she's from Boston, it's six hours earlier than she's used to. She sits up and crosses her legs in front of her… and I like the view. At least until she throws the sheet over her lap.

"Let's go do something."

I rest my hands behind my head and lift an eyebrow. "Or we could just stay in bed and do something."

She grins and even in the dark, I can see the crimson creep into her cheeks. She looks away and as she focuses on the storm outside, her eyes narrow. I follow her gaze and realize the storm has died down a little. She pats my chest and says, "Let's go outside, play in the rain."

"Really?"

She's up and out of bed before I can say anything else. I sit up and watch as she searches for something to wear. With a shrug, I get out of bed and throw my clothes on.

"Let's do it."

We rush out the back entrance to the resort, near the beach and beach path, which runs nearly the entire length of Kaanapali shores. It's still raining pretty steadily, but the wind is bearable, and it's pretty warm. The ocean's calmed slightly too. There are still some swells, but not enough to make the beach unsafe. The crashing sounds are hypnotizing. I could listen to that sound forever and never tire of it.

There are lanterns lighting the path and in the glow I can clearly see Emily's ear-to-ear grin. We head down the path together and she's laughing as she lifts her face to the rain. I glance around to see if we're the only crazy people out here and I'm thrilled to find we are. She skips down the path, looking like she doesn't have a care in the world.

Now this isn't the same woman I met yesterday in the business suit, spiked heels, and tight bun. No, this woman is enjoying life. Hair down, mouth open to catch the raindrops, and spinning around like she's standing under a beam of sunshine. I chuckle as I watch her and when she hears me, she tilts her head in my direction.

Her joy illuminates her entire face and I love it.

"I'm ridiculous, right?"

"Adorable. Not ridiculous."

She hops over and plants a kiss on my cheek. "Thanks for indulging me." I grab her before she can get away and hold her against me. I push the wet hair off her face and take her lips with mine. The heat between us is intense and I'm tempted to take her right here, on the path. I lift from the kiss and check for other people.

"Want to go sit on the beach?"

Her body tenses and she shakes her head, her eyes changing from joyful to sad. What did I say? I kiss her again, hoping to take the sadness away. When I pull back this time, I see something else in her eyes. Something I can't decipher. I sway with her in my arms and dance her around a little, hoping to make her happy again.

It works. She's beaming as she mutters, "We're dancing in the rain."

We stay like this for several minutes and we're completely soaked, but I don't care.

"Winter, spring, summer, or fall?"

With her eyes locked on mine, she says, "Spring."

When we're done we continue hand in hand for a while. There are small puddles of water on the concrete path and Emily joyfully stomps her feet, splashing water on both of us. Again, I'm reminded of my little Hannah. After another half an hour or so, I see Emily yawn and I turn her back toward our resort and we wander back slowly.

When we're inside her room, we strip off our wet clothes and crawl into bed, our bodies heavy with exhaustion. Within seconds, Emily's breathing levels out and she's asleep.

I listen to her for a long time, enjoying the warmth of her plastered against my body. Within a few minutes, my body reacts to her lying naked next to me. I don't wake her though, I want her to rest. Besides, letting her sleep gives me time to figure out how I'm going to get her to tell me where she's from. I want to find out as much as I can about her. I'm sure I could Google her, but Thomas is a very popular name. There could be a million Emily Thomases out there.

Shifting to my side, I wrap an arm around her and nuzzle into her hair with a sigh. It's nice to fall asleep with someone. It's been a long time. Sex is one thing, but having someone to laugh with and enjoy my days with is priceless. Could Emily become that? I have until the end of the week to find out...

# CHAPTER ELEVEN

## Emily

*What is that?*

I squeeze my eyes shut, trying to block it out. Then my eyes pop open, and I hear Drew's voice say, *Good morning, Hannah*, and see him buttoning his cargo shorts and slipping outside with his cell phone to his ear.

Damn, he looks good without a shirt on. So tanned and he's sporting a perfect trail of hair down the center of his abs. He turns toward the ocean and gives me a view of his broad shoulders and narrow hips. It should be illegal for men who look this good to wear shirts. I stay still and watch him as I'm trying to wake up. The noise I heard must have been his ringtone. Then it occurs to me.

*Who's Hannah?*

*He told me he wasn't attached.*

*Do I want to know?*

*Of course, I want to know!*

Son of a bitch. If he's married, I'll kill him! I'll call Hannah myself, whoever she is, and tell her what he's done. But why would he spend three weeks alone in Maui if he's married?

I close my eyes again and realize that this is all too much to think about without coffee. I make my way to the bathroom and throw on a robe.

Just as I get the coffee brewing, Drew comes back into the room.

"I'm so sorry if my phone woke you."

I brush a hand and say, "I should get up anyway."

"Why? You're on vacation."

I stare at him and consider that.

"Honestly, I don't know."

He chortles as he approaches and leans in for a kiss. I draw back a little, staring up at him with a raised eyebrow.

"Who's Hannah?"

His eyes widen, and it looks as if he's trying to decide whether or not he wants to lie about it.

"Do you really want to know?"

"She's not a girlfriend, wife... lover?"

"None of those things, I swear."

I'm not sure I believe him.

"Yes, I want to know who she is."

He inhales deeply, his eyes blinking rapidly, and I almost feel like he's trying to come up with a story.

"Hannah is my roommate."

I withdraw a little more.

"Roommate? Really?"

"Yes, really. I only went outside because I didn't want to wake you."

"Roommate?" I ask again. "Do you and your roommate share a bedroom?"

"I don't share a bedroom with either of my roommates, but I do share my house with them."

I start to pull away from him.

"You live with two women?"

His faces twitches as if he's confused.

"No, Emily! I have two roommates, Hannah and Kyle."

I stare into his eyes, waiting for some proof that he's lying to me. I don't know what I'm expecting, but I pray he's being honest.

"Roommates, huh? Why two?"

"Um… well, I have the space and I don't like living alone. Why does it matter? The point is, I wasn't lying when I said I wasn't attached. I'm not in a romantic relationship with anyone but you."

My heart leaps when I hear this, but I don't react because this *isn't* a relationship. I have to remember that. I nod and set out two coffee mugs. "Drew, I hope you're telling the truth. I couldn't forgive myself if I found out I was sleeping with a married man."

"I'm not married, and I haven't been in a relationship in over a year and a half."

"What happened?" I ask, interested now.

"You want to know? That's against the rule."

"I'm just curious. You don't have to be specific."

He shrugs. "It was short-lived. We met at a friend's barbeque, we hung out for a few weeks, we had a lot of fun, and when reality set in, we ended it."

"Reality?"

"Yeah, you know, everyday life."

Oh, I know.

"I'm sorry. My attitude is oddly overbearing considering I don't really know you. I just…"

"I understand. I wouldn't appreciate being lied to about that either. I'm not interested in wrecking homes." He steps toward me again, and this time I let him kiss me. "However, you got to ask a personal question, now I want one too. It's only fair."

I swallow and feel heat blush my checks.

"That's a dirty trick. I didn't know we were playing quid pro quo. But okay, go ahead."

"Without specifics, I want to know how long it's been since your last relationship."

I raise an eyebrow at him. "How am I supposed to answer that without being specific? I already told you it's been a long time."

"Days, months, or years?"

Hell. I really don't want to think about Tucker when I'm with Drew. It's hard enough to fight the guilt without the reminder. I sigh and pour myself a cup of coffee now that it's done brewing. Then I lift my mug, walk to the small table, and sit near the open lanai door. Drew pours a cup too and follows me over. Watching me. Waiting for an answer.

He looks at me pointedly.

Staring into my mug, I say, "Years."

Drew doesn't say anything. When I glance up at him, he's looking into his own cup now too, with a frown on his face, but then he meets my eyes.

"Why did it end?"

"That's two questions, and I don't want to talk about it."

"You don't have to be specific, just tell me how."

"That's ridiculous." I huff in aggravation, but Drew doesn't care how uncomfortable I am. He's waiting for an answer. I swallow the lump in my throat. It's been nearly four years since Tuck died, but that doesn't keep me from tearing up when I think about his death. Not to mention all the feelings I'm dealing with about being with another man. "Badly," I mumble, turning my face away from him. "It ended badly."

"I'm sorry, Emily."

I'm still trying to fight my emotions, so I don't speak. I inhale then let out a slow breath before sipping my coffee, savoring how strong it is. I don't know if Drew can tell I'm upset, but I don't want to look at him.

"It must have ended badly if it's been years and you're still this affected by it."

I nod because there isn't really anything I can say to that.

He stands and paces the room. Is he angry? He finally stops in front of me and squats down so that we're eye to eye.

"Emily, were you hurt? Did someone do something to hurt you?"

I'm confused at first but after seeing the fire in his eyes, I understand. "No, not like that. Nobody has ever physically hurt me." I see the instant relief in him, but he's still watching me, and I feel like he's reading me. Like I'm an open book, which I am not. I know that about myself. That's the one thing my friends and family complain about. I don't talk about myself... or my feelings, or anything personal at all.

Suddenly his eyes change, and I'm not sure how to describe his new expression. "Was it divorce... no." He shakes his head, examining me like I'm a puzzle that needs to be solved.

I brush him aside and stand to get some space between us. "You know, Drew, maybe you should go."

"What?" He's standing now too and approaches me. "No, don't do that, Emily." He draws my name out in a plea, and I feel bad, but I don't think I can do this. It's too much, too soon.

"No, I don't think this was a good idea. We should've stuck to the rule."

He reaches out for me, but I can't help pulling away, the emotion building in me.

"Why?" he asks, and his tone has changed. I think he's mad now, but I'm not sure.

"I told you I don't want to talk about it, but you keep pushing."

"I'm sorry. I'll stop. Don't make me go. We have three more days. If you don't want to continue with this after we leave, at least spend the next three days with me... or let's take it one day at a time. Okay?"

I drop my head and nod, but I know I won't be able to go through with it if I'm constantly trying to dodge questions about Tucker. Questions that make me doubt what I'm doing. Questions that remind me of my loss. When I feel his hands touch my face, I lift my head to look at him.

His eyes don't hold pity. They hold hope. I'm not sure that's much better.

When he kisses me, I lift up and into his embrace. I miss being held like this. I miss the feeling of being wanted and desired. I realize I'll never be able to repay Drew for giving me that again. But this conversation is a perfect example of why this won't work long term. I want this. I fucking want to feel these things again but I also hate myself for it, even though I know it's *not* wrong.

Moving on is hard. Fighting to keep from drowning in my guilt and emotions over the next few weeks is going to be tough. No man wants to deal with that in a new relationship. Add God knows how much distance to that relationship and you have a recipe for disaster.

No, that's just not in the cards for me, which makes this deal we've made perfect. I need this… *fling.*

"Emily, spend the next three days with me. I promise you won't regret it." His golden eyes are so sincere, and looking into them, I have no doubt I'm going to have some regrets when this is over.

*

I've only known Drew a few days… well, technically four days if you count my first day here, but I feel like I've known him much longer. He's so easy-going and so much fun to hang out with. I'm not sure what this trip would have been like without him.

On Thursday, we agree to spend the rest of the day on the beach after our morning helicopter tour of the island. It's a perfect day, with the sun shining brightly and the sky is completely cloudless for the first time since I arrived. We rent a cabana and to be honest, I didn't want to visit the beach, but once I'm settled in and enjoying the sounds of the ocean lapping the sand, I'm glad to be here.

I used to love the beach. Beach trips were a regular thing for Tucker and me. We actually met on a group surfing trip in Southern California. We had mutual friends, and after a weekend with each other and our friends in Huntington Beach, we were inseparable.

After we were married, surfing in the Pacific and rafting in the river were our favorite pastimes. We both loved the water, and even when I couldn't find the time to go with him, Tucker would spend his free time outdoors, and usually in the water.

I should have been with him for every trip, savoring every single moment. I worked too much when I should have focused on my family, focused on him. Instead, I spent most of my time working on my career.

Since his death I've completely avoided the beach. This week, I would have been perfectly happy admiring the ocean from my lanai. I had a lot of reasons for not wanting to come to Hawaii for my vacation, but thanks to Drew, I'm actually enjoying myself.

I lay my head back and close my eyes. It's really a perfect day... if only I could keep the memories away. When I hear Drew approach the cabana, I open my eyes. He has a huge grin on his face.

"What are you smiling about?"

He points to his chest. "Me? I'm smiling at my awesome luck."

"What are you talking about?"

"My luck. You know, because I get to spend the rest of the day on the beach with the hottest babe here."

I have to laugh at this. "It's been ages since someone has called me a hot babe."

"Oh, I'm sure someone has. They just didn't do it when you could hear them." He holds up a net bag full of some kind of equipment. "How about some snorkeling?"

The smile drops from my face. I stare at him, praying he's joking.

"Snorkeling," he says again, and I sense he's hoping for a different reaction.

I shake my head. "Great. Have fun."

"No, you're going with me. We can do it here, that's why I picked this beach for us."

"Drew, I can't snorkel. I don't like the water."

I swallow hard, trying to tamper down my reaction. Everything in my body is rejecting the idea of getting in that water, but I'm fighting pretty damn hard to keep from showing it.

He looks perplexed. "Seriously? You're in Hawaii. Why did you come here if you don't like water?"

I lift from my resting position to lean in closer. "My brother planned this trip. I told you that."

He sits down and turns to face me. "You don't like the water..." He shakes his head and asks, "Are you afraid? Did something happen to make you fear the water?"

Pulling my sunglasses from my face, I meet his confused eyes. I stare at him, wishing he understood without actually having to tell him. I don't know if I can bear to form the words. I can see from his expression that he wants to understand, but he doesn't.

"I'll be right next to you the entire time. I'm a great swimmer... I promise you'll be safe, Emily. I wouldn't put you in danger."

Yeah, Tucker was a great swimmer too. So great a swimmer he thought he could risk his life without consequences... until he *lost* his life.

The weight of this is heavy. Too heavy to bear right now. I drop my head and give myself a little pep talk, trying to shift this awful, all-too-familiar feeling. I can't spend my life going through this over and over. I need to move forward, I need to move on. It's what I want. It's what Tucker would want... but the idea of getting in that ocean has me shaking.

I lift my eyes and look at Drew again. He's trying so hard to understand, I can see that. He grips my jittery hands. "Emily, this should be part of moving forward for you. Even though I don't know why, I feel like I need to push you to do this. My instinct is telling me." He waves at the equipment. "Maybe not snorkeling, but I feel like you need to get in that water. You need to beat whatever this is."

I know he's right. I don't get how he knew or what outside force is at work, but he's absolutely right. I blink away the emotions that are fighting to show and mumble, "You're right. I do need to do this and... purge this"—I motion outward with my hands—"Purge this awful shit from my system... or at least I need to try."

He takes my elbow and pulls me from the lounger.

"Come on."

When we reach the edge of the water, I stop. My entire body is vibrating from the stress and my heart is heavy. I feel the weight of what I've been through for the last four years. Every second of every minute of every day I've spent without Tucker in my life. There must be some sort of a spiritual exercise involving the ocean and grief that applies to moments like these, but I'll be damned if I can think of one.

I glance up at Drew, and he's patiently waiting for me. I must look like a serious idiot. I turn to look around, but he's the only person watching me. I meet his eyes and say, "I'm sorry for being so ridiculous."

"Stop it. You don't need to be sorry about anything. You be whatever you need to be, and if that's ridiculous, so be it."

This makes me laugh. I love how he didn't deny my ridiculousness but embraced it instead. "You're incredible. Do you know that?"

"Nah." He shakes his head. "I'm just trying to be here for you."

"Thank you."

He reaches over and takes my hand.

"Ready?"

I chuckle, and it sounds funny because I'm feeling emotional again. We step into the ocean together, my heart thumping, and I breathe in, then out.

The farther into the water I go, the lighter I feel, as if I'm shedding something. I go as far as waist-deep, and as the waves roll over and past me, I feel better. I keep going, and I can feel Drew's presence next to me the entire time. He still has my hand gripped in his and I turn toward him.

"It feels good," I say, and I feel a sense of relief flow through me. I never thought this could be possible.

His smile is full of pride and again, I'm reminded of just how wonderful he is. The poor man has no idea why this is hard for me, but here he is, right next to me, my rock nonetheless. I reach out for him and pull him against me.

"I'm so lucky."

"Why are you lucky?"

"Because I'm with the hottest babe on the beach."

Drew drags his lips to mine in a deep, slow kiss, and as I sink into him, I wish so much that I could keep him.

# CHAPTER TWELVE

## Drew

I'm not sure what wakes me. Maybe it's the loss of Emily's heat next to me or the sound of crashing waves streaming in from the open windows but I'm surprised to find myself alone in her rumpled bed and still naked from making love with her.

I lift my head and glance around. That's when I see her, sitting alone outside in the dark, wrapped in a robe with her chin resting on her knees as she stares out at the dark sea.

I slowly creep out of bed and dress in the matching robe. When I peek my head out, she turns to look at me. It's dark, but I can still see her sad expression. She quickly wipes the tears from her face.

"Everything okay?"

She nods but doesn't speak.

"May I join you?"

She nods again, but then says, "Of course."

I sit in the chair next to hers and stare out. There's not much to see, except the lighted beach path several floors below and a hint of the surf hitting the sand. It's barely illuminated from the path lights, but just enough to highlight the whitecaps.

I lift my face to the breeze and inhale the sea air. It's an odd mix of salt water and the natural flora of Maui... and even the distinct scent of Emily lingering on my skin from earlier. After giving her a few minutes, I tilt my head over and say, "Are you upset about today at the beach?"

She takes a deep, steadying breath then blows it out slowly. "Yeah, but probably not for the reason you think."

"Do you want to talk about it? I'm a good listener."

She reaches over and links her fingers with mine. "I believe that about you."

I lift our joined hands up and kiss the backs of hers. "I'm here and you can say anything to me."

She blows a strand of hair off her face and looks back out to the ocean. "I wouldn't know where to begin."

"Well, the beginning is usually a great place. But I can take a guess if you want." I have a feeling I understand more than she could possibly imagine—I know because I've been where she is.

She glances over and lifts a doubtful eyebrow so I accept the challenge.

"Did you lose someone, Emily… are you a widow?"

Her eyes widen in surprise and she shifts slightly in her chair. "How could you possibly have guessed that?" Her voice is heavy, but I think she's too surprised to care about hiding her emotions.

I shrug, not really surprised my guess was spot on. "The bellman called you Mrs. Thomas, you didn't correct him." When she gives me an incredulous look, I say, "That and you're out here, alone and crying, after a couple of rounds of really great sex. I certainly don't want to believe you're crying because you didn't enjoy it, so I can only assume it's guilt."

She drops her chin, letting her gaze fall to the sea once more. "Well, you're right." She's quiet now so I give her time to get her bearings. "He drowned almost four years ago."

Hearing this feels like a punch to the gut—I wasn't expecting it. Now the entire day comes into focus and I get it. *Jesus Christ.* I shift in my seat so that I'm facing her.

"I'm so sorry, honey. If I'd known that, I wouldn't have pushed you at the beach today."

"No, you were right, I needed to get in the water. I used to love the beach. Still do, but I've stayed away since losing him."

"So, you really were crying the other night when I picked you up for dinner."

"Yeah, and you're ever so perceptive."

"Is he the reason you're sticking hard and fast to this rule of not sharing personal information?"

She nods and I see another tear slip down her face. "I have many, many reasons. I could sit here and list a dozen reasons why this is a bad idea." She looks pointedly at me. "I realize four years is a long time to still feel like this; the stuff I'm dealing with didn't die when he died. For one, this entire vacation is hard for me. I was so wrapped up in my career, I never took the time to travel with him. And now I'm doing it alone. I took him for granted while he was here and now he's gone and it's too late. That's something I have to live with every day."

"It's not too late for you to have a life."

"I know that. My head knows that, but my heart is still trying to cope. My real point here, Drew, is that I don't think the next few weeks are going to be easy for me and I'm not willing to put you through my mood swings or force you to put up with my emotional baggage."

"What if I told you I don't mind?"

"I'm sorry, but it just won't work, Drew. I like you, I'm loving the time we're spending together. I can't begin to tell you how wonderful it was to swim in the ocean today, and you gave me that. I've had fun and I've really tried to come out of my shell of grief. But if I'm being honest, I'm not sure I'm ready for something more permanent. I don't want to ruin this. I want to go home with my good memories of you, and of this trip, intact."

"Or, just maybe, I'm exactly what you need when you get home?" I squeeze her hand and say, "How do you know if we don't try?"

"And what if we live on opposite sides of the country? How is that going to help me?"

"What if we don't?"

"What if we do?" Her voice raises and her tone is heavy again. "I can't take on a long-distance relationship. It would be like going in reverse when I'm trying so hard to move forward."

I can't argue with that. I understand too well what it's like to lose someone. I think of Kayla and I want to tell Emily about her, but I can't, not here and not now. I wouldn't dare try to throw my grief in her face when she's clearly trying so hard to cope with hers. I also can't argue with her reasoning. She's right about a long-distance relationship, that would be incredibly hard for me too, but at least I'm willing to try.

I blow out a breath, knowing exactly what that means: I get to be her vacation fling. The one who helps her move on from her marriage and her grief. I did the same thing two years after losing my wife. I came to Maui and screwed everything and anything in a skirt. Several nameless women who were all interested in having a good time and nothing else.

It helped… for a while. Months after returning home, I realized I needed something more steady, but if it hadn't have been for those weeks of sowing my oats, I don't know if I could have had a real relationship. Of course, none of those real relationships have worked out. I'm not sure what I was expecting, but I thought I'd eventually find someone who was interested in having a relationship with my kids as well. Apparently, Emily isn't that person either.

Emily pulls our entwined hands to her lap. "Are you terribly disappointed?"

I try not to frown when I say, "I am disappointed, but I can't pretend I don't understand. I just want to make sure *you* understand that I'm not looking to escape the difficult time you're having. I'm willing to put in the time and help you work through it. I'm not afraid of that. So, don't pretend you're doing this for my benefit."

"I appreciate that, more than you know, and I recognize that this is something I've decided. I own that decision. I promise I won't blame you later if I have any regrets."

*If.*

I guess I'd better step up my game to ensure she has some regrets about losing me. I refuse to go down without a fight. I don't want to be some fleeting memory of a past vacation. I want to be someone she can't live without.

With my eyes locked on hers, I lower myself to the ground in front of her and pull her feet off the chair, then I push open the robe and spread her knees. I move in between her legs and grip her hips, pulling her rear closer to the edge of the chair. Then I drape her legs over my shoulders and lean forward, licking inside her. I feel the tension ease and her body relax in the chair. A moan escapes and I devour her, using my tongue and grazing my teeth gently over her clit.

"Oh God, Drew, what are you doing to me?" She starts moving with the motion and her legs tighten behind my head as her fingers snake through my hair and grip it.

Jesus, she tastes good. What am I going to do when she's out of my life and I'm alone again? I dread that day. I dread the day I can't hear her voice or taste her skin or smell her sweet scent.

*

I'm all packed and what I haven't shipped home already is loaded into the trunk of my rental car. As much as I miss the kids, it's hard to leave Maui. It's fucking killing me that I still don't know anything about Emily. But that's not true. I know a lot about Emily, about her likes, dislikes, I can tell when she's holding something back, and I know when she's totally over-the-moon happy. I know what heartbreak she's been through. I just don't know things like where she's from, or what she does for a living. What her family is like or her actual phone number. I even feel like I know her better than a lot of people might, but that hasn't gotten me closer to being able to contact her once I leave this island. Leaving her and knowing I have no way of reaching her is just torturous.

I've fought hard not to get too attached over the last few days but some things are inevitable. I've lightly touched on the idea of staying in contact a couple of times, but she's steadfast. I get it too. She doesn't want to be in a long-distance relationship. It's too hard. She needs time to adjust to being a single woman. She needs to date and experience life without strong attachments. She needs time to come to grips with her grief and with the guilt she's going to experience now that she's dating again and moving on with her life. I understand because I've been there.

But, *what if…*

*What if* keeps repeating in my head. What if it's not long distance? What if we live close? What if she and I together are right? What if this is what we both need?

Unfortunately, it's the *what ifs* that keep her from continuing this relationship. What if it *is* long distance? What if she never comes to grips with her grief? What if we try to stay in contact and it ends up ruining our relationship?

Like I said, I get it. I slam the trunk closed with a little extra force. It doesn't help release the frustration I'm feeling. I ran six miles this morning, hoping to work through it, but that didn't make a difference either.

Tonight, we're having dinner and spending the evening together before I have to leave for the airport. When I planned my trip, I purposely booked a red-eye so I could sleep on the plane and arrive at my in-laws in time for lunch. After lunch, I'll take a nap and then leave in the evening for my ride home with the kids. With traffic, it's usually an eight-hour drive home, and the kids withstand it a lot better when they're sleeping. Monday morning, it's back to the grindstone. But tonight, tonight, I get her all to myself.

I make my way back into the resort and stop at the floral gift shop. I ordered a lei... well, several leis, for Emily. I wanted to leave her with something. She can dry them and keep them forever if she wants. And if she doesn't, she can toss them. I also grabbed a greeting card.

If Emily won't let me tell her where I live, I'll stash the information in her suitcase. That way, if she changes her mind, she'll have the option. Of course, *I* won't have the option, but what else can I do?

In addition to feeling like shit for having to leave her, I'm riding a wave of guilt over my lies, but it's a double-edged sword. She didn't want me to tell her anything personal about me, but she wanted to know about Hannah. I did what I had to do. Emily might have ended this days ago if I'd told her the truth. If not because I have children, she would for *telling her* that about myself and breaking the rule. Now I'm torn between wanting her to cave and agree to see me again and fear that she'll find out I've been lying all week about my kids.

I'd risk her finding out the truth if I could just have a chance with her. Honestly, I'm leaving this island with a very heavy heart. I want her. *I want her every day.* I take the bag from the clerk and step out of the gift shop, following the path to our building.

Stopping at a table near the outdoor bar, I ask the waiter for a pen. I pull the greeting card from the bag and smile wryly at the *I miss you* printed in script on the cover. The card has a beautiful image of a Hawaiian beach, complete with a setting sun and palm trees. Maybe it's corny, but I don't care. I lift the cover and the inside is blank, which is perfect because I have a lot to say to her.

It takes me half an hour to figure out what I want to write and then to spill my guts inside this card. I start second-guessing myself, but then I remember I have nothing to lose at this point. I might as well put it all out there.

When I'm finished, I slide the card into the envelope. Once it's sealed, I turn it over and write:

*When you've decided you can no longer live without me, open this. Love, Drew*

I stare at it for a couple of minutes, feeling unsure. I'm trying to respect her wishes…I'm trying not to feel hurt that she doesn't want me, but it's hard—even when I understand why.

Finally, I walk back to our building. When I enter my suite, swinging the door wide, I'm surprised to find her smiling. It's a grin, really. Like she's keeping a secret. My gaze travels down her body, and that's all it takes for my dick to jerk in my pants. She's in flip-flops and a knee-length red dress that hugs her curves perfectly.

"Hello, beautiful."

"Hi." She does a quick little twirl. Her hair is down, and it sprays out when she spins. "What do you think?"

"The question is, what do *you* think?"

"I love it. Thank you, again, for buying it for me."

"You're welcome. I'm happy to see you wearing something that makes you happy."

"It does… very much. Especially the flip-flops."

The difference between her now and the first time I laid eyes on her is striking. She's beautiful, without a doubt, but now she looks so much happier and more relaxed, with none of that buttoned-up, stressful air about her. I motion for her to come closer. "Come here." She steps forward and slips into my embrace. When her arms circle my waist, I pull her toward me and take her mouth with mine. She tastes sweet, and she feels comfortable in my arms. She feels right. I take a moment to breathe her in. I know this is coming to an end, and I'm trying really hard not to dwell, but I can't help it.

"Dog person or cat person?" I ask.

"Dog," she answers with a smile. "But I don't have anything against cats. I like them too." Then she inclines away, her eyes meeting mine, and she frowns. "What's wrong?"

"Nothing's wrong. Why do you ask?"

"You're lying."

"Yep, I'm lying." I take a step back and fight to shrug it off.

"Drew, don't be like this."

"I'm trying, Emily. I'm trying really hard to be a good sport about this."

I walk over to the bag that's holding the leis I bought for her. Taking the box out, I remove them one strand at a time and hold them up.

"What are those?"

"These are from me to you." I step toward her and gently rest a lei around her neck: "Monday." I drape another around her neck: "Tuesday." Another: "Wednesday." And then: "Thursday and Friday. It's a lei for every day I've known you."

"Drew…" She lifts one to her nose and closes her eyes as she breathes in their beautiful sweet floral scent. "They're so beautiful. Thank you, but you don't have to keep buying me gifts."

"I know that, but I like seeing you smile."

Her eyes lock on mine. "*You* make me smile." She lifts the leis again and looks down to examine the flowers.

"That's a pikake lei."

"The scent is incredible. Is pikake the name of the flower?"

"It's some sort of jasmine. The scent is supposed to be relaxing… and it's also rumored to be an aphrodisiac. They're supposed to be a sure way to a woman's heart. According to tradition…"

"I absolutely love them. Thank you so much."

"I'm glad you like them." I give her another quick kiss. "So, what are we doing this evening?"

"I thought we'd have a picnic on the beach and watch the sunset. Is that okay with you?" She glances over at my carry-on bag. "I'm just not in the mood for being around a bunch of people."

"I can't think of anything better."

*

She's thought of everything. I'm not sure why I'm surprised. If I've learned anything about Emily this week, it's that her attention to detail is impeccable. The grilled chicken skewers, fruit, and the white wine are perfect for our beach picnic. Being with her on the shore and watching the sunset together makes me so thankful to have been able to spend the week with her.

When she sits up to pour herself another glass of wine, I'm pulled from my thoughts. The sun hasn't completely set yet, and the sky is streaked beautifully with orange, red, and pink. Emily's silhouette against the sun is just as stunning. I take the chance to pull out my phone and snap a photo.

"Thank you for the picnic. It really was a great idea," I say after getting my shot.

"You're welcome! I slaved all day to prepare this meal for you."

I snicker and say, "I bet you picked the grapes for the wine too. How are your feet after all that stomping?"

She laughs and winks at me. "The café offers packed dinner just for this type of occasion. Pretty smart marketing on their part. And I'm so happy we got such a beautiful sunset." She turns toward me and says, "I have something for you."

I sit up to face her. "You do?"

"Yeah, but I left it in my room. I thought we could stop by there on the way to the airport."

"What do you mean? You can't go with me to the airport. I have to return my car to the rental company."

"I'm spending every minute I can with you and that means I'm riding with you to the airport." She lifts a shoulder in a shrug. "I can Uber back to the resort."

I want to argue with her, but I can't—I'm happy to get every second I can with her too. We're staring at each other as the sky darkens and once the sun has completely dipped into the ocean, I slant forward and kiss her bare shoulder.

"Thank you."

"You don't have to thank me, Drew. This is hard for me too."

I lift my head to look at her. "Then why are we doing it?" I sit up straight. "Seriously, Emily, let's talk about this."

When her eyes close, I know she's going to refuse again.

"I'm sorry."

Now I feel bad for bringing it up. The look on her face breaks my heart. I reach over and grab her hand. "I'm not trying to make you feel bad. I just don't want to say goodbye." I squeeze her hand and say, "I hate it, but I understand. I really do."

Wrapping my arms around her, I pull her into my lap.

"Thanksgiving or Christmas?"

"Thanksgiving."

With my chin resting on her shoulder, I hold her. That's all I want right now. This moment, on this beach, with her in my arms.

# CHAPTER THIRTEEN

## Emily

The ride to the airport is quiet—very quiet. Drew is holding my hand in a tight grip, and I know it's because he doesn't want to let go. I can't ignore his desire to continue whatever we have, but I just don't want to ruin the experience. I'm afraid I'll hear something that will kill it.

He's given me so much this week. I'll never be able to thank him enough and I feel like walking away now is the best way to preserve this time and these feelings. I don't want things to get messy with Drew and I believe if we try to continue this, it *will* get messy—I like him too much for that.

The truth is, I need this right now. I need fun without strings. I want to preserve these moments forever in my memory as new and exciting and uncomplicated. I don't want real life or... what was it that killed Drew's last relationship... *reality*... to ruin it for us. Maybe it's stupid, but I don't care.

After dropping Drew's rental car keys in the provided drop box, we head into the airport. He has ninety minutes until his flight leaves and the time is flying by way too fast. I'm fighting to keep the sadness from my expression.

After he checks in, we walk toward security. I can't walk through there, so we sit in nearby chairs. Once we're seated, Drew sets his ticket on his knee and I spare a glance. When the letters LAX jump out at me, I gasp.

"Do you live in Los Angeles?" I ask before I can stop myself.

He glances at me, and I can see the dejected expression on his face.

"Stop. Don't tell me where you live, just say yes or no."

He shakes his head. "LA is just a stopover. I don't live there."

I feel disappointed. Why, I'm not totally sure—LA is too far from Sacramento anyway.

"Emily, do you live in LA?"

"No. I don't live in LA either… or even in Southern California, if it helps."

"If it helps? Emily, please." He shifts in his seat to face me. "We're running out of time. Let's just… Let's just do this, okay? Please, just give me your phone number. Please."

My heart aches. He looks so disappointed. Just like I'm disappointed.

"Drew, think about this, okay? We tell each other where we live, okay, and what if we're not actually far—maybe three hundred miles?"

"That wouldn't be so bad," he says. "We could make that work."

"Could we though? Really?" I give him an earnest look. "Driving back and forth while also working full-time? Trying to have social lives and relationships with our families *and* commuting to see each other?" I grab his hand and say, "What if it's four hundred miles? Would you be okay with driving a round trip six or eight hundred miles every other weekend to make this work?"

"What if it's only one hundred miles?" he asks.

"The problem is, if I tell you where I live and it's not a hundred miles, if it's four hundred miles, we're still going to want to try. That's not far enough to say no, but it is far enough for us to try and make it work… But it *won't* work. We'll end up hating each other in a few months. I really don't want to hate you." I close my eyes, trying to find a way to make him understand. "I'm afraid if

I tell you, it will either be much too far away or not far enough away for us to keep from trying."

He taps my chin so that I open my eyes again. "I understand. I get it… But, Emily, once I walk through that security line, it'll be too late—it's now or never."

"Why don't you stay until Sunday?" I blurt, without really considering what I'm asking for.

"That's not fair. You know I can't. We've talked about this."

I close my eyes and fight the tears that are desperate to break free. I hate myself for this, but it doesn't change my mind. Once he's through that security line, I'm going to have so many regrets that I'm not sure I'll be able to live with my decision, but those regrets won't be as bad as the ones I'd have after a few months of trying to make a doomed relationship work.

"Movies or TV?" I ask as I open my eyes.

"Movies."

"Action or drama?"

"Action."

"Hmm… Sports or theatre?"

He laughs and his hold on my hand tightens.

"Sports."

When both our smiles fade, I say, "I'm sorry."

"I'm sorry, too. I wish more than anything I'd never suggested that stupid deal in the first place. That first night when you got falling-down drunk, and I had to put you to bed." He draws me into a kiss and says, "Please don't do that after I leave. Promise me you'll look after yourself."

I nod and feel the heat of embarrassment warm my cheeks.

"I promise."

He stands and pulls me into a tight hug. I don't want to let go, and he's made it clear that he doesn't want to let go either. I'm not sure how long we stand there, holding each other, but I have to hold my breath to keep from crying.

"One more question… Milk chocolate or dark chocolate?"

My chest bounces up and down with my silent laugh.

"Dark."

He nods against me approvingly. "Good. Me too." Then he whispers, "I'll never forget this week, Emily. I already miss you. Please take care of yourself and…" He doesn't finish, but I understand.

"I miss you already too. I'm not sure how I'm going to spend the next two days without you."

"Take the time to enjoy your own company, you know, like you were planning before I came along." We both laugh at that and then I remember I have a gift for him.

"Oh, I almost forgot!" I untangle myself from the hug and pull an envelope from my purse. "Here."

He takes it with a furrowed brow. "What's this?" He tears the flap and takes out a picture we took minutes before our helicopter tour of the island. "Oh, wow! When did you pick this up?"

"I had a brief window when you weren't paying attention. I got us both one. Now you have something to remember me by."

"I love it. Thank you so much." He reaches out, wraps an arm around me and holds me close again. "I hate to go."

"I know, Drew." When he steps back to look into my eyes, I can see the sadness lingering there. "Thank you for such a fun week and thank you for respecting my wishes. I really do appreciate it. You're such a gentleman, and I hope someone finds you and sees you for the wonderful person you are."

When his lips touch mine, I squeeze my eyes closed and fight the emotions building in my chest. His kiss is gentle and long and achingly familiar. I never thought I'd want to kiss a man again after losing Tuck, but thanks to Drew, I've figured out that I have a long life ahead of me, with lots of frogs and princes to kiss along the way. He ends the kiss, meeting my eyes.

"I gotta go."

I nod and take a step back. Reluctantly, he turns and walks toward the security line. I stand and watch him until he's all the way through and out of sight. Then I drop down into a chair and just sit there, unable to move.

I don't know what I was expecting but now that he's gone, I'm sure this is going to hurt a hell of a lot more than I thought it would. When I finally stand, I have no idea how long I've been sitting there, but I get up, and I move forward, and I order an Uber to take me back to the resort. When I arrive and enter the lobby, there's nobody around. It's well past two in the morning, and most people are in bed. I ride the elevator up and stop in front of the door to my room. Turning around, I look at Drew's door, staring at it for a long time, remembering the first time we met.

I finally enter my room and go straight to the minibar. I promised to look after myself but I didn't promise I'd stay sober. I grab all six little bottles of vodka and two bottles of orange juice. I take the bottles, cradled in my left arm, grab a glass from the bar and carry everything to the lanai, where I proceed to get smashed... all by myself.

\*

I wake under the bright but misty sky. I'm covered in morning dew... not cold, but damp from the misty Hawaiian rain. I'm still outside, still in the red dress Drew gave me... I'm also still wearing the leis. I lift them to my nose and fight to keep from crying. I miss him. Badly.

After a minute of self-pity, I stretch and slowly get up. Inside, the bed is still rumpled from when Drew and I made love yesterday afternoon. I remember his possessive hands all over my body, the tender way he kissed my skin, the way he had me crying out in pleasure, and I hug myself. I don't want to sleep there until after the sheets have been changed. It smells like him, and I need to purge him from my system. Even though that kills me.

I throw my hair in a ponytail and change into my swimsuit before grabbing a towel, cover-up, book, and my room key. I need to be outside.

I wander down to the outdoor bar and pay for a cabana rental for the entire day. It's ironic, given that before Drew, I didn't want to be anywhere near the beach. My cabana is oceanfront, and it comes with bar service. Good thing because I don't want to be sober—not at all.

The ocean is surprisingly soothing. The sky is bright, and just like my first day here, rainbows shine in the distance. I can smell the plumeria as the scent drifts through the heavy, humid air. I've never been anywhere that's smells as good as Maui. Back home, I can walk past a bed of jasmine or an orange tree and smell the sweet blossoms, but here, the air itself smells good, all the time. It's truly wonderful.

Staring at the shore, I'm forced to think about Tucker. After spending the last few years avoiding the beach, I feel like a lost love has returned, thanks to Drew. No, not the love of my husband—which will always be there—but the love of the sea. Being here with Drew was refreshing… a gift, really. He gave me a moment of freedom; freedom from grief, freedom to get back to something I used to love. But that freedom was short-lived because sitting here now, it's hard to ignore the fact that my husband drowned in this same ocean. I want to forget it, I want to move on, but I'm not strong enough.

I told Mac I didn't want to come here. I didn't want a week in paradise. I'd much rather spend a week in the mountains *alone*.

Isn't life funny like that?

If he had planned the vacation I'd asked for, I never would have met Drew and I never would have had these last few days of freedom. So, now what? Drew isn't here to distract me.

I sigh as I sip the vodka tonic the waitress delivered, and then carry it to the waterline. With a deep breath, I step in… three or four more steps and the warm waves are brushing my thighs. It feels good. I can't deny, I want to do this. I want to get back to life before death—it's just coming to grips with doing shit like this alone.

My drink splashes a little as I drop into the water. I don't care. I'm sitting in the sand, and the waves are now grazing just below my shoulders. I lift my knees and rest my hands on them. The water is perfect, and I find myself smiling, looking up toward the beautiful blue sky.

*I love you, Tucker. I really do, but I need to move forward without you.*

# CHAPTER FOURTEEN

## Drew

I've been home for nearly a full week and I still can't keep my mind from wandering. Wandering? Ha! No, not wandering: I straight up can't stop thinking about her. I cannot get her off my mind. I want to know if she made it home okay. I want to know how she's doing. Fucking Christ, I want to touch her.

I knew this would be hard, but I seriously underestimated just how distracted I'd be. It's crazy. I glance up at the clock. This time last week, I was sitting on the beach, watching the sunset with her in my arms, preparing to say goodbye. Now I'm back to reality and it's just not the same.

When I hear the screeching alarm, I fight the instinct to cover my ears.

"Dad! What is that?" Hannah has her little palms over her ears and she's running in circles. Kyle has his head on the table, laying among the scattered Lego pieces, and he also has his hands over his ears.

"It's the smoke alarm. Hold on, it'll stop in a minute." I pull the smoking pan from the oven and throw it in the sink, then I grab a pot holder and run over to the blaring alarm. After a few minutes of fanning, it finally stops.

"Dad, did you burn dinner?" Hannah asks as soon as the alarm stops sounding.

"Go turn that fan on. Kyle, open the front door so we can blow out some of the smoke."

I walk back over to the range and click the vent fan on, fighting to keep from cussing in front of the kids. How in the hell did I manage to burn something so damn simple? Kyle walks over and glances into the sink at the black chicken nuggets.

Then he shrugs. "That's okay. I didn't want chicken nuggets anyway."

An instant laugh bursts out. "I didn't either. How about pizza?"

He looks at me thoughtfully and finally nods. "I can eat some pizza."

Hannah starts jumping up and down. "Yay! Pizza!"

I snatch the page of coupons off the fridge and dial the number listed, walking into the living room to escape the smell of smoke. Stopping in front of the fireplace, my eyes land on the photo. Maybe I should just put the damn thing in a drawer. Looking at it every day only makes me feel worse. Not to mention the questions it's raised. Between my mom and the kids, I can't escape the reminders.

I finish my pizza order and end the call. Staring at the photo, I know I need to stop this. I haven't had any luck in my search for her, which makes me think I need to work at getting her out of my system. I can't help but wonder if she found the card I stashed in her suitcase. Did she find it and throw it away? *Would she?* I find it hard to believe she isn't missing me too. Glancing down, I see Hannah watching me.

"Do you miss your friend, Daddy?"

I fight the frown as it tugs at my lips. "Can you tell?"

She reaches her hand up and motions to the photo. "Can I look too?"

I pick up the picture of Emily and me standing next to a helicopter and give it to Hannah.

"She's pretty." She whispers it, like it's a secret, and that makes me smile.

"I think so too."

"Are you okay, Daddy?"

Her question makes me chuckle. She's pretty damn observant for a six-year-old. "I'm fine, honey. Thank you for asking."

"It's hard to say goodbye to friends."

I bend down and kiss the top of her head. "Yes, it is, but we don't want to let that keep us from making new friends."

"I miss my friends too," she says.

"I know, but don't worry. You'll be back in school real soon."

"How many days?"

This is a new thing for her. She's really learning to grasp time and distance. It amazes me, the changes between this time last year and now. Entering first grade is a huge step and watching her grow really makes me miss her mother. Kayla is missing the milestones she was so looking forward to.

"Do you remember how many days it was yesterday?" I ask, testing her.

"Um…" Her eyes drift to the right, then they shift back to me. "Yesterday was twenty-eight days… so today is twenty-seven days."

"That's right. School starts in twenty-seven days."

"Ugh. Don't remind me," Kyle blurts from the kitchen table.

I lift my hands in question and look over at him. "I thought you liked school."

"I have Mrs. Woods this year. She's horrible, Dad, and like a hundred years old."

"Give her a chance before you judge, you may end up really liking her. And who cares how old she is?"

Hannah tugs on my belt. "But, Daddy, what about the school fair? Are we going?"

"School fair? What school fair?"

"Auntie Jennie put the flyer on the fridge. Remember? It's the Saturday before school starts."

I vaguely remember something about the school's renaming ceremony. I walk over to the fridge and read the flyer. Lifting my phone, I add it to my calendar, so I don't forget again. "You guys really want to go to this thing?" I glance around and say, "You know it's not your typical fair?"

"Yes! Yes!" Hannah jumps up and down. "My friends might be there." Her eyes widen in excitement, and she points. "Dad! Maybe your new friend will be there too."

And just like that, my Emily-free mind is filled with her again. I shake my head.

"I really doubt it, honey."

After the pizza's been eaten, the kitchen is clean, and the kids are in bed, I grab a beer and my laptop before heading out to the back patio. After a full day of kids' stuff, I need a place to clear my head and relax. I drop into a patio chair and open my laptop. This is how I've spent every evening since returning home. I open my laptop and search for Emily.

Before I have time to get the machine booted up, I hear, "What's up, Drew?"

I pop my head up and look over toward the side fence just as the gate opens. My neighbor is sneaking in through the gate quietly to keep from waking the kids.

"Hey, Jake, what's happening?"

He clicks the gate closed behind him gently and lifts two beers. "Brought you a beer."

"Thanks, but you're too late," I say, gesturing to my bottle. When my computer prompts, I go straight to Google.

"How's work?" he asks. "Glad to be back at it?"

"Busy, but that's what I get for taking three weeks off."

"You're not one of the construction crews working on that new commercial building on K Street?"

"No. That's not us. We put in a bid, but didn't get it." I shrug and say, "Probably a good thing, I don't have enough guys right now for a huge job like that."

Jake sits in the patio chair facing me and gestures toward the laptop. "You find your lady yet?"

I press my lips together and shake my head. "No luck yet."

"That's a raw deal."

"I know, but maybe I'll get lucky."

"Weird she isn't on Facebook. Isn't everyone on there?" He lifts his beer and swigs before saying, "Or Instagram. That seems to be more popular these days. My sister can't stay off that shit. She's constantly posting her workouts and food." He shrugs. "And what's up with that? Why the fascination with people taking pictures of their food?"

I laugh at that because I don't get it either. "I wish I knew."

Jake's laughing too and as I type the words "Emily Thomas California" into the Google search bar, he says, "You know, Drew, we have this hot new receptionist at work. Why don't you let me set you up?"

That really makes me crack up.

"Hell, no! The last time you set me up, it was a disaster."

"What are you talking about? Mandy was a great catch, you're the one who blew it."

I whip my head around to stare at him. "Blew it? You're kidding. That woman couldn't run away fast enough when she found out I had kids."

He points to me. "That was your fault for telling her."

"They're two small human beings, they're a bit hard to keep secret. Besides, I don't want to be with someone who doesn't love my kids."

"See." He points my way again. "That's your problem. You're too freaking honest and nice. Too damn transparent."

"Bullshit! I just spent a week with a woman without even exchanging phone numbers. I couldn't be less transparent."

"And that's another point. You should have forced it on her. You should have just told her where you live. Dude, she could be from around here."

"I couldn't do that. She had her reasons for not wanting to know. I couldn't force it on her." I start checking links before saying, "I'm pretty sure she's from California though."

"What makes you so sure?"

"She specifically said she wasn't from *Southern* California." I lift a shoulder in a shrug. "If she wasn't from California at all, she would have just said she wasn't from California but because she added Southern, I'd bet money she's somewhere up here in NorCal."

"That's a fair point. But may I suggest that when you find her, you try some discretion? Don't tell her about your kids until you're tired of her."

"That's a dick move, Jake, and you know it."

He laughs sardonically. "Yeah, but it's also a dick move you've already made with her. Might as well keep up the lie."

"That was different and you know it." I glare at him and say, "I'm not going to lie about my kids, not on purpose. I didn't tell her before because she asked me not to."

"I'm just saying, you should use the tools you have. Hang out with a chick until you're over it and then spring the kids on her. It's an easy out."

I tut. "You know what? I feel sorry for you when you fall in love. Because that girl, she's gonna rip your heart out—but then again, I guess you need to have a heart before it can be ripped out."

Jake stands, chuckling. "Whatever. I'm not looking for love anyway." He taps my beer with his. "See you later."

"Yep." Just before he leaves, I say, "Come over tomorrow if you want to catch the Giants game with me."

"Will do."

He slowly clicks the gate closed behind him, and I'm alone again. Too bad it's not what it used to be. Too bad I can't stand it anymore.

# CHAPTER FIFTEEN

## Emily

I hit the ignore button on my cell phone again. I just don't have it in me to deal with Grant today. Standing, I walk across the room to get a drink of water. Rebecca and I still don't have our offices settled yet, and I know that's my fault. When we left Tate, Brown, and McKennon together, we bought this Victorian in the Mansion Flats district downtown with big plans. It's a beautiful building too. We both immediately fell in love when we did the first walkthrough.

Now, we can't get started on the remodel because I keep delaying the meeting with Grant and the contractor. As if reading my thoughts, Bec walks into my office. Her platinum-blonde hair drifts off her shoulders with the motion. She's removed her jacket and rolled up the sleeves of her blouse. Her tanned skin is glowing and if I didn't know any better, I'd think she's the one who spent a week in Hawaii. She brushes a loose curl off her face and points to me. "Tomorrow morning. We're doing it. I can no longer stand the smell of the hundred-year-old carpet in my office." She sits across from me. "I know you don't want to deal with Grant, but the best way to get him out of our lives is to meet with the contractor he's recommending. I also think it's important to acknowledge the fact that he's possibly saving us thousands and thousands of dollars."

"Yeah, I know. I appreciate that…"

"Emily, we've put this off for three weeks. We're doing it tomorrow. Period."

"Has it really been three weeks since I came home from vacation?"

"Yep, it was three weeks last Sunday." She sizes me up for a moment and then asks, "How are you doing with... all of it?"

"I'm... fine." I purse my lips. "I'm not saying I don't have regrets, but I'm doing okay."

"I can get Richard on the phone, have him start looking for the guy. Seriously, if we're going to keep a private investigator on retainer, we might as well send some work his way. It's one of the best perks of running your own law firm."

My head shakes immediately. "No... no. I'm trying really hard to stick to my guns on this, Bec."

"You're so full of shit! Just stop, Emily. Just cut it out."

I draw back and look at her. "What the hell are you talking about?"

"Stop being a martyr. I can see how unhappy you are. You're even more unhappy now than before you left for vacation."

"Jesus, Mac said the same thing. He actually feels guilty for sending me on vacation."

"Did you tell him about Drew?"

"Yeah, I had to so he wouldn't think my mood was his fault."

"Okay, I have an idea." She holds her hand out. "Hear me out, okay?"

With my arms crossed over my chest, I recline in my chair, waiting to hear what scheme she's cooked up to fix me.

"I'll call Richard and let him do a search. He can send me the results, and if your guy is too far away or if he has some criminal history or some other awful thing, I'll trash the information and never share it with you."

My eyes drop to my desk. It's not a bad idea, but just considering it makes me feel weak-minded. Who am I if I can't stick to my resolve? But damn, I miss Drew. Painfully so.

"You either let me contact Richard or I'm building you a profile on a dating website."

"Absolutely no dating website." With a bob of my head, I waver on the rest. "Fine. If you want to hire Richard, do it, but I don't want to know anything about it. Keep me completely out of the loop, okay?"

When my eyes pop back up to hers, she's smiling from ear to ear. "Okay. It's a deal." She slides a piece of paper toward me. "Write down what you know about him, and I'll get the rest."

I can't believe I've agreed to this. I write everything I remember about Drew, including the names of his roommates. I also mention that he spends the same three weeks in Maui every year. Once I have it all down, she takes the information but doesn't get up to leave my office.

"Now, what are we going to do about Grant?"

I roll my eyes and groan. "I guess I just need to be clear with him. What choice do I have?"

"The longer you delay, the worse it'll be."

"I know. He's just so pushy, and he doesn't seem to hear me when I speak. He has, like, selective hearing."

Rebecca sits up straighter. "Em, you need to be frank with him."

"I know. I'll do it tomorrow. It's just weird that he can't take the hint. I only had dinner with him twice. I can't believe he's going around telling people we're in a relationship. Jesus, it's been weeks. He can't still believe I'm interested."

"Have you talked to him at all since you've been back?"

"Yeah, we've had a couple of brief conversations, but I keep putting him off."

"Tomorrow, then. We need to get the work done on this building."

"Agreed."

Bec gives me a firm nod and leaves my office. Standing up, I walk over to the window and look down on the street. City noise drifts up from below. I hear a car door slam and the bass bump of a car stereo. The tree-lined street is well shaded, but I can feel the Sacramento heat seeping in through the glass.

I'm in the right place. I'm where I want to be. I like the slower pace. Working for myself, alongside Rebecca, and getting to choose my clients and cases is a dream come true. So, why don't I feel happy? Why do I feel like something's missing?

I glance down at my watch. Six o'clock. Time to head home, to my empty house. Inwardly, I groan. Just as this thought lingers through my head, Bec peeks back into my office. "Drinks?"

I turn toward the sound of her voice. "Nah, go ahead without me. My stomach's been bothering me too much lately to drink."

She frowns and looks me up and down. "How about a good healthy dinner?"

"Hum… maybe. What did you have in mind?"

"Let's see… healthy. How about Sinclair's? They only serve locally sourced, organic food." Her voice sounds like the commercial and I have to laugh at her.

"That sounds very boring and probably just what I need."

Before I can grab my purse, Eddie, our office manager, steps into my office.

"Hey, Emily, Grant Russell is on the phone. He wants me to confirm a nine am meeting tomorrow with someone from DK Construction and the two of you."

"Confirm it!" I smile and say, "We're all getting new offices." When Eddie turns to leave, I stop him. "Hey, Eddie, please make sure we have pastries and coffee before the nine am."

He winks at me and does a little spin as he steps out of my office. As Rebecca and I descend the stairs, I can hear him on the phone with Grant.

"Mr. Russell, you're confirmed for tomorrow." There's a pause, and then he says, "Yes, sir, she's been swamped since returning from her business trip, but I got a firm confirmation from Ms. Baldwin. Okay, that's great. We'll see you in the morning."

On the way out, I stop at Eddie's desk and say, "Thank you, darling. I owe you one."

He grins. "That's what I'm here for."

With a final wave, Rebecca and I head to dinner.

When we enter Sinclair's, I look around at the crowd. For a Tuesday, it's pretty busy.

"Do you look for him?" Bec asks over the murmur of the crowd.

I shift my focus back to her. "Look for who?"

She lifts her dark sunglasses from her face to the top of her head. "Your guy—Drew?"

The question surprises me. "Why would I look for him? Do you know what the chances are he's from Sacramento?"

With a flick of her wrist, she waves away my question. "I'm sure they're astronomical, but do you look for him anyway?"

I shake my head. "No. It never occurred to me that he could live here. Honestly."

"When you imagine him living somewhere, you know, in your head, what do you see?"

"I try not to think about it." I stop talking when the hostess calls us for our table. Once we're seated, I say, "I tried to guess with him. His first flight out of Hawaii stopped at LAX, but he said it was just a stopover."

"Oh, but that's something." She opens her menu. "It could have been a stopover to Sacramento. Maybe even San Francisco."

The words San Francisco ring a bell with me. I narrow my eyes to focus, trying to remember. Why does that stand out in my head? Closing my eyes, I try to recall conversations we had, even the first in the hall outside our rooms. I snort a little when I remember how I thought he was the maintenance man. He just looked so at home in his ball cap and flip-flops. My eyes pop open.

"What about San Francisco?"

"What about it?"

"The first time I saw him, he was wearing a San Francisco Giants ball cap."

Her eyes grow wide. "That's not too far, is it?"

I frown at her. "Isn't it?"

"It's a ninety-minute drive." She closes her menu. "It's like, what? Less than a hundred miles." She lifts her water glass and then blurts, "Also, the entire Bay Area is full of Giants fans. It doesn't necessarily mean San Francisco. Hell, half the state loves the Giants."

I get a flutter in my stomach at the thought, but I know it's ridiculous to hope for something like that. "True. I guess that's something you can add to your list of things I already know about him."

"I'm calling Richard after our meeting tomorrow. Should we set some parameters?"

"Like what? Distance?"

"To start."

We both order when the waitress approaches the table again, but I'm not in the mood for much. I've had zero appetite since returning from Hawaii. After I order the wild arugula salad, a bowl of soup, and a glass of ice water, I get a funny look from Bec.

"Seriously, no drink?"

"No. I'm trying to cut back, and I'm really not feeling myself the last week or so."

"Why's that?" She anchors her gaze on me. "Besides that first night, did you drink a lot in Maui?"

I shrug, afraid to give her an honest answer.

"Is that a yes?"

I shake my head. "Not too bad until the last two days."

"Oh, so you drank a lot after he left?" She crosses her arms in front of her. "I guess you're feeling a little guilty about that now, so you're taking a break?"

"Maybe. Really though, I haven't been feeling good. I think I'm fighting some flu."

She giggles. "Yeah, the heartbreak flu."

I laugh too, but it's not funny. "I just don't remember ever feeling so tired and I'd love to blame my state of mind, but I've been through horrible times, and even then I didn't feel so lethargic."

"What else? You mentioned your stomach."

"Yeah, I've been nauseous a lot the last few days. I don't have much of an appetite."

She slaps a hand on the table and guffaws. "Wouldn't it be hilarious if you were pregnant?"

I feel the heat drain from my face. "Hell no. That wouldn't be funny at all. Don't even say that out loud."

This just makes her laugh harder. "You guys were safe, right? I mean, it's not like you could be pregnant. Didn't you and Tucker try for a few years and nothing?"

My stomach plummets at the reminder and my heart races at the thought. Surely I couldn't be. God wouldn't be that cruel to me. "No. We didn't really. Tucker wanted to, but I wasn't ready. I wanted to work on my career first."

The laughter dies, and she gives me a serious look. "You did use protection, right?"

"Of course we did!" I rest my head in my hands. My mind is spinning, and I feel like I want to throw up. "Please, God. Please let this be the flu."

"Oh, my God, Emily, I was kidding." She leans forward and says, "You don't think you could be, do you?"

"I don't know, Bec, but anything's possible. It's only been a couple of weeks. Would I already be showing symptoms?"

"Fuck if I know. I've never been pregnant."

"Okay. Okay. Stop." I take a deep breath and pull my phone from my purse. "I'll just Google it."

"Emily, exactly how long has it been since the first time you guys slept together?"

"It was Tuesday. Hold on, I'm still Googling."

I hear a slight giggle. "That's right, you guys didn't waste any time." I glance up at her, and she's got her phone out too. "Tuesday? That's four weeks ago today!"

"Google says women usually don't get the first signs until their period is late, but for some women, early signs can come within weeks of fertilization."

"Emily, did you hear what I just said? It's been four solid weeks since you first slept with Drew. Holy fuck, Emily, you're pregnant!"

"Shut the hell up," I hiss.

She starts giggling, and I want to punch her. "This isn't funny. Why are you laughing?"

"I'm sorry, I'm just in shock." She inhales to fight her laughter. "It's been four weeks... if you haven't had a period, you're late."

I feel my face get hot and I want to cry. This can't be happening. This cannot be happening. "Bec, this can't be happening."

She drops her hand and reaches out for mine. "Emily, honey. Oh my God."

"Don't. We don't know for sure. Don't jump to conclusions."

"Let's go buy a test. Right now."

I shake my head vigorously. "I'll probably start in a day or two. It's just PMS."

"Denial isn't a reliable form of birth control, you know. Don't you think you'll feel better once you know for sure?"

"No, Bec. I'm not ready." I brace my head in my palms. "What am I going to tell my mother... shit, everyone?" I close my eyes. "Gee, Mom, I'm pregnant, and I don't know who the father is."

"That's not fair. You know who the father is. It's not like you've been with more than one person."

I scoff at her. "Do you think 'I don't *know* the father' is better than 'I don't know *who* the father is'?"

She beams at me, and I know it's because she can't help it. Of course, she's excited, she's not the one in trouble. I can't believe this. I just can't believe I let this happen.

"Should we get back to those parameters for my search for Drew?" she says with a snarky tone.

"I'm sorry, but I need to go throw up now." I rest my face in my hands and mumble, "Am I really destined to be a single parent—to be just like my mother?"

"Oh, hon." Her eyebrows draw together and her lips purse into a frown. "Regardless of Drew, you won't be alone. I'll be here every day. You have Mac and Kelley, your mom, and Eddie. It'll be okay, Em. Besides that, your mother was single by choice. She could've moved on from your dad, but she chose not to. It's not the same. Your parents made a choice."

I think about that and feel even worse. I didn't want to do this backwards. I had a plan: marry my soulmate, build my career, then have a family with him. Nothing is going according to that plan. I wanted to be better than my parents—who never married because my dad didn't believe in marriage. He travelled so much we never saw him and then he died, and my mom is still alone.

"It's true. I'm turning into my mother."

"No, you're not, but even if you did, she's amazing."

"And alone, Bec."

"Emily, stop. You're not your parents." Her head wags back and forth. "You're getting yourself worked up and we're not even sure you're pregnant. We could be jumping the gun."

I exhale slowly. "You're right. No panicking until we're sure."

"I'll give you until Friday. But if you don't start your period, you have a date with a pregnancy test. Until then, remain calm."

Easier said than done. I'd love to say I'm not worrying, but my insides are in knots. What am I going to do if I'm pregnant? How can I bring a child into this world without a father and how will I live with myself if I can't find him? And what about him? What is *he* going to think when I do find him? He's a single guy living in a shared house with roommates. He's not interested in being a father…is he?

# CHAPTER SIXTEEN

## Drew

"I gotta go, guys. Be good for Celia, okay?" I say, looking toward the babysitter.

"Bye, Daddy." I bend down so Hannah can wrap her arms around my neck, and at the same time, I lift her off her feet and spin her around.

"Listen, Celia is going to drop you off at Nanna's later. Behave yourselves this week, okay?"

"Are we spending the night at Nanna's?" Kyle asks.

"Yeah, I told you this. Nanna is taking you down to Santa Cruz with Aunt Jennie." I set Hannah down on her feet and lean over, so I'm eye to eye with Kyle. "Celia is going to help you guys get packed up, and you're leaving with Nanna this evening before I get home. Don't forget your swimsuit and please be helpful, okay?"

"Oh!" Kyle jumps up, and his eyes widen. "Dad, can I surf?"

"No, sorry. Not this time."

He crosses his arms over his chest. "Why not?"

"Because Nanna can't surf with you and you can't do it by yourself. It was different when you were in LA—you had Gramps and Uncle Milo with you *and* a surf instructor."

"So, come with us then. You can surf with me."

"I can't this time. I'm starting a new remodel job this week."

He slaps his hands down at his sides. "But, Dad!"

"Kyle, stop. You're not surfing."

He ducks his head. "Okay, gosh."

"I'll call you before you leave for Santa Cruz, okay? Don't be pouty with Celia just because you're mad at me."

He snickers. "You said pouty."

I chuckle too and spread my arms out for a hug. He lifts up and wraps his arms around me in a tight embrace. "Sorry, Dad."

"Hey, it's okay. I love you. Have fun."

"I will… At least I can swim."

I glance over at Hannah and say, "You guys are going to have so much fun."

She starts hopping up and down like a flea. "If Aunt Jennie is coming, are Amy and Connor coming with us too?"

"Yes, your cousins are going with you guys." I plant a kiss on her forehead when she calms down. "Now I'm late. I'll see you guys on Saturday morning. We'll have breakfast, okay?"

"Bye, Daddy."

I glance at Celia and nod toward the door. Once we're outside, I say to her, "I really need to go, but I'll call you later about the packing. You can also call my mom. Her number's on—"

"On the fridge. I know, Mr. Whitney. Don't worry about us."

"Thank you so much, really."

"No problem. Oh, but hey, can I go with you to the school fair? I'd like to get familiar with the school since I'll be dropping off and picking up this year."

"Absolutely. I'll call you when I know what time we're leaving, or feel welcome to come by Mom's on Saturday morning and have breakfast with us."

"Great! Thank you for the invite. I'll see you then."

"Okay, gotta go."

I rush to my truck as I'm flipping through my phone for the address. Once I find it, I plug it into my maps app for the directions. With morning traffic, it's a twenty-minute drive. That's going to make me about five minutes late, damn.

When I turn down the street, in the center of Mansion Flats, I'm taken by how different every building is in this area. It's zoned for business, so many of the older homes have been converted into offices. In between the older-style buildings are more modern homes, apartment blocks, and even some mid-century buildings mixed in. There's a beautiful old Victorian down on the left that I used to drive by all the time. I follow the numbers until I'm in front of that very building. No way. I'm excited now and my heart's racing. I didn't even know this place had been sold. I'm excited I get to work on it. I hope they want to restore it.

I park on the street and look around at the front. There's a beat-up old wheelchair lift next to the front steps that needs to be updated but at least there's accessibility. As I'm inspecting the railing and the steps, I hear Grant's voice.

"Drew, hey, I didn't realize you were here. What's up?"

I turn and stick my hand out to shake his. "Grant, good to see you." I throw a thumb over my shoulder. "I love this old place. I'm glad to see it get updated."

"It's great, isn't it? How about that original stain glass? Gorgeous."

"Are they keeping it residential?"

"No, no. Law firm. So, you haven't met Emily or Rebecca yet?"

My ears perk up when I hear the name. "Excuse me, did you say Emily?"

"Yes. Emily Tucker and Rebecca Baldwin bought the building. They left Tate, Brown, and McKennon to start their own law firm."

I feel the dip in my stomach. It takes me a minute to absorb what he just said. Tucker, not Thomas. When I get my thoughts together, I say, "That's ambitious, but it seems like a small job for your group."

"Oh, no, I'm not designing for them, just helping them find someone. I can't do it on my own time, and my firm would charge them too much overhead. I'm just helping Emily out."

"Thanks for thinking of me."

He waves dismissively. "Are you kidding? I wouldn't have called anyone else. You're the best carpenter in town, and I know you can handle the design as well."

"Thank you, I'm looking forward to it."

"Let's walk around back and go through the kitchen." Grant leads me around to the rear of the house and into the manicured backyard. There's a beautiful little picnic area on a covered patio and at the end, near the ally, is a small parking lot. We go up the stairs to the back door and onto a redwood deck, which has an assortment of potted plants and flowers. I examine the wood siding and the planks under my feet. It looks good and sturdy.

"This deck has been replaced recently," I say.

He nods and looks at the wood under our feet. "Yes, I believe Emily said it's only a couple of years old."

Every time he says the name Emily, my heart skips a beat. I'm trying to ignore it, but it's hard. I rub my hand along the custom handrail. The detailed design is beautiful, and someone took the time to install lighting along the stairs. It's not true to the era of the house, but it's nicely done.

When we enter the kitchen, we're walking on what looks like original penny tile. It's old but in pretty good shape. The cabinets haven't been updated lately, and that surprises me considering the detail that has gone into the deck and the backyard.

I chuckle and look up at Grant. "So, whoever owned the place put all their time and energy into the outdoor space and never got around to the inside."

"Exactly. The interior has had very few upgrades." He points to the walls. "At least not since the seventies."

I start laughing. "Oh, yeah, that wallpaper is horrible."

"Yes, so now you see what we're dealing with. Let's head upstairs, and I'll introduce you to the ladies."

I'm fascinated with the space as we wander through the kitchen, dining room, a drawing room, and to the stairs. After driving past this old place for so many years and admiring it, I've always wanted to see the inside. When we enter what used to be the drawing room, there's a reception desk staffed by a young man.

"Good morning. I'm Eddie, do let me know if you need anything while you're here." He points up the stairs. "There's coffee and other refreshments in the lounge upstairs. Rebecca and Emily will be with you in a few moments."

We both head up to a landing that's been turned into a seating area. Pastries, coffee, and water are displayed on an antique sideboard. It's a nice space and works well as a waiting area between the two offices. It makes me wonder if they plan to expand by adding more attorneys to their practice.

On either side of the room is a door. It looks like they used to lead to bedrooms, which have since been converted into offices. The door on the right is open, and the door on the left is closed.

An attractive blonde woman about my age steps out of the open door and extends her hand. "Good morning, I'm Rebecca Baldwin. You must be the contractor Grant's been bragging about the last couple of months." She turns to Grant and gives him a big smile. "Grant, how are you? It's good to see you."

"Rebecca." He leans in and kisses her cheek. "You too. How are you?"

"Oh, fine. Ready to get started on this remodel. Emily's on the phone with a client, she'll be with us in a few minutes. Come on in and get comfortable."

We enter her spacious office, and Rebecca says, "You look familiar, but I'm sorry, I didn't get your name."

I shake my head. "I'm sorry, I'm being so rude… it's just, I've admired this building for years and I'm excited at the prospect of working on it."

She raises her eyebrows, and that's when I realize I still haven't given her my name. "I'm Drew Whitney."

As this sentence escapes, I hear my name being repeated from the open door.

I turn, and my eyes meet hers. "Emily!"

# CHAPTER SEVENTEEN

## Emily

When our eyes lock, I'm instantly light-headed, and I feel the blood drain from my face.

"Drew?"

He's staring at me, his expression going from surprise to excitement to confusion.

"Emily?"

Rebecca approaches me, and I can see the concern on her face. I'm not sure if I'm going to pass out or vomit so I turn and walk to the bathroom. As I close the door behind me, I hear Rebecca say, "I'm sorry, Emily has been fighting a migraine all morning. Let's give her a minute."

*Migraine*... if only, but I'm thankful for her quick thinking. I sit down on the toilet lid and bend forward, so my head is between my knees. Drew is here...in my office. If it weren't for the fact that I feel so completely sick, I'd be thrilled. The thought makes my heart race. It's Drew. It really is Drew, and he's here, in my office. I'm not sure how long I sit like this before I hear a knock on the door.

I hesitantly say, "Who is it?"

The door creaks open, and Rebecca asks, "Are you okay?"

"Holy shit, Bec. That's Drew!" I whisper-shout, and my eyes must look like saucers.

"Yeah, I figured that out. Again, are you okay?"

I nod. "Nauseous, but I'm getting past it slowly. What's happening?"

"They're exploring the rooms downstairs. They're both super concerned about you, but, oddly, Drew also looks a bit angry. Any reason he'd be angry about seeing you?"

"Grant probably told him we're in a relationship. And I promised him in Maui I was completely unattached."

She drops her hands to her hips in aggravation. "Because you *are* completely unattached."

"Bec, what do I do?"

She inhales deeply then exhales slowly. "Do you think you should tell him you suspect you're pregnant?"

"No!" I whisper. "I'm not even sure it's true. I don't want to tell him until I'm sure. Besides, we were careful."

Rebecca snickers. "I think you're *seriously* in denial, but you're right. There's no point in telling him until you're sure. Just hold off until Friday, then we'll find out and figure out what to do."

"Until then." Her eyes focus on mine, and in a strong, confident voice she says, "You're going to stand up, exit this bathroom with your head held high, walk downstairs, and greet your guest as if you're completely unshaken." She reaches out for my hand and hauls me off the toilet. "You're Emily freaking Thomas, get out there and act like it."

Jesus… *This* is why this woman is my partner. She's absolutely right. I grip the bottom of my blazer and tug it into place, lift my chin, and move to exit the bathroom—but first, I stop to examine myself in the mirror. "Hold on… I gotta…" My hair is tightly knotted on my head, swoop bangs in place. Just enough cleavage to make men notice but not enough to keep them from looking into my eyes. I turn my face and check out my make-up… it's also on point. I nod at my reflection. "I got this," I mutter to myself as I pass Rebecca.

"You're fucking fabulous, and don't you forget it."

This makes me grin, which is exactly the way I want to look. When I reach the bottom, Eddie points toward the back room. I walk down the hall and look at the two of them from behind. They're absolutely nothing alike. Grant is dressed in an expensive grey suit and shiny shoes. He's not as tall as Drew and even his blond, sleeked-back hair contrasts with Drew's darker, messier style. Drew's wearing jeans and I think it's the first time I haven't seen him in shorts. The jeans are well-fitting and I appreciate that, flattering him in all the right places. His polo shirt fits snugly around his broad shoulders and my mouth waters a little when I remember him shirtless and standing on the sunny beach, the ocean water glittering on his skin. I enter just as Grant turns to look for me.

"Emily, how are you feeling?" He leans down to kiss me, and I turn my head so his lips land on my cheek.

Remembering that Rebecca said I was fighting a migraine, I push out a nervous laugh and say, "I'm sorry for my quick exit earlier. I'm fine now that the meds have kicked in."

I turn toward Drew and my smile widens. "Fancy meeting you here." I reach for his hand and hold it in both of mine and squeeze. Warmth spreads through me and memories of Maui flood my mind. "Sacramento," I say. "I can't believe it."

A relieved look washes over his face. "It's good to see you." He tugs on my hand to pull me into a hug, and I'm so glad he does. I press against him. I can't help it. I rest my head on his shoulder, and I want to stay there forever, but he withdraws too fast.

"So…" Grant tosses a glance between the two of us. "You two know each other."

Drew says, "Yes, we're… old friends, but I know her as Emily Thomas."

"I don't understand, what other name would you…?" Then it occurs to me. I turn toward Grant and say, "My actual last name is Thomas. You know that, right?"

He snaps his fingers. "Oh, right, your ex-husband's name was Tucker."

That really makes me frown. *My ex-husband?*

I hear Rebecca clear her throat behind me. "You mean her dead husband, right?"

I glance at her with my *see, he doesn't listen* expression on my face. "Sometimes it's like talking to a wall," I joke, but it doesn't matter because Grant didn't hear that either.

He snaps again, then frowns. "I'm sorry. I don't think I knew your ex died."

I roll my eyes and turn back toward Drew. *How could he forget something like that?* "Anyway, I take it you're the recommended contractor who hopefully wants to work on our building."

He's not smiling, and I'm having a hard time reading his expression. "I would love to work on this building. I've admired it for a very long time."

I tilt my head as I take in what he said, but before I can respond, Rebecca interrupts, "So has Emily. She's loved this house for years."

I nod. "We're lucky it was available."

"Excuse me? Luck had nothing to do with it." She gestures toward me. "My girl here gets what she wants. She pursued the owner persistently until he had no choice but to sell to us. Emily isn't great at taking no for an answer."

One side of Drew's mouth tips up. "I believe it."

I rest my hands on my hips and say, "It'd been sitting empty for too long, neglected. I couldn't live with myself if I didn't try."

Grant pulls the attention back to himself when he claps, then rubs his hands together. "I'm going to get out of the way and let you guys finish the tour." He points to me. "Emily, lunch?"

"Sorry, I'm not available."

He gives me a strange, almost disbelieving look, but I don't care. "Okay, I'll call you later."

I wave as he exits. "Yep, okay."

"Ah, I'm just... going to walk him out," Rebecca says, leaving Drew and me alone together.

When she's gone, I turn toward Drew and I can't fight the smile on my face. "I can't believe you're here. Did you know, or were you surprised to see me?"

But he's not smiling, and that's disappointing. My heart sinks at the look on his face.

"I'm completely surprised. Grant kept referring to Emily, which I questioned, but he said your name was Emily Tucker."

"Tucker was my husband's last name, but it was also a nickname. His name was Charles Tucker." I drop my gaze as I say, "When we got married, I never legally changed mine but I informally started using Thomas Tucker. The law firm is Thomas Tucker and Baldwin."

He looks me up and down, as if examining my suit. "Lawyer."

"Disappointed?"

His eyes widen. "Not in the least. Impressed, actually."

I cross my arms over my chest and say, "You're very perceptive. Have I told you that?"

"I thought I was, but..." His eyebrows lift, and he lets his words trail off.

Our eyes meet, and I'm waiting for him to finish his sentence, but then I realize what's bothering him. "Grant! No, Drew, we're not together."

"He thinks you are."

"No. I went to dinner with him twice before my vacation, but that's it. I'm not in a relationship with him, and I don't want to be. You saw him, he's completely self-absorbed, and he doesn't hear anything I say."

"So, your husband... He *was* your husband, not your ex-husband. You weren't divorced?"

I shake my head, and I'm fighting not to be hurt by the question. "I didn't lie about my husband, Drew. Tucker and I were very much married."

"I'm sorry," he says in a whisper.

With a shake of my head, I try to brush off my feelings, but I can't. I want Drew to hold me. I want him to be happy to see me. It bothers me that he didn't trust what I told him to be true, and it makes me angry at Grant for misleading him.

"I am sorry." He reaches for me and the next thing I know, he's got his arms around me. I don't want to cry, but I can't help it. In his embrace, the stress I've felt for the last three weeks hits a peak and then everything melts away. He just does that for me. I didn't realize this before, but it wasn't Hawaii that relaxed me, it was Drew. He's like a drug, lulling me into a sense of calm.

"Drew, I'm so sorry I was adamant about not exchanging information. I'm so stupid. The last few weeks have been miserable."

I feel his chest quake with his laugh. "It's been difficult for me too." He releases me and drops his hands to my waist. "When I saw you upstairs, I couldn't believe it. I thought my heart was going to pound out of my chest. You looked so beautiful, but then when you saw me, you lost all your color, and I thought you weren't happy to see me."

I shake my head vigorously, and when I do, tears drip down my face. "No! I really have been sick… I think I'm fighting some flu or virus." And the reminder that I might be pregnant makes me tense up again. I pause and fight to push those thoughts away. "When I heard you say your name and then I saw you, I was shocked. Genuinely shocked. But I'm so happy you're here."

He leans in for a kiss, and when his lips touch mine, they're gentle at first but then possessive and firm. He grips my upper arms and he's holding me against him. It feels so good. Natural and familiar. Then he wraps his arms around my shoulders. "Emily, damn, I missed you so much. So many days I suffered though believing I'd never see you again. I hated it."

When I hear Rebecca's shoes click along the wood floor in the hall, I turn away and wipe my face clear of tears. She enters with a smirk on her face. "Well, Drew, thank you for saving me from paying that private investigator I hired to find you." I laugh at that and flash a nervous glance at him.

He chuckles too. "I never thought of hiring a PI. I'll have to remember that next time I need to find someone who refuses to give me her number."

"Emily, I've asked Eddie to cancel all of your appointments today." She gestures to the two of us. "Let's finish this tour, and then you can get out of here."

"Oh, ah," I stutter. "Thank you, but I have a few things I need to take care of first."

Rebecca focuses on me for a long moment. "You're not feeling well. I really think you need to get some rest."

"Maybe we should postpone the walkthrough for a few days until you're feeling better," Drew offers.

"No, no. I promised Bec we would get started on the remodel this week. We can't put it off because I'm not feeling well."

He nods. "How about I'll do a walkthrough on my own while you finish up what you need to do and then I'll take you home?" He looks over at Rebecca. "I'll make sure she gets some rest."

Rebecca relaxes and gives him a look of thanks. "That sounds great. Thank you, Drew."

"We can regroup tomorrow, and I'll share my impressions about the building, and you guys can then tell me what you want to do with the space."

"Perfect," Rebecca replies, then she nods to me. "I'll meet you upstairs."

As she retreats with the clicking of her heels on the hardwood, I turn to face Drew and say, "I'm going to go finish up. You don't have to give up the rest of your day for me."

He laughs heartily. "You're kidding, right?"

"Drew, I'm sure you didn't plan on dealing with me today. You must have things to do."

"You're crazy if you think I'm letting you out of my sight."

# CHAPTER EIGHTEEN

## Drew

After Emily leaves the room, I take a minute to get my bearings. I feel like I've been on an emotional roller coaster. First, the euphoria of finding her, but then the confusion over her relationship with Grant. Of course, I felt sheer helplessness when I watched her retreat from the room, white as a ghost. And I'm still not so sure about Grant. I know she said they're not in a relationship, but *he* obviously doesn't know that.

I do a thorough walkthrough with a notepad, taking copious notes. After spending an hour or so on the downstairs, I head out onto the back deck and call Celia to check on the kids. Thankfully, they're doing well. Celia's the fourth nanny the kids have had, and so far, she's the best. The kids love her, and my mom seems to really like her too, and if there's ever a sign I've found the right person to help with my children, it's their approval.

Now that I've found Emily, I'm thankful the kids will be gone for a few days. That gives me time to make things right with her. I lied about them in Maui when the subject came up, and that doesn't sit right with me. Am I afraid she won't want to continue a relationship with me once she knows I have children? Yes, terrified, but I don't have any control over her reaction. I can only control when, where, and how she finds out. I'm not a liar. It's not who I am, and things won't be right until we clear the air.

I head back inside and up the stairs. Emily is in her office on the phone, so I take the time to check out the other rooms upstairs. Walking to the end of the hall, I inspect the bathroom. It's spotless and in pretty good shape if you can ignore the rose wallpaper. When I step out, I run into Emily.

"Hey," she says, and I get the impression she's nervous.

"How are you feeling?" Out of concern, I lift my hand to her forehead to check for a temperature. She doesn't feel warm, but with her hooded eyes and flushed checks, I can tell she's not feeling well. After checking her forehead, I slide my hand down her arm before letting it drop.

"I'm almost done, just another few minutes. How's it going?"

I look around and exhale slowly. "This place is amazing. I can't wait to get to work."

Finally, she smiles. "I love it too."

"How long have you guys been here?"

"Not long. We signed the papers about eight months ago. Before that, we worked out of my house for a few weeks after we left Tate, Brown, and McKennon." She hesitates then stammers, "Drew, I'm sorry but do you think... what I mean is, would you be horribly offended if I *did* have lunch with Grant? I just realized you're right. I need to set the record straight with him. I tried once before, on the phone, but he obviously didn't listen. I've been avoiding him since I got home from Maui, and I feel I need to make things clear with him, so he understands that he and I, that we're—"

"You want to make sure he knows you're not his girlfriend."

She dips her head as if she's embarrassed. "Yes, exactly. I don't want any hard feelings, but I also don't want him to continue to tell people we're seeing each other." Her brows lift. "We were never seeing each other."

I grin at her and realize she's worried about what I think. "I promise I won't be offended if you have lunch with him, provided you're up for it. If you're not feeling well, you should go home."

"I'm fine. At least, I feel okay enough to eat lunch."

"Okay, that works out since I have an errand to run too. Do you want me to meet you somewhere after lunch?"

She looks perplexed but then clears her face. "Right... you have roommates... So we probably shouldn't go to your house if we want to be alone." She lifts her wrist to look at her watch. "How about meeting at my house?"

"That's fine... but Emily, I need to tell you something about those roommates."

Her eyes widen and I'm wondering what she's thinking, but I'm sure whatever it is, it's not the actual truth.

"Can we save this?" Her eyes drop to the floor and then slowly lift to mine. "I know we both have some things we need to share, but I'd love to wait." She closes her eyes for a moment. "I just need a day to have this... to have you... without those truths."

"It's not what you're thinking."

She lifts her hand. "Please, let's wait. Please."

I feel like I'm missing something vital. Something she doesn't want to share, and in return, she's keeping me from telling her everything. My heart sinks. I don't want her to tell me something that will ruin this, but what could? I can't think of anything she could tell me that would turn me off. I want her. Regardless.

I nod at her, understanding. "You can have two days if you like. Three, even... just as long as I get to share those days with you."

She reaches out and hugs me. "Thank you. I just want to enjoy a day with you without everything else getting in the way, okay?"

When she tries to let go, I keep a hold on her. "Is everything okay? Why do I feel like I should be worried?"

Her shoulders drop, and she shakes her head. "You don't need to worry. I'm fine. Just really happy to see you." She glances down at her watch. "I'm going to go call Grant. When you're done looking around up here, come into my office, and we can swap numbers. Finally!" she says with a laugh.

"Okay. See you in a few minutes."

When she retreats back to her office, I rest against the door frame and watch her walk away. She's rocking that business suit, with a perfect little ass, but I have to admit, I can't wait to see that thick, silky hair tangled around her shoulders. How did I get so lucky? I lift my eyes to the ceiling, praying nothing ruins this. I want her... I need her. The last weeks without her have been torture.

I move into the next room, which I expect to be empty, but it's been turned into a storage and copy room. Filing cabinets line the walls, and a couple of them are locked up with padlocks. I fight to focus on the job as I inspect the molding and then bounce up and down on the squeaky floor. The floorboards are loose under the ancient carpet. I pull out my notebook and add it to the list. I keep catching myself grinning. Grinning like a freaking loon.

*Please let this be as good as it feels.*

After finishing up in the copy room, I walk down the hall to Emily's office. She's signing off her computer and locking her desk drawers. As quietly as I can, I walk to the windows and look out at her view. She has a smaller office than Rebecca, but she's also got the beautiful window seat with the beveled stain-glass window.

"I'm ready. How about you?"

Her voice is so pure and sweet. Hearing her reminds me of our whispered conversations while lying in bed, listening to the ocean in Maui.

I turn toward her and nod, taking my phone out to enter her number. She gives me a business card with her office and cell number listed. I enter those in and then say, "Address?"

She calls it out, and when I hear it, I mutter, "Shit. Are you serious?"

Her eyes pop up to meet mine. "Yes. That's my address. What's wrong with it?"

I close my eyes and shake my head. "If I'm not mistaken, we're practically neighbors. I only live about six blocks from you."

Her blue eyes light up, and one side of her mouths tips up into a grin. "Stop it. You're joking."

"Nope, not joking."

We stare at each other for a moment, but then her eyes drop back down to her phone. "I'll see you there in about an hour, maybe closer to an hour and a half?"

"Sounds good. I'll see you there. I hope the lunch goes well." Once I'm in my truck, I sit there for a while, trying to get my bearings.

*I can't believe this day.*

With a huge, stupid smirk on my face, I head over to my mother's house. I want to hug the kids one more time before they leave, especially after arguing with Kyle this morning. Also, I want to make sure my mom knows he's not allowed to surf. He's a sneaky kid, and I wouldn't put it past him to try and talk her into letting him do it.

When I arrive, they're packing the car.

"Perfect timing," my mom says, smiling at me when I get out of the truck. "Now you can help load the car."

"First, you don't invite me to go away with you guys, now you're trying to recruit me to load the car," I laugh as I lift Hannah off the ground to hug her.

"Hi, Daddy."

"Hi, doll, are you all ready for the trip?"

She nods with a toothy grin.

"Thank you for helping Celia pack. She said she couldn't have managed without you."

I hear a snort behind me and turn to see my sister, Jennie, carrying out two duffle bags. "Celia's very kind, and probably a liar," she grumbles this last part as I set Hannah down, grab a bag out of Jennie's hand, and toss it in the trunk.

"You guys better hurry or you're going to hit a lot of traffic."

Jennie rolls her eyes. "Have you tried loading up the car for a trip with four little kids running around your feet?"

"Nope, but that just proves I'm smarter than you."

"Hmmm," she hums as she drops the other duffle into the car.

"You should have asked Celia to come along. She could've helped with the kids."

"Oh, stop. We can handle these kids just fine. Jennie's just upset Rob isn't coming along."

Jennie raises a finger. "I am indeed irritated that my husband backed out at the last minute." She cocks her head. "Maybe you two should hang out while we're gone. I'd hate for you both to have to eat alone."

I laugh at that. "I'm not babysitting your husband. Besides, I have plans." Again, I can't erase the grin from my face.

"Really?" My mom narrows her eyes at me. "I thought you were dead set on finding that gal from Hawaii.'

"I was… and I did."

Her eyes stretch, and she gasps. "Oh, my gosh, Drew, that's wonderful. How on earth did you find her?"

"She's my new client. She and her partner bought that huge house in Midtown I've been wanting."

"No way," Jennie says. "That's crazy."

"Yep. She even lives in East Sac, just a few blocks from me."

"Partner? What does that mean?" Mom asks.

Jennie rolls her eyes. "Mom, it doesn't mean she's gay. It's probably a business partner."

Before the bickering can start, I interrupt. "She's an attorney and yes, it's her business partner."

My mom stops glaring at Jennie long enough to pat my arm. "I'm so glad, Drew. Really. I hope everything works out. I can't wait to meet her."

This stops me dead in my tracks. Maybe I shouldn't have told my family about Emily. What if she doesn't want to continue this relationship after she finds out I have kids? It's possible. Then I'm going to have to tell them, and they're going to judge her for it. Of course, then I can count on them talking about the lawyer who didn't want a relationship with my kids for weeks after. As if losing her over it won't be enough. It wouldn't be the first time, and I really dread it. There's nothing like being constantly reminded of what you lost because of what you have. But that's the story of my life.

As if reading my thoughts, Jennie says, "Don't worry, if she's really into you, it won't matter that you're a single father. She'll want you *and* your kids."

I meet her eyes, and I'm thankful for her kindness. We've been through this before, and she knows the struggle. My mom and Jennie have been my champions since losing Kayla. They've been here every day for my kids and me. I'm not sure where we'd be or how we would have survived without them.

"Thanks, Sis." I wrap an arm around her and kiss the top of her head. "I need to say bye to the kids and get out of here. Have fun though. Oh, and no matter what Kyle says, he's not allowed to surf."

"Right, we know," Mom replies. "No surfing."

"We've already heard all about how mean you are for not letting him surf," Jennie says. "Go, quick and give them a hug so we can get out of here."

"Oh, and Drew, there's a sandwich in there for you. I grabbed you one when we stopped at the deli earlier."

"How'd you know I was stopping by?"

They both look at me like I have three heads. My mom drops her hand on her hip. "We're taking your kids away for three days. I had no doubt you'd drop by to say goodbye."

I shrug as I head into the house. "Thanks, Mom, but one of these days I'm going to do something truly unpredictable just to throw you off."

As I step inside, I turn to look at the family photos along the entry hall. I do it whenever I enter this house, I can't help myself. Seeing Kayla pregnant with Hannah and her smiling face gets me every time. It was such a magical time. We were happy, all of our dreams were coming true… and then Hannah was born, and everything fell apart.

"What are you doing, Daddy?" Hannah asks, watching me from her perch on the couch.

"Just looking at Mommy." I turn to face her. "I need to get going. Come give me a hug goodbye."

I bend down as she runs over and wraps her arms around my neck. When I lift her off her feet, she squeezes and holds on for a long time. This child gives all her love unconditionally, just like her mother. She is her mother in so many ways.

"I love you, Hannah Banana."

"I'm sorry you miss her, Daddy."

My heart breaks a little every time Hannah says something like this. She has no idea how her mother died, but one day she's going to ask… I dread that day. I've been dreading it since the day we lost Kayla. It's the reason I hide my grief from them. It's why I can't let them see how much I miss her. The day Hannah asks about her mother will be the day she loses her innocent spirit and I hate that I can't hide it forever. I pat her arm so she'll look at me. When our eyes meet, I smile at her.

"You don't have to be sorry, sweetheart. I miss her, but I have you." I poke her nose. "And you are my heart."

*There's nothing like a constant reminder of what you lost because of what you have.*

"I love you too, Daddy." She makes a little heart with her fingers. Then she plants a sweet kiss on my cheek. As I set Hannah back on her feet, I realize my sister is absolutely right. Any woman who couldn't find room in her heart for these two incredible little beings doesn't deserve them—or me.

# CHAPTER NINETEEN

## Emily

As I sit waiting for Grant, I'm running through a script in my head. It's not working though. No matter what I say or how I say it, it doesn't come out right. It irritates me that I have to break up with someone I was never actually seeing. But I know I need to be kind. Yes, he's self-absorbed. Yes, he's arrogant. But he's probably not going to take this well, and I don't want to burn the bridge. So… *I must be kind*.

When I feel a hand rest on my shoulder, I nearly jump out of my skin.

"I'm glad to see you were able to make time for me." He leans down to kiss me. I turn so his lips land on my cheek. He doesn't seem to notice, which doesn't surprise me. The calm that settled over me in Drew's presence has evaporated completely. With Grant, I feel incapable of relaxing. I guess that's one more huge difference between the two. Drew hangs on my every word. He's perceptive and caring. Grant… isn't. At all.

"Thanks for making time for *me*," I reply. "I know I told you I wasn't free, but I wanted to talk to you about something."

"I've wanted to see you too. We've barely had time for each other since you returned from your business trip."

I fight the blush. Forgetting that I lied about my vacation. Now I feel a little ashamed, but it passes when he says, "I'm sorry about Drew today. I can't believe his behavior."

"What do you mean?" I shrug, truly baffled. "What did he do wrong?"

"Hugging you like that, getting so close. Acting like you were actually glad to see him."

Now I'm really surprised. "Grant, I was as happy to see him as he was to see me."

"You don't have to say that." He looks up as the waitress approaches our table. "Can we have a bottle of Vermentino. Also, I'll have the lasagna, but start with the spinach salad… and make it for two. Emily, you like the spinach salad, don't you?"

I glance up at the waitress, trying not to look annoyed. "I'll just have the soup of the day and a glass of water."

Grant nods. "Go ahead and bring the salad first." He holds up two fingers. "Remember, for two."

The waitress writes it down and then rushes away. Seriously, it's like I don't even exist. What can he possibly see in me when he knows nothing about me?

"Grant, I'm not trying to be nice. Drew and I—"

"Listen, Em, I'm sorry. He may be a bit odd, but he's a brilliant craftsman. If you can bear to be around him, I still think he's the perfect choice for you."

I hold up my finger, ready to defend Drew. "First, he's not odd. Not in the least. Second, please stop talking and actually listen to what I have to say."

He lifts a single brow, and I think he may have actually heard me. But then he says, "Oh, I forgot to tell you, an associate at work offered to let us use his cabin at Lake Almanor. It's available the week after next. What do you think?"

"No."

He tilts his head, and I can't help but compare him to a confused puppy. It makes me wonder how many times he's actually heard the word no.

"I'm sorry?"

"No, I'm not interested in going away with you."

"Okay." He sucks air through his teeth. "You don't like the mountains… What about spending the weekend in San Francisco?"

"No, Grant."

Again, with the cocked head. "Is someone having her monthly?"

"Excuse me!" I scoff. "Actually, I'm not having my *monthly*! But that's none of your damn business." If only he knew the truth about that. Dropping both of my hands on the table with a bang, I slant back in my chair, fighting to control my reaction. I want to rage at him, but I exhale slowly and struggle to keep from embarrassing myself. "I can't believe you just said that to me." I take another deep breath. "Grant, this isn't going to work. I can't see you anymore."

Finally, he looks at me as if he's really heard me.

"What are you talking about?"

"I'm talking about how you keep telling people that we're involved when we're not. We only had dinner twice and I'm sorry to break it to you, but we are not actually dating. If you keep talking without listening, we won't even be friends much longer."

"I apologize if I've offended you. I've only had good intentions. Inviting you away for a few days was meant to be a kind gesture. I didn't realize it would offend you."

"Inviting me away wasn't offensive. Asking me if I'm having *my monthly* was offensive. Not hearing a word I've said was offensive. Calling Drew *odd* was offensive. Nearly every other thing you've said to me since we sat down has been offensive."

Of course, this is the moment the waitress brings over the salad and the wine. She sets down two glasses, but I immediately place my hand over my glass before she can pour.

"I'm not drinking, but thank you."

Grant is staring at me like I just killed his favorite Marvel character. I can't believe he didn't see this coming. How could any person be so clueless? When the waitress walks away, he takes the salad tongs and plates some for both of us. I fight with everything I have to keep from rolling my eyes.

Once he's done, he says, "I was only trying to be thoughtful."

"Word to the wise, Grant. The most thoughtful thing you can do is actually listen to people when they speak to you." I gesture to the salad. "You haven't heard anything I've said to you since I met you."

"Of course I have. You don't need to exaggerate."

"Really?" I ask, crossing my arms over my chest. "If that's true, tell me something you've learned about me. Anything."

He stares at me for a second. "I know you're divorced."

I want to slap him. Really slap him. "No, Grant. I'm not divorced."

"You're still married? You told me you were divorced."

I shake my head and close my eyes. "No, I didn't. I would never tell you I'm divorced because it simply isn't true."

"So, what then? Just today you told me your ex-husband died. Or was that my imagination too?"

I open my eyes and glare at him. "My *husband* is dead, Grant. He died. I'm widowed, not divorced."

He shrugs. "So, then you're not married."

I reach to grab my purse off the back of the chair and stand.

"Goodbye, Grant. I hope you enjoy your lunch."

By the time I reach my car, I'm exhausted, physically and emotionally. I can't help but second-guess myself. Did I tell him about Tucker? I think back over our friendship and try to remember. Yes, I told him. I've told him more than once. It was the reason I wouldn't go out with him last year. He'd started inviting me out regularly a year ago, but I wasn't ready. I told him that; I told him exactly why I wasn't ready to start dating. It wasn't until a few weeks ago that I accepted one of his invitations. I shake my head and turn out of the parking space.

There's no going back now. I may have just burned the bridge, but does it really matter? If a person can't show enough interest in me to remember that I lost my husband, is it worth the effort of maintaining the relationship?

When I get home, I barely have the energy to get out of the car, so I sit there for a few minutes, wondering how long it'll be before Drew arrives. As this thought pops into my head, he drives up in a huge Chevy truck with the words "DK Builders" printed across the door.

He hops out and as he strides toward me, my hand drops to my stomach. God, what if I am pregnant with this man's child? I haven't even had time to consider how I feel about that, much less how he's going to feel. I have no idea how I'm going to tell him.

As he approaches my car, I pop the handle.

"Perfect timing," I say as I lift myself out of the driver's seat. I grab my work bag and my purse, but Drew quickly takes them from me. My stomach does a little flutter at the reminder of what a gentleman he is. Always so thoughtful. So unlike Grant.

"Thank you," I mutter when he takes the bags from me. I grip my keys in my right hand as we approach the front door. Then I stop. Damn. I wasn't expecting company, and I know my house is neglected at best and disastrous at worst. I've been so depressed since getting home from Maui, and that reflects on my living space. I know it does. I turn toward him and lean against the door. "I have to tell you something."

Nothing inside this house screams happy woman, and as soon as he enters, he's going to know just how bad I've been. I'm fighting hard not to frown, but I can't help it.

He gives me a sincere look, and I can tell he's trying to help.

"Go ahead. You know you can tell me anything."

"Do I… and can I?"

"Just because we're no longer in Maui doesn't mean I'm a different person." He gently kisses my lips. "You can tell me anything."

I'm surprised by the tears that slip from my eyes. I cry so easily these days. What the hell is wrong with me?

"You are starting to scare me. I thought I didn't need to worry."

I take a deep breath, and I'm trying with all my might to get myself together, but the words won't come. I roll my eyes then throw my hands over my face. I'm freaking pathetic. He should run away while he still can.

"Start from the beginning. It'll help."

I drop my hands. Looking into his golden eyes, I almost feel like we're still in paradise. With another deep breath, I say, "My first night alone in Maui I drank every drop of vodka in my minibar and then slept in a lounger on my lanai because I was afraid I'd smell you on my sheets." My voice dips when I say this last part, and I have to close my eyes because I'm so embarrassed.

He rests a hand on my upper arm. "I was completely miserable too."

"I stayed drunk until I boarded my flight home," I added.

He squeezes my arm this time. "You promised me you'd look after yourself when I left."

With a nod, I whisper, "I know... but there's more."

When he doesn't respond, I rest my head against him, and it feels so good. So comforting... I stay there and enjoy the feel of him for... well, for too long.

After a few minutes, he says, "Do you want to talk about it inside?"

"No." I vigorously shake my head. "Since I've been home, I've been a complete mess. Literally. My house has been horribly neglected. Drew, I haven't even unpacked."

"Wait!" There's a hint of humor in his voice. "Are you seriously upset because your house is untidy?"

I nod, and that makes him laugh outright. He rests a finger under my chin and lifts it until we're eye to eye. "I don't care what the inside of your home looks like."

"I just need you to understand, okay? I want you to know that this isn't me. I'm not a crier. I'm not a messy person. I'm not *this* person. I've just been in a bad place." I take a deep breath because I need to get this all out of my system before we go inside, but I'm not ready to tell him everything. "Listen, Drew, I told you in Hawaii this was going to be a difficult time for me. I told you I'd be an emotional mess when I returned home. This is why I didn't want to stay in contact. I didn't want to drag you down the rabbit hole with me."

"And I told you I wanted to be there for you. I told you that in Hawaii and it's still true. I'm not afraid of this. I'm not afraid of the *messy* side of your life. I understand who you are. Okay? I know enough about you to understand how difficult this is. I knew enough about you *yesterday* to not give a shit about you being emotional or sad or depressed, or whatever this is. And I certainly don't give a damn what the inside of your house looks like."

# CHAPTER TWENTY

### Drew

When she opens the door and we enter the dark house, it takes my eyes a minute to adjust. Emily rushes over to open the blinds in her living room. When she does, I squint at the light shining through. I glance around as she quickly collects some dishes from her coffee table and rushes away with them.

"Just keep your eyes closed for a few minutes, okay?" she blurts from the other room. I do as she says, even though I really don't care how messy her house is. Although I must admit, she was the exact opposite of messy in Maui. She's definitely the *make your bed every day* type of person. Which she proved by making her bed every day before Housekeeping could do it.

I hear her moving around, and after a few minutes, I feel her standing near me, very near. I reach out, and my hands collide with her hips. I grab them and tug her against me.

"You can open your eyes now," she whispers. I do, and I'm staring into her brilliant blue ones. She's got a slight smile on her face. "You're a really good sport. Thank you so much for your patience. If you want to leave now, I'll understand."

I laugh as I bracket my arms around her. "Why on earth would I want to do that?"

"Because I'm crazy... if not way too emotional this week." Her eyes go from amused to apologetic. "I'm sorry."

I lean in and take her lips with mine. How can I even tear my eyes away from her to look around her house when she's standing here in front of me... here, in the flesh? Fuck, I'm happy about that. I lift my hands to cup the back of her neck as my tongue dips inside her mouth. I want her so much. I grasp her lip between my teeth, wishing I could mark her. Wishing I could prove to everyone, Grant and the rest of the world, that she's mine. Her arms come around me, and her little fists grip my shirt, and I know she's feeling exactly the same.

"I'm not sure what you're worried about, this place looks totally fine."

She grins. "You haven't even looked around yet."

I see all I need to see. Just as I'm about to kiss her again, my phone rings.

"If that isn't shitty timing, I don't know what is. I'm sorry." I release her and glance down to see Celia's number. "Hello?" I answer.

"Hey, Mr. Whitney, I just wanted to let you know I dropped both kids off at your mom's house."

"Yeah, I know. I already stopped by there. Thanks for letting me know though."

"Oh, okay, great. I'll see you on Saturday. Enjoy the rest of your week."

"Thank you, see you, Celia."

I end the call and look up at Emily, who's watching me with a hesitant expression. "Everything okay?"

"Yeah... Celia works for me," I say, feeling guilty.

She closes her eyes. "Am I that obvious?"

"No, I just wanted to let you know." I point around the house and say, "This is a great place."

"Thank you, but it's terribly cluttered. I haven't done any housework since I've been back from vacation. I've basically worked nonstop since I got home. I didn't want to stop because I knew I would just end up feeling sorry for myself."

"Why?" I ask as I survey her space. The room is decorated in beach tones: blues and greens, with whitewashed wood furniture. In the center of the coffee table is a large round bowl filled with sand and several seashells. There's a beautiful deep blue chenille blanket draped over the back of her white couch, and all I can think about is how my kids would have the pure white fabric ruined in a matter of hours. Jesus… I have to tell her about them. I cannot put it off much longer.

"Because I was so damn mad at myself for not getting your number."

"I was pretty mad at you for a few days too, but then I was just missing you." I walk around a little as I take things in. "What about now, though?"

"What do you mean?" she asks.

"Is it safe to assume you regret not staying in contact? Is this chance meeting a good thing for you?" I'm reminded of the card and note I hid in her suitcase. I guess she hasn't found it yet, since she hasn't even unpacked.

"It's perfect," she says, smiling. "I'm so happy to see you. I'm so relieved. Not getting your information was quickly becoming one of my biggest regrets in life."

I smile at her. "I hate to say I told you so, but…"

She laughs at that and I'm happy to see her relax a little.

I take a few steps toward the mantel to look at the framed snapshots displayed. There's a shot of her on the beach with a man, and they're both wearing wetsuits. "Where was this taken?" I say as I point to the photo.

Her shoulders drop. "Huntington Beach." She exhales a long and slow breath. Then she shakes her head. "I don't want to talk about it. You already agreed I can have today without"—she pushes her hands out—"Everything else."

"Right. Sorry." I watch her for a moment, then my brows furrow. "Can you tell me why you don't want to… share things yet?" I gesture between us and say, "I can't help but feel like you're hiding something important." When I finish saying this, I have to wonder if it's my own guilty conscience talking.

"No... no bombshells." She bites the inside of her mouth and that makes me question whether she's telling the truth. Either way, I'd rather get to spend some time with her before dropping my bombshell too so I'm not going to look a gift horse in the mouth. "I just don't want to worry about anything today. I think it's a good idea to enjoy each other and get reacquainted before bringing real life into this."

I know she's trying hard to be light-hearted, but there's clearly something on her mind. Something heavy. I make a mental note to ask her properly about it when the time's right.

"How are you feeling?" I ask.

"I'm fine. You don't have to worry." She drops down into an armchair, then bends forward to unbuckle her shoes. "If I'm being honest, Drew, I've been so wound up the last couple of weeks. You have a way of calming me. I realize it wasn't Maui that mellowed me, it was you. You just have a way of relaxing me." Once her shoes are off, she sits upright. "I need that so bad today."

"Listen, Emily, there is something we need to talk about."

She glances up at me, and I can see the reluctance in her expression.

"It's not... anything off-limits, I promise. I just want you to know I'm here, okay?" I sit down across from her and lean forward, taking her hand. I know what she's going through, I've been there, and I just want to be there for her now. "Whatever is happening with you today, I'm here without hesitation and without a bunch of questions and without judgment."

She nods but doesn't speak so I push forward. "I guess I just want you to know that if you're worried about me, don't be." I rest my hand on my chest and say, "I don't have any deal-breakers.

I can't think of one thing you could tell me that would keep me from wanting this."

Her blue eyes are intense, and it's as if I can see her thoughts turning in her head and I sense a tremor pass through her. Proof that she's seriously worried about something.

"I mean that, so stop, okay? We have plenty of time to learn each other's stuff, good and bad." As I say this, I realize that our pact in Maui wasn't such a bad thing. It gave us leave to enjoy each other without the outside world getting in the way. I guess it was both a blessing and a curse, but I can understand why she wants to enjoy the anonymity for another day.

She rests back in her chair. "I'm sorry."

"Stop that too. Do not apologize again."

"Okay," she whispers. "Thank you for being here. Did you get some lunch?"

"I stopped by my mom's place on my way to the office and had a sandwich. How about you?"

"Not a bite."

"Wait, you haven't had lunch?"

"No, I didn't eat."

I stand and walk toward her kitchen. "Let me fix you something."

"Oh!" She jumps to her feet and follows me. "Wait! Um... the kitchen hasn't been cleaned."

I click the light switch and look around, then I turn toward her in mock horror.

"Oh my God, what a slob."

She laughs at my exaggerated expression and lightly stomps her foot. "Don't tease me."

I open the fridge and now I really am horrified. "Emily, your fridge is nearly empty."

"I also haven't been shopping since I got back."

I grab the carton of eggs and I'm relieved to see she has three left. "How about an omelet?"

"You don't have to—"

"An omelet it is," I say, cutting her off. "And I know you like eggs since I've had breakfast with you a few times."

"Yes, smartass, that's a safe assumption... and thank you."

Emily's kitchen is galley-style, with a long island in the middle, dividing it from her small dining room. She sits on a stool across the bar from me as I whisk together the eggs.

"So, what happened with Grant? I thought you were having lunch with him."

"Oh, I met him, I just didn't stay to eat."

I suck air through my teeth. "It went that badly, huh?"

"The man doesn't hear a word I say. I literally had to get angry for him to pay attention." She locks her hands in front of her. "At first, I felt bad about it. I didn't want to end the friendship, but then I realized there wasn't really a friendship at all. If the guy cared about me at all, he'd have listened when I told him I'd lost my husband. At the very least he should have heard me when I explained the most painful event of my life."

"I completely agree."

When I turn to glance at her, she narrows her eyes at me. "How do you know Grant?"

"We've worked on projects together. The first was about five years ago." I turn back toward the stove, then say, "I'm not sure I understand exactly what happened with you two. You went out with him a couple of times, but that's it?"

"Yes, exactly. I met him last year when I represented his firm. We stayed in contact mostly because we run in the same circles. The week before my vacation, Bec and I met with him about the remodel on our building. He was very nice, very generous. He could have done the design himself, through his architecture firm, and charged us an arm and a leg, but he very graciously offered to help us find a more affordable contractor who could do the design and construction. After our meeting, he asked me out for drinks, and I accepted. He actually asked me out for the first time over a year ago, and that's when I told him about my husband's death. Back then, I explained that I didn't think I was ready to date."

"Wow. This morning he acted like he'd never heard that before."

"I don't know if it's because I'm a woman, or because he's just too damn arrogant to listen to other people in the room… I really don't know, but after the second date, I knew it wasn't happening. As a matter of fact, when I left for Hawaii, I didn't tell him I was going on vacation. I asked Bec to tell him I was on a business trip."

I grin at her. "Gee, Emily, you didn't want to spend the week with him at his condo in Maui?"

She drops her head back with a groan. "My God, you've heard about the condo too?"

"Oh, yeah, he manages to bring it up in almost every conversation."

"He's so busy bragging about himself, he can't listen to other people."

I shrug. "Fine with me. His loss is my gain."

"I just can't be with someone who doesn't see me… do you know what I mean?"

"Yes, I do. I'll also add, what an asshole."

"Right? I didn't tell him about us, not that it would have mattered since he wouldn't have heard it. For some reason, he felt the need to apologize for *your* behavior."

I turn quickly. "What did I do wrong?"

"I guess he thought your hug was inappropriate, but he couldn't have been more wrong. That just pissed me off even more."

I scoff at that. "He should just be glad we didn't start making out right there."

She laughs and then leans back in her stool with a sigh. When I turn to put the plate down in front of her, she says, "Thank you so much, but you really didn't have to."

She picks up her fork and takes a bite then glances up at me through lowered lashes. "I can't believe you're here."

I tap my chest and say, "I'm just floored. So happy though."

"Me too."

"Oh, and congratulations on starting your own firm. Rebecca seems fun."

"She's incredible. We both got passed over for a promotion. They offered the partnership to a younger and less experienced man. After that, we got angry and then we did a lot of soul-searching. That's what prompted us to leave. We realized we didn't want to devote our lives to a firm that didn't appreciate us… We didn't want to devote our lives to our careers at all, we wanted more."

"And with your own, smaller firm, you can have that?"

"Yes. My vacation, for example. I never would have been able to take that much time off."

I grin at her and say, "Maybe next year you can take the full three weeks with me."

"That would be amazing." She sets her fork down and rests her head on her hand. "It took losing Tucker to realize I wanted to have a life outside of work. He always wanted me to travel with him, and he always wanted to do fun stuff like camping… he wanted to have a baby… but I…"

She trails off and I watch her, waiting to hear the rest, but she doesn't say any more. I think she's fighting to keep from crying. She lifts her eyes to me and finally says, "I didn't want to talk about this today."

"But you obviously need to talk about it."

She clears her throat. "Yeah, but that's probably because you're so easy to talk to. Why is that? My friends and family usually complain about how I don't like to talk about myself, but when you're in the room, I just spill my guts."

"Ha! If that were true, I would have gotten your address in Maui." I shake my head and fight to keep the smile off my face.

"No, your friends and family are right, you're not good at talking about yourself."

"Well, thank you for listening and for the omelet. It's delicious." Then she pushes her plate away. Only half has been eaten, but I know Emily is a light eater so I don't push. When she gets up and walks back to her chair in the living room, I click the kitchen light off and follow her.

As I sit on the couch across from her, she says, "I guess the main reason I want you to understand this is because it's part of the reason I didn't want to stay in touch when we left Hawaii. I'm honestly not sure if I'm relationship material, at least not yet."

"Let's just go with it and see what happens. We don't need to define what this is. Not yet. There's no reason to put more pressure on yourself right now." I let my eyes drift down her body and say, "As long as you want me here, it's all good."

"I want you here, for sure, but I have a hard time flying by the seat of my pants. You should know that now."

I give her a curt nod. "Duly noted." I wait a beat then try again to tell her about the kids. "There is something you should know, Emily."

After a long look, she gets up and moves over to straddle my lap. I'm surprised but not disappointed. Not at all. I scoot back to make room for her as she hikes her skirt up and places her knees on either side of my hips. Pressing against me, she places her lips on mine, and through the kiss, she says, "I missed this so much." The sultry tone of her voice makes my dick grow between us.

"I need to tell you…"

"No, you don't. I'm sorry to have dumped all of that on you but I think sharing time is over. I have something else in mind."

It's incredibly hard to argue with her in this position, so I give up and focus on getting her clothes off.

I unbutton her blazer and slide my hands over her shoulders to push it off. She flings it aside, and I'm only one cotton blouse away from touching her bare skin.

"Have I told you how incredible you are?"

She shakes her head. "Feel free to fill me in on that later."

I chuckle through our kiss, and I can feel her lips tip into a smile too. Then she leans forward and rests her face on my shoulder. She smells deliciously like jasmine and something else... something I can only define as pure Emily. I nip at the inside of her neck and mumble, "You're supposed to be resting. I promised Rebecca."

Her fingers start moving through my hair and tickling the back of my neck. "I guess you'd better take me to bed then."

With the agility of a teenager, I lift us both off the couch. She whoops as I spring up with her in my arms. "Don't have to tell me twice. Point me toward the bedroom."

# CHAPTER TWENTY-ONE

## Emily

When Drew sets me on the bed, I avoid looking around. My brain recognizes that I've brought a man into the room I used to share with my husband, but my heart wants Drew in ways I never thought possible. I've already fought through this guilt when I was in Hawaii, and I refuse to let it hold me back for another second. We both deserve to explore where this goes... all I can do now is hope Tucker would have been okay with it.

Drew leans over me, and I can feel his breathing against my hair, then his lips land on the space below my earlobe. His hands are jerking the pins out of the coil of hair twisted on my head. Once he's yanked the third out, he shakes my hair loose, buries his face in my neck, and moans quietly. "I missed this so much," he mumbles as he runs his hands through my hair.

I reach down to work at the button on his jeans, and that's when he freezes for a moment. He lifts up and says, "I need to go grab something, have these damn clothes off before I get back."

I want to laugh because as intimidating as he tries to be, I know he's just a big softy really. When I hear his footsteps retreat from the bedroom, I'm curious, but I quickly strip down to my panties. I'm fine with a little male dominance in the bedroom, but that doesn't mean I'm going to follow all his orders. I heave back the blankets on my bed, noticing the sounds from the neighborhood.

Someone is mowing their lawn, another seems to be running a saw of some kind. I almost feel sorry for them since I know I'm about to have so much more fun than they are.

When Drew pads back into my bedroom, I realize he's stripped off his shoes and socks. Through the light filtering in from the hall, I can see that he's carrying something. "What is that?" I ask.

"Condoms. I stopped at the drug store while I was out."

"Oh, smart thinking."

"Yeah, I had a feeling you wouldn't have any and I don't have a reason to carry them on me... especially since I wasn't expecting to run into you when I left the house today."

I grin at the thought that he doesn't walk around expecting to get laid on an ordinary Wednesday. "Well, I guess that's gonna have to change."

His laugh is muffled when he tugs his shirt over his head. "I'll leave these here, so we'll have them handy."

I run the tips of my toes up the inside of his leg and say, "You're assuming we're not going to use them all today."

The bed dips as he crawls in next to me and I hear him say, "Fuck, that's hot."

And then he's there, his warmth against me and I revel in how good it feels to have a man in my bed again. I've spent many, many nights alone in this room.

Drew's tongue swipes into my mouth, and his hands explore my body. I love the way he feels, I love the way he touches. He's so in control and confident. I admire that. I want a man who knows how to touch a woman and a man who can sense what I need and what I like. When his hand makes its way down my body, he freezes when it grazes over my panties.

"You're not naked." Then he travels further down, his lips pressing against me in random spots as he goes. When his kiss lands on my abdomen, he stops and rests his head there. I freeze, feeling suddenly unsure about myself. Can he sense I may be pregnant? Can he somehow tell? *No. Of course not, because I'm not pregnant.*

We were careful, just like we're going to be careful today.

"I told you to strip these off," he mutters from under the blankets.

He lifts up, pressing his palm against my clit, and now I'm seriously regretting keeping my panties on. His movements are teasing, and damn, I hate the barrier between us.

"I'll take them off."

But when I lower my hands to take the panties off, he gently smacks me away.

"Too late, now I get to do it." He grips the fabric tightly, and before I can stop him, he rips them away. I gasp in surprise, but I guess that's what I get for not stripping completely when he demanded it.

I feel him tear away the remnants of my underwear and then he lifts my knees, spreading them slowly, and a long, torturous moment later, his tongue is inside me. I gasp again but in pure pleasure this time. He feels incredible and, oh God, he's not going to need to do that for very long… I'm so close to losing all control, but then he pauses.

"Drew, oh God, don't stop."

A finger dips inside me, painfully slow, an inch at a time, exploring, but it's not the same as his tongue, and when he pulls out, I know he's teasing me on purpose.

"You're not nice, sir."

He swipes again with his tongue, but then leaves me wanting again. I'm so close to exploding, I can barely stand it. I would complain, but my mouth won't form words. My entire focus is on him and what he's doing to me… or *not* doing to me. His finger enters me again, and I push down, begging for more. But he continues to tease me.

The man is a monster.

I'm panting now, desperate to have any part of him inside me. When his lips circle my clit, I lift up, but he just hovers gently, giving me barely a hint of his tongue… then the gentle graze of his teeth.

"Oh God," I mumble. "Next time I'll get completely naked."

I feel his mouth turn into a smile, and then he's pushing two fingers inside me, and his tongue gets to work. It takes seconds for my body to react and I'm crying out as the orgasm flares wild and hot, a quick flash that leaves me panting in relief.

Before I realize what's happening, he slides his sheathed cock inside me, and I'm riding the wave again. I wrap my hands around his hips, afraid he's going to tease me and stop like he did before. I curl my body around him, lifting my feet around his waist to make sure he doesn't.

The sound of our bodies slapping together is almost as loud as our cries and groans. It's as if it's been a decade since we've done this, and if my stupidity had gotten its way, we might have lost a decade together. That thought makes me want to cry, even as he's pushing inside me. I just can't imagine not having this with him. He's become a part of me. I don't want to know the other version of how this could have gone.

I want him to feel this too, and when I open my eyes, I get a glimpse of his, and I know in my heart that he does. He does feel it. I can't hold back, so I close my eyes and let go of everything. All sense is gone for a couple of solid seconds, and then I feel Drew tighten, his body going rigid as he thrusts one last time, groaning as he does.

He's unmoving for a long time, and I'm not sure if he's breathing, but then he sucks in a lungful of air, and his body goes limp. As he drops to the bed, he pulls me with him so that I'm on my side and half over his body. It's quickly becoming my favorite spot in life… next to him, skin on skin. He's breathing hard, and his grip on me is tight, and all I can think is that he's shaken to the core the same way I am.

My heart is full and my belly fluttering with nervous energy. I should be scared at the intensity, but I'm too sated for that.

After a few minutes, Drew mutters, "Fucking Christ, Emily." He's still holding me against him, and when my grip on him tightens as well, I feel his lips on the top of my head. It's ridiculous that I'm fighting tears and I hold my breath for a long moment, hoping it'll pass. I'm not sad, I'm joyful, and it's been a hell of a long time since I've felt this.

As if he senses something's up, he loosens his grip finally. "Are you okay?"

I nod, afraid to use my voice. If I could talk, I'd tell him the same thing he told me. I'd tell him there are no deal-breakers when it comes to him. I am willing to forgive anything, willing to accept whatever part of him I can have.

*

I wake to the dark. There's a heavy arm draped over my torso and heat against my back. The reminder makes me sigh. I snuggle closer, and this makes Drew stir. I didn't mean to wake him up, but I also didn't realize it'd be so easy. Within a few heartbeats, I feel his erection against my rear. I press back against it and then hear a muffled moan that sounds full of sleep. I have no idea what time it is, but I truly don't care.

I roll over and push him onto his back. He's still limp with sleep and, damn, he's warm. I straddle him, his firm cock resting between our bodies. Then I lie on top of him, snuggling closer. Once I'm there, the rise of his chest lifts me, then lowers. He's so strong. His shoulders are so broad, and I feel tiny, resting on him like this.

When his arms encircle me, I smile and press my pelvis against him. He smells so manly, musky. I inhale deeply, enjoying everything about being pressed against his firm body. His heartbeat is calm and rhythmic, but strong like him. I feel so secure within his embrace. It's been a lifetime since I've felt so content. A quiet moan sounds in his chest, and the vibration rumbles under my cheek. His hands slide from my back to grip my ass and now I know he's fully awake. I want to regret waking him, but my need is stronger than that. I ease over and reach out for the box of condoms sitting on my nightstand.

Once my fingers find purchase, I bring the box closer, then rip off one from a strip. With it gripped in my hand, I grind up and down until he's lifting to me. Aha, it's my turn to be in control. I sit up on my knees, and I can feel his length pressed against me, sliding back until it springs forward. I can't see much, but when my hand wraps around it, Drew's head pops up, and a grunt rumbles from his throat.

"What are you doing?" he mumbles, his voice still sounding sleepy.

"Be still," I say, rubbing my hand up and down until he's rock-hard.

His hips lift against me, and a long moan sounds around me. "It's literally impossible to be still when you're doing that." Now he sounds awake. I almost want to giggle, but I hold it back. Before he can do anything else, I rip the condom wrapper open and slip it on.

"Oh, that's what you're doing."

"You got a problem with this?" I ask, and I'm sure he can hear the smile in my voice.

"No, ma'am. I like having my hands free to explore," he says, as his hands reach out to my breasts.

"Did you just call me ma'am?" I mutter as I rest myself over his standing erection and wait.

"No, ma'am—I mean, no, I would never…" I lower myself an inch and feel Drew's anticipation vibrating through him. "Oh, damn, slide down, please slide down," he whispers, holding absolutely still. Maybe he's trying to give me control, or maybe he likes the torture. I lower myself slowly, inch by inch, and it's a tease for me too. Once I'm fully seated, we both take a deep breath.

I drop my hands onto his chest and feel a flick of his hips. I push down, trying to control the experience. *Trying* being the key word here. I'm barely able to move without a million sensations pulsing through my body, but I lift myself anyway and lower myself again.

"Christ." His hands move from my breast to my hips. He lifts me again and tugs me down hard. "Now who's teasing?"

"What do they say about payback?" I ask, and my words are breathy, proving to him that this isn't easy for me either.

With strong hands, he lifts me then lowers me back down again. The sensation forces my hands into fists against his chest. I'm not sure how long I can hold out, but I know he's running out of patience. He lifts me again and pulls me back.

Unable to wait, I raise my hips and lean forward so that my breasts are dangling over him, brushing against his hard chest. He grips the back of my head and drags me down for a kiss. His teeth capture my lip, and now I'm thrusting for all I'm worth, his hips lifting at the same time to meet my thrusts. He takes my hands in his and links our fingers together, pushing against them, giving me the leverage I need to ride. My body tenses, coiled like a tightened spring, and I can't breathe.

My lungs heave as I cry out his name.

His hands squeeze mine. "I've got you, Emily. Let go, babe, I've got you."

With his words, I drop my head and arch my back, vibrating with the force of my explosive release.

I barely recognize the movement when Drew shifts and flips me onto my back. Then he's close, and I can feel his breath. I lift into a kiss, and a split second later, he's inside me again. It feels incredible, and I have to wonder how I went so long without this feeling. Without connecting to another human in the most primal way. Drew is moving achingly slowly, and our lips are locked, our tongues fighting for control. He wrenches away from the kiss and then his hot lips surround my nipple, sucking it into his mouth and then nipping with his teeth.

I can feel him pulsing inside me as his hips glide against me. I'm so sensitive after my orgasm, intensifying every movement, but when he reaches down and draws one of my knees up toward my chest, I'm opened even further and he's deeper than he's ever been.

He begins his climb with quicker movements and harder thrusts, his grunts coming in spurts. My entire body is shaking with the weight of him pressed against me.

"Emily, Christ, oh God," he cries, and the intense expression on his face pushes a surge of power through me. I did that. I reach up and drag my hand through his hair, and that forces his eyes to open and land on mine. Then he finally lets go.

# CHAPTER TWENTY-TWO

## Drew

We lie still, our bodies entwined tightly. In this pitch-black room, I have no clue what time it is but the shaft of light that was shining through the gap in the curtains has dimmed considerably. I'm so glad I don't have to worry about the time today. Emily and I needed this day together. But I can't deny how thrown I am by the intensity of my connection with her. Judging from her silence, I'm sure she's just as affected. We were good together in Maui, without a doubt, but now that we're home, the level of emotion between us has increased ten-fold.

I reach up to rub a hand up and down her arm. Emily is so still, I'm not sure if she's awake. When she inhales deeply, I draw her closer and feel her shudder as she exhales. Is she crying? I tilt my face down so my lips land on her forehead.

"Emily…"

The sound of her name stirs her, and when she stretches out, my hand travels to her mid-section. I wrap it around her and press her flush against me. I love the way she feels; I love the heat between us. It's been so long since I've been intimate with someone… and I mean truly intimate. I could stay in this bed with her forever if only that were possible.

When she reaches up and presses her lips gently against mine, I mumble, "How are you feeling?"

"I'm hungry. How about you?"

"Starving. Do you have any idea what time it is?"

"Not a clue… do you need to be somewhere?" she asks.

"Absolutely nowhere but here… if that's okay with you."

She stretches and inhales heavily, then exhales as her body relaxes again. "I like you here."

She slants away from me, and a second later, I see the light from her phone brighten the room. "It's almost eight."

"No kidding? I guess that explains the darkening sky."

"Close your eyes."

I do as she says and a moment later, red is burning behind my eyes. I lift the sheet over my head and groan. "No, don't do that. With the light comes real life."

"Nope. I still have several more hours without the interference of real life. I haven't forgotten."

Chuckling, I say, "Okay, all right. We can eat though, right?"

"Absolutely!"

I poke my head out from behind the sheet and glance at her with narrowed eyes. Her hair is tousled, her cheeks are flushed, and she has a bright and genuine smile on her face. She's the most beautiful thing I've ever seen. My heart jumps in my chest, and I fight to keep from blurting this out to her. The happiness I feel sobers me, and she must sense it because her smile fades too.

"What's wrong?" she asks.

"Nothing's wrong. The opposite. Everything feels right."

She nods, her eyes wandering away from me, and I can see she's considering this. "What if I said the same thing? What if there's nothing you could tell me that would be a deal-breaker?" Her eyes close and she says, "As long as you're not married. You didn't lie about that, did you?"

I grab her hand. "No, I didn't lie about that. I'm no longer married."

Her eyes pop open. "But you were? No, wait. No. Drew, it doesn't matter. I don't want any of that to interfere with tonight."

I link our fingers. "I don't want anything to interfere with tonight either."

She bites the inside of her mouth. "Why don't you stay with me for the rest of the week? Do you need to be home for any reason?"

"Nope, not this week. I have something happening Saturday morning, but I'm good until then."

"If you're here, I'll be forced to stop working. I'll have to come home."

"Aha, I see your plan now and I like it."

"How about Saturday evening? Let's have dinner or something." Her hand rests on her stomach and her eyes close. "I'm seriously going to need a distraction."

I wiggle my brows. "Distraction, huh?" I'm trying to be playful but when she doesn't laugh, I know I've missed something. "What's happening on Saturday that's going to require a distraction?"

Her expression grows serious and I get a glimpse of the sadness I recognize when she thinks about him. "I have a… thing… and I have to give a speech…" Her eyes dance around the room then lower to the bed. "But that's not something I want to think about right now." I glance around too, noticing the open suitcase that hasn't been unpacked.

I consider telling her about the note I left her, but then decide against it. Hopefully, it'll be a happy surprise when she finds it. My eyes drift around her bedroom again and land on the photo on top of her dresser of us standing next to the helicopter. Draped over the photo are the leis I gave her in Maui, now dry but still very pretty.

My eyes scan the other photos and then the little details I couldn't see in the dark, including the empty nightstand on the other side of the bed and that's when it hits me. Jesus. I feel like such an ass. This was the room she shared with her husband. This can't be easy for her, but I can see that she's trying so hard to keep from letting it get to her. She's so strong… too bad she doesn't realize it yet.

"Emily, I'm always available to be your distraction."

Her sultry but droopy eyes meet mine. "Perfect. Now let's go get something to eat."

She hops out of bed, and I watch as her sweet ass saunters across the room. I think about how incredible she is… and how this is a sight I hope to get the chance to see every day.

# CHAPTER TWENTY-THREE

## Emily

I'm floating on air. It's the only way to describe the way I feel. Last night was incredible and this morning in the shower was heavenly. I can't wait to talk to Rebecca. When I get upstairs, she's there, outside her office, waiting for me.

As soon as she sees my face, her gray eyes widen. "I guess you had a good night. You certainly look better than you did yesterday."

"I had a great night," I gush as I walk over and pop my office door open. "How are you this morning?"

"Oh, don't you try to act all normal and nonchalant with me," she says, following me.

I put my bags away and drop down into my chair. "I cannot believe this has happened. I'm absolutely stunned."

She lets out a deep laugh. "I bet! Understatement of the year." Then she sits in the chair across from me. "I take it you haven't started your period either."

I press my lips together and shake my head.

"Did you tell him you suspect you're pregnant?"

"No. Of course not!"

"Emily, maybe we shouldn't wait until tomorrow to take the test. This isn't something you can ignore. It won't go away… you know what I mean?"

"I don't think I'm pregnant. We were really careful in Maui, so I'm sure it's just the stress of missing him the last couple of weeks."

"Oh, yeah." She lifts her perfect brow. "You're not in denial at all, right?"

I sigh and drop my shoulders. On Tuesday, when I thought I'd have to face this without Drew, I was scared, but now, the idea of having to tell him I'm pregnant is daunting as hell.

"I know and I'll deal with it in my own time. I just want a little uncomplicated happiness, just a few freaking days of normal. Can you believe I went home yesterday and didn't do any work? This is a good thing, but it's hard not to feel like something is going to ruin it."

"I'm glad you took the night off, you needed that, but, Emily, don't assume a baby will ruin this. You don't know how he feels about having kids. Stop looking for the tragedy that lies inside your happiness. Just enjoy the happiness while you have it." She lifts up a finger as if to stop me from interrupting. "We'll stick to our original agreement. I'll give you until tomorrow morning, but then we have an appointment with a pregnancy test if your period still hasn't come."

As she's talking, I'm reminded of my conversation with Drew last night.

"Oh, yeah, and guess what? He's divorced."

"Really? He told you that?"

"He told me he was no longer married, but then I stopped him from telling me more. I didn't want the details."

"Jesus, Emily. How is it you manage to learn something so important about him, yet avoid asking for details?"

"It's baggage that will ruin my high. I just said this. Besides, if she's out of the picture, she doesn't matter to me."

"Divorced, huh?" She purses her lips for a moment. "Any kids?"

I freeze, my eyes locked on her. "No. No kids."

"So, you asked?"

"No, but he would have told me that."

"How, when you stopped him from talking about it?"

I think about all the time we spent together in Maui. "No, I would have figured it out in Maui. I'm sure I'd know if he has kids. He's divorced with two roommates. Besides that, he was with me all night last night. If he had kids at home, he couldn't have done that."

She gives me a perplexed look. "Most divorced dads only see their kids on the weekends, Emily."

I consider that, but nah, I don't see it. He would have told me that. How could he not have? "No, I'm sure. There's no way he could have kept that from me. I'm sure. No kids."

"Okay, well, that's good, since he's divorced. You don't have to deal with baby momma problems."

"Exactly. And why force him to talk about a painful experience if we can avoid it?"

"Hey," Rebecca says, sitting upright in her chair. "Did you invite him to the ceremony on Saturday?"

I shake my head. "No. I mentioned it briefly but I don't think it's a good idea. I don't want him there to see that. I'm sure he wouldn't be comfortable."

"So, how does a renaming ceremony go? And why this random elementary school when Tucker was a high school teacher?"

"The district's upgraded the school. They've built a new gymnasium, new administrative offices, and fully repainted it. They've even changed the mascot and they wanted a new name." I link my hands together and say, "It's sort of a rebranding… and since Tucker was a former district teacher and he died saving two lives, they picked his name for the school."

"I can't argue with that. The man died a hero, he should be honored."

"I agree. They've asked me to speak, so I'll be talking about Tucker, and I believe a couple of his former students are also going to give speeches."

"Will Mac and Kelley be there?"

"Yes, they're coming. Aren't you?"

She draws back, surprised. "Of course. Eddie will be there as well. We're coming to support you. What about your mom? Is she going to make the drive out?"

"Um, I don't think so. I mentioned it to her, but she didn't say she was coming."

"Hey, speaking of your mom and Mac, do they know about Drew?"

"Mac knows. I texted him an update this morning so he'd stop worrying about me. I haven't told my mom anything."

"But you're going to, right? I mean, you probably should tell her about Drew before you tell her you're pregnant."

I narrow my eyes, not sure how to handle my mother. "I don't know… I'll have to figure that out after I take a test. I just can't worry about that right now."

"If she shows up on Saturday, it might get a little awkward. You realize that, right?"

"Yep, just what I need, my mom showing up unannounced. Thank you for putting that worry in my head. I do appreciate it. Now…" I throw a thumb over my shoulder. "Get out of here so I can get some work done."

# CHAPTER TWENTY-FOUR

## Drew

When I enter the office the next morning, I'm running late. This gets me the stink-eye from Maggie, my office manager. "Sorry. I… ah… had a long night."

She looks me up and down. "Did ya now?" She winks at me, and I get the sense that she knows something she shouldn't.

"Yes, I did," I reply, smiling. "Why's it so quiet?"

With a wave of her tattooed arm, she gestures toward the controller's office. "Paula took the day off and Manny's out inspecting the Grainger place. The crew finished it up yesterday."

"Wow, they weren't due to finish until tomorrow, that's awesome work. Any messages for me?"

"Nope. You're in the clear."

"Thanks," I grumble before stepping into my office. After waking up at Emily's house and spending a solid forty-five minutes with her in the shower, doing *a lot* more than just washing, I had to rush home for clean clothes, then I called and checked in with the kids. After our long nap yesterday, neither Emily nor I got any sleep last night. We did, however, almost run out of condoms. This thought makes me smile.

After spending the entire evening in her space, I feel better about our future but I'm still nervous about telling her about the kids. She said she didn't have any deal-breakers and I want to believe her, but my history with women goes against that. Thinking about the next couple of days, I'm thankful they're out of town. It gives me time to ease her into it.

Yesterday, I got the impression there was something specific she was hesitant to tell me, but now I just think she doesn't want the honeymoon phase to end. I can't blame her—if I could stay in paradise with her forever, I would. But I can't.

I step into my office and click the switch on. Once I'm settled in with a fresh cup of black coffee, I log onto my computer and navigate to the county's online records library in search of all the permits and blueprints for Emily and Rebecca's building. I have some great ideas for the space, and I can't wait to get started.

Without much thought, my eyes drift over to the framed family photo that's sat on my desk for the last seven years. It's a photo of our family before Hannah. Kyle was so small, and his huge grin was electric... still is. Kayla and I had just started DK Builders and we were celebrating our first winning bid on a commercial property in West Sacramento. We were ecstatic that day. We dreamed about the success DK has gained since she's been gone. Yet another thing she didn't get to experience in her short but sweet life.

I have another picture of the kids and me, without Kayla. It was taken just a year ago, on the day Hannah started kindergarten. Her big smile shows off her missing teeth. She happened to lose both front teeth that summer when she was visiting her grandparents in LA, and she was so proud of it. This year was the first time I've come back from vacation without being threatened by Kayla's parents; the first time they let me pick up the kids without criticism or threats to take them away. It's been a long road, but I think they're finally coming to terms with the fact that I will always fight for my children.

I pick up the photo with Kayla and run my fingers over the surface. God, I miss her. Just because life has settled and we've found normalcy in the midst of grief doesn't mean I don't think about her every single day. But I need to move on. I need to love someone else… someone who will also love my kids. Is that person Emily?

I sure as hell hope so.

# CHAPTER TWENTY-FIVE

## Emily

On Thursday afternoon, we're sitting in our makeshift conference room, and thanks to Eddie, we have fresh coffee and ice-cold water. The room is warm because this old building doesn't have a powerful enough air conditioner to cool every room. And in Sacramento in August, air conditioning is must. As hot as the room is, and as weird as it smells with the old, faded carpet, it's still a beautiful space, with hand-carved moldings and a gorgeous antique chandelier. Yeah, it's a bit over the top, but it fits the space and it's still not the centerpiece of the room. That would be the fireplace, with the carved beams that reach the ceiling.

Rebecca and I haven't taken the time to pick our official conference room furniture so we're sitting at a folding table in folding chairs while Drew presents his ideas. Midway through our meeting, I stop to remember him in shorts and flip-flops. The difference between that Drew and this one is crazy. He's so professional. So smart... and his design plans are so freaking intuitive, I can hardly stand it. It's as if he was in the room with Rebecca and me when we talked about what we wanted.

He's definitely not in shorts and flip-flops now, but I'm glad he doesn't feel the need to be in a suit. I like him relaxed. I like how confident he is, no matter what he's wearing. Not that he's not incredibly sexy in his fitted Henley and jeans.

"Earth to Emily." Rebecca snaps her fingers in front of my face.

I nearly jump out of my skin. "Oh, sorry. Did I miss something?" I look up to see Drew smiling at me, then I turn toward Rebecca. "What's the problem?"

"Did you hear Drew's suggestion?" She waves toward him. "He suggests we have two downstairs conference rooms."

"Why? What's wrong with one upstairs and one downstairs?" I ask.

He points to the upstairs. "There's no disability access to the second floor. If you have to meet with a client who needs special access, they won't be able to get up there. Unless you want to pay to install an elevator."

"If we have two available rooms downstairs, we have an office space option if we hire someone who can't get upstairs. Which is actually a great idea," Rebecca says, annoyed with my inattentiveness.

I feel the heat in my cheeks but try to shrug it off. "That sounds fine to me. Drew, I can't believe how quickly you were able to draw this up," I say, gesturing toward his notepad.

He cocks an eyebrow. "Did I mention I've been in love with this building for years?"

"The plans are really great," Rebecca agrees. "Can we meet again on Tuesday for an update, same time as today?"

"Absolutely. I'll add it to my calendar. Thank you, ladies, for your time." As he says this, he stands and collects his notes.

Rebecca and I stand too but before I leave the room, I turn toward Drew. "Can you stop in before you take off?"

He nods, "Of course, let me get everything in the truck first."

I head up the stairs with Rebecca, and when we reach my office, she follows me in. "I just want you to know, I'm picking up a pregnancy test tonight and bringing it with me tomorrow, so you don't need to worry about it."

"Thank you." I blow my bangs off my face and say, "I'm so nervous."

"How are you feeling? Still nauseous and tired?"

My stomach drops when she asks this but it's pointless to continue to ignore the obvious. "Yeah." I feel the tug of a frown pull my lips down. "And my boobs hurt. There are too many symptoms to ignore now."

"Oh, crap!"

"I know. I'm trying not to freak out about it, but when you look at me like that, it's really hard."

"Emily, how do you feel? Are you happy about it?"

"I'm too freaked out to know. I think I am, but it's hard when I don't know what his reaction is going to be."

"Are you going to tell him?"

"Not until after I take a test tomorrow and I need to get through this event on Saturday first. I don't know, but I'll figure something out after that."

I can tell Rebecca is trying to hide her smile, and I'd like to feel happy about it too, but I'm too scared. She finally says, "It'll be fine, you'll see." Then she stands and as she's leaving my office, Drew steps in.

"Everything okay?"

"Of course, why?"

"You look flushed." He lifts his hand to my forehead, and my stomach immediately starts to flutter. He's always trying to take care of me, which makes me think he'll be a great dad one day. My stomach somersaults... maybe even sooner than *one day*.

I wonder if it's time to test the waters. "Have you ever considered having kids?" I ask, but when I see his expression change, I immediately know I made the wrong decision. *What the hell is wrong with me?* The concerned expression melts away and he pulls back like he's been burned. Discomfort and confusion are clear in his eyes.

*Dammit, what was I thinking?*

"I have... why?"

I shrug, trying to act nonchalant. "I don't know, I was just thinking you'd make a great dad someday... you know, because you're such a good caretaker."

"Oh, ah, thanks. I think." He looks around as if he's trying to find an escape. "I need to get back to the office. I have to work late tonight. Do you mind a late dinner? Probably eight or nine."

I'm fighting not to feel hurt by this, but I'm not sure what I was expecting. My stomach bottoms out. What the hell am I thinking? We barely know each other. Of course he doesn't want to think about having kids with me, much less talk about it.

*Is this pregnancy going to scare him away?*

I stare at him as I think about that. If he's the type of guy to break up with me because I'm having his baby, then he's not the guy for me. I don't see him acting like that, but I really don't know. I mean, I've never even been to his house.

"Emily, you okay?" he asks, reaching out to touch my shoulder. "You're awfully distracted today."

"Um, sorry. Dinner... yes, that's fine, but if you want to skip it, that's okay too." I step back from his touch and walk around my desk to sit down.

He watches me with a tilt of his head. "I don't want to skip it, but I don't want you to wait for me if you'd rather not... But I want to see you... you know I do, right?"

I nod but avert my eyes. "I would understand if you didn't want to spend the night again. I'm sure you have other obligations."

"I'm working late to clear up those obligations, but what do you want, Emily?" he asks. Then he sits across from me and leans forward. "I'm getting a weird vibe."

I take a deep breath and lift my eyes. "I would like to see you tonight, I'm just not sure where your head is at."

He stands and walks around my desk, then takes my elbow to guide me out of my chair. "My head has been with you since the moment I laid eyes on you. Since the moment I saw you with your hair tightly bound in that bun and your cute little ass stuffed into that business suit." He takes my lips, and his kiss makes my knees weak. I'm so distracted, I don't realize he's pulling the pins from my hair until he's removing the third.

I twist away and laugh. "I have another meeting today, you know."

He flashes me a sexy grin. "No, I didn't know." Then he shakes my hair loose, so it drapes down my back. "But don't worry, they're going to like you like this." Then he drops the three bobby pins into my palm before laying a light smack on my ass and walking out of my office.

# CHAPTER TWENTY-SIX

## Drew

I head to my house to work on the design for Emily's building. I need to check the mail and get a change of clothes for tomorrow. Although, after this afternoon, I'm not so sure I'll be spending the night with her. She seemed… off. Why did she ask me about kids? And why the hell didn't I tell her the truth about Kyle and Hannah?

*Dammit, what the fuck is wrong with me?*

I step out of my truck and walk over to the mailbox, removing the stack of junk mail and folding it under my arm to flip through the bills as I unlock the front door.

When I walk into the house, it's so quiet, it's almost sad. It's not the same without the kids. I miss them. I grab my phone and read over the last few texts and pictures I received from them and my mom. They're having so much fun, and even though Hannah is too small for most of the Boardwalk rides, in the photo she's smiling wide on the beach.

Kyle's looking just as happy, with sand in his hair and a sunburned nose. I flip to the next photo, of Kyle and my nephew Connor, building a sandcastle with a moat. They must have spent hours on it because their shoulders are red and the thing spans several square feet. I look at the text under the picture, and it says, "It's our beach lair, Dad!"

I chuckle and click my phone off as I drop it on the coffee table. Sinking into the couch, my mind turns to Emily. *What the hell am I going to do—and what the hell have I done? Not telling her this afternoon was a mistake, I know that.*

I can't continue to pretend I don't have children. It's not like Emily and I are only dating. It's bigger than that. I know it's early but I also know, somehow, that this is deeper than that. Besides, the kids will be back on Saturday morning, and after that, I can't hide them. I need to tell her tonight. That gives her time to get used to the idea before they're here. I feel so shitty about it. Having not told her makes me feel dirty. Pretending is wrong—it's wrong to her and wrong to them.

I hear a tap at the back door and peek out to see Jake there, holding two beers. I step out and take one from him. "I guess it's break time," I mutter as I sit in one of the patio chairs.

"Where you been, man? I thought we were watching the game last night. Everything okay?"

"Oh, shit, sorry. I completely forgot. The kids are out of town with my mom, and I stayed with a friend last night."

"Really?" He looks me up and down. "So, you met someone? I thought you were set on finding the chick you met in Maui."

"I was, and I did."

"No way! You're shitting me."

"Nope. She's my new client."

"Wha… you're pulling my leg."

"It's true. She's a lawyer with her own firm in Midtown, and she lives about six blocks from here."

He sits down in a patio chair and rests back. "How the hell did you find her?"

"We have a mutual friend. She needs a remodel done on her new offices and he recommended me. Crazy, really."

"So, you stayed at her place last night?"

"Yeah. The kids were gone, so why not?"

"Speaking of the kids, what did she say when you told her?"

I take a long swig of beer then press my lips together for a moment, not sure what to say.

"Oh shit! You haven't told her yet?"

I shake my head, too embarrassed to speak.

"Oh, finally taking my advice, huh?" He points his beer at me. "I told you it would work. All you have to do is keep it a secret until you get tired of her."

I clear my throat, slightly offended by his macho bullshit. "I'm not going to get tired of this woman, Jake. I'm pretty sure I'm in love with her."

"Fuck, are you serious?"

I nod, the words getting stuck in my throat. "It's crazy, I know that, but I can't pretend it's not happening, and she's probably going to end it when she finds out about Kyle and Hannah."

"You fell fast, man. Are you sure?"

I chuckle at that. "Yeah, too fucking fast, and I'm not totally sure about anything right now, Jake." I lift my beer again and swig. "It's been a long time since I've felt like this about a woman, but this isn't something I have control over."

He nods, then shrugs. "Well, I guess you'd better pray she's interested in being a mom."

"I'm telling her tonight. I have no choice."

"What happens with the job if things don't work out?" His knee starts bouncing around when he asks this, and it's making me jittery as well. "I mean, if she breaks it off, is she still going to hire you for this remodel job?"

I hadn't thought about that. Could I continue to work there without having Emily? I want this job but not as much as I want her. I lift my hand in defeat. "I have no clue, honestly, but I can't keep lying. She's going to find out eventually. Besides, I can't be with someone who doesn't love my kids." I get up out of my chair. "Listen, thanks for the beer, but I need to get some work done."

I give him a wave then head back into the house, grabbing the plans I brought with me and heading back to the office. Laying the plans out on the drafting table, I'm relieved to have a few hours. Sometimes work is the only thing in my life that makes sense. Sometimes, it's the only thing I feel I have complete control over.

When Kayla and I started this business, we had a plan to build our dream home on the river. We wanted a house full of kids and looked forward to hordes of grandkids after our retirement. So far, the only dream that's been realized is the success of our business. Yes, we were blessed with two of the most precious kids a couple could ask for, but what is a realized dream without the partner you planned to enjoy it with?

Instead of the large family *we* wished for, I'm alone with two living reminders of what I've lost. I work every day to make sure they don't feel like they're missing something, but they are. They're missing the love and perfection that was their mother. They're missing the softness and affection mothers bring to life. Not once since losing Kayla have I thought I needed to find another wife. Not once have I felt that my kids needed a replacement mother. Because there is no replacing Kayla. But for the first time since losing her, I feel that undeniable connection to someone else. No, I don't need a partner, but I do feel a strong need for Emily in my life and in my bed every day. I want her to be a more permanent part of my life—of *our* lives.

The more I consider this, the more afraid of being with her I become. Having her as mine is almost as frightening as losing her.

Losing Kayla was hell on earth. I'm not sure I could go through that again. I know Emily dying isn't something I should worry about, but I can't avoid it. It's instinctive for my mind to go there after the grief and loss I've experienced. Not only that, but what if I tell Emily I have kids, and it doesn't end in disaster? What if she's excited about getting to know my children? What if it all works out?

Maybe I'm a little paranoid, but when she asked me about kids today, my heart nearly jumped out of my chest, but it wasn't because of Kyle and Hannah. It was because, for the first time since meeting her, I saw a real future in her eyes and what that might look like for her.

She doesn't have children. She's going to want one of her own someday. She's going to want to get pregnant and have a baby.

I'm not sure I can do that. I'm not sure I'm willing to go through another pregnancy.

I think about it and realize, I'm sure. I'm sure I can't do that again. I can't sit by, hopeful and happy for months and months, watching another woman grow my child, just to lose her. My heart couldn't take it.

# CHAPTER TWENTY-SEVEN

## Emily

I purposely left work early so I could cook for Drew. It took me over any hour on the internet to find the perfect meal, but once I found the shrimp scampi recipe, I rushed to the grocery store. Now my fridge is stocked and I'm out of my work clothes and ready to start cooking. I glance at the clock. "Crap, it's already after eight o'clock."

I get all the fixings for the salad washed and chopped, and just as I'm about to finish up with the tomatoes, I hear a knock at the door. I shout out, "It's open, come on in."

Drew comes inside, whistling. "What smells so good?"

I laugh at him and look down at the tomatoes I'm slicing. "Um… salad?"

"Oh, okay." He enters the kitchen with a confused expression. "We're having salad for dinner?"

"Salad and shrimp scampi, but I haven't started on that yet." I point to the bottle of Pinot Grigio. "Will you open that for me? Oh, and I also got beer, if you'd prefer that. It's in the fridge."

He looks over at me and wags his eyebrows. "Someone went grocery shopping."

"Yes, finally. Of course because of it, I got a late start on cooking. I thought you were working late."

With a chuckle he says, "I am late. It's nearly nine o'clock. Although, to a workaholic like you, that probably isn't late." He pops the cork on the bottle and takes a glass down from the cabinet. As he's pouring my wine, someone else knocks on the door. We glance at each other, confused.

"Are you expecting someone else?" he asks.

"No. No one… Do you mind answering?" As he's walking toward the door, I say, "Feel free to get rid of whoever it is. I'm not interested in buying or subscribing."

A minute later, I hear a loud guffaw. I rush to the door to find my mom standing on my front porch. She looks over at me. "Well, isn't he cute?"

*Oh. Shit.*

"Mom! Hi! What are you doing here?"

She's smiling wide and wearing a teasing expression behind her round, red-framed glasses. It's been several weeks since I've seen her. She looks rested and happy.

"It's lovely to see you too, daughter." She reaches in and gives me a tight hug. She's about an inch taller than me and her long arms snake around me and hold on for a long moment. Then she withdraws and takes me in with her startlingly blue eyes. "Who's the hunk?"

I give Drew an apologetic glance and fight the blush that wants to bloom on my cheeks. "Um, Mom, this is Drew Whitney. Drew, this is my mother, Marilyn Mackensey."

My mom holds out her hand to shake Drew's. "Lovely to meet you. I'd like to say I've heard a lot about you, but I haven't."

Drew's smiling and I'm glad he's so laid-back. Anyone else would be freaking out right now. "It's very nice to meet you too, Marilyn. I'm equally confused because Emily hasn't mentioned you either."

Of course this makes my mother laugh again.

"I'm sorry. I haven't exactly had the chance to call you since I returned from Maui, Mom."

"Yeah, yeah, I know. You're an uber-busy and important lawyer with no time for family. I know, I know."

"So, Mom…" I look at her little overnight bag and say, "You're here for the night…?"

"Yes, just tonight. I'll stay with Mac tomorrow night." She holds her hand up before I can respond. "Don't worry. I'll take the couch."

"I didn't know you were coming."

"I didn't mention it?" She slaps her hands to her sides. "I'm so sorry—but of course I want to be here to support you on Saturday. Unfortunately, I have to leave right after, though. I hope that's okay?"

"Oh, Mom, thank you. I just… it's not a big deal. You didn't have to drive out just for that."

"I didn't just for that. I also wanted to check in on you." She glances at Drew, who's politely listening to our conversation as he's bringing her bag inside and closing the door. "Thank you, Drew. Emily, I didn't know you'd have company."

"I was just cooking dinner. Are you hungry?"

"You're cooking? Really?" She follows me into the dining room and sits at the bar, facing the kitchen.

I turn toward Drew and try to whisper an apology. "I'm sorry to ambush you. I really didn't know she was coming. She usually stays at Mac's since he has a guest room."

"I do. It's true," Mom says, without even trying to pretend not to have heard me. "But it's too late. I didn't want to get him out of bed."

Drew glances at his watch and lifts an eyebrow.

"Mac works really, really early in the morning so he goes to bed super early."

Drew chuckles. "It's okay. I don't mind having dinner with your mom." He looks thoroughly amused by this development and it makes me wonder if he's realized this means he won't be able to spend the night. That news is surely going to wipe the grin off his face.

I pour my mother a glass of wine and hand it across the bar to her. She gets up out of her chair. "I almost forgot. I brought you something."

She goes back into the living room but I keep working on dinner since it's getting so late. When she returns, she's carrying a huge scrapbook. My heart sinks. Please don't tell me she's brought baby pictures. Jesus. It's as if she knew I had a man here.

"Mom, what are you doing?"

"I made this for you and I made one for Mackensey. It's a scrapbook with all the photos I had of your dad."

"Oh, wow, Mom, that was nice."

She sits at the table this time instead of the bar and shifts the book so that she and Drew can look at it together. I keep working in the kitchen, fighting the urge to walk over and join them.

"He's a musician?" Drew asks.

Mom stops midway through turning the page. "Well, at least I know she didn't tell you about him either."

I roll my eyes and say, "He passed about ten years ago."

"Oh, I'm sorry. I didn't realize…"

I drop my shoulders with a sigh. "We weren't that close. Mac and I were raised by my mom."

My mother bounces slightly in her chair. "He traveled a lot, but he loved you two so much."

"Yeah, I'm sure he did." I think about that, trying to remember spending time with him as a kid. He was always the coolest guy in my eyes. I loved him so much and I was always in such awe of him. Of course, now, as an adult, I realize he wasn't that cool. He was just an absent father.

My brain immediately stalls on the fact that I'm pretty damn sure I'm pregnant. I glance up at Drew and wonder how on earth this is going to turn out. Will he be there every day for our child, or will he be an absent father too? I drop my chin and close my eyes. God, I hope not. I don't want that for my life or for my baby. I don't want to be my mother, always making excuses for my child's father. Always trying to be both mother and father.

I loved my dad, I really did, but my memories of him are clouded in a fog of disappointment and regret. I spent most of my life missing him and wishing he'd surprise me and show up out of the blue. He did… sometimes, but not very often.

I catch snapshots of their conversation as I'm cooking. My mom is telling Drew how she met my dad. How he left us to tour the country with his band. They didn't marry—because my father didn't believe in marriage. I remember what she went through with him. She tried moving on, she tried seeing other people, but she never stopped loving my dad. When he'd come back to town, she'd drop everything for him—then he'd just turn around and leave again a few weeks later. As I'm listening to her story, all I can think about is how I have to take a pregnancy test tomorrow… and how much that's potentially going to change my life.

"He toured with his band every year so we didn't get to see him that much," my mom explains. "He called pretty regularly though."

I want to make a snarky comment about how often he really did call, but I don't bother. The man is dead, I don't need to rehash the past. I pick up the salad bowl and walk over and place it on the table. I lean in to see the photos and my heart skips when it lands on a particularly great picture of my dad on stage. His long hair is all over the place and he's smiling so wide.

"At least he was happy," I mumble.

Drew points to the photo. "You look like him."

"Yeah, I do, don't I?" I stare down, trying to remember the last time I looked at a photo of my father. I glance around the house and realize I don't have any pictures of him displayed.

"Thank you, Mom. This is such a great gift."

"You're welcome. I didn't see any point in holding onto them so I made copies for both of you and put these books together."

"Mac's going to love it too."

"Wait, is Mac's first name Mackensey?" Drew asks with a puzzled expression.

"Yes." My mom nods and says, "Mackensey Thomas. We gave him my last name as his first name and then his dad's last name, Thomas. We both thought it had a nice ring to it."

Mom flips the page and the first thing I see is my father holding me as a newborn baby. For me it hits so close to home that my eyes instantly tear up. I realize that's another thing my child won't have: my dad as a grandfather. Am I crazy for bringing a child into this weird, unsettled situation? Is it a mistake? My hand drops to my stomach at the thought and I know, deep down, that if I'm pregnant, it's not a mistake. Drew and I are magical together. We really fit, and while I'm not sure what his reaction is going to be when I tell him, I know the connection we share is real. It's tangible and beautiful, even if it doesn't last forever.

I look over at my mother with a new understanding. I lean down and kiss the top of her head before walking into the kitchen. I get it now. I see why she always defended my dad when he wasn't there for us. Why she always made excuses for him while we were growing up. Why she wasn't resentful about being a single mother. Without my father, Mac and I wouldn't be who we are. Without their relationship, her life would be completely different. If I know anything about my mother, it's that she loves her life and she loves her kids. I've never doubted that. If she considers her relationship with my dad as beautiful as I consider my relationship with Drew, then I understand. And just as she felt about me and Mac, there's no way I can't regret—much less question—bringing our child into this world, with or without him.

When we sit down to eat, I let Drew tell my mom the story of how we met. I'm grateful when he leaves out the part about me getting drunk and him putting me to bed.

My mom loves it when Drew tells her about how I corrected the bellman when he called me "ma'am". I smile too; it's hard not to when I see Drew's dimples and I'm reminded of how hot he looked in his aloha shirt and flip-flops. Besides that, I'm not such a snob that I can't laugh at myself. Drew reaches across the table and lays a hand on my arm before saying, "It was a great week."

Mom's face brightens and she beams at me. "Oh, honey, I'm so glad." She glances at Drew, her expression thankful. "I'm so happy you were there and you two met—and what a coincidence that you live so close."

Drew's eyes lock on mine. "I'm glad too." When he says this, a warmth spreads through me. I'm as thrilled about it as Mom is. I couldn't have asked for more... and to think, I almost screwed it up. I just pray this is still where he wants to be once I share the news.

When we've finished eating, my mom heads off to the shower so Drew and I take advantage of our alone time and curl up on the couch for a while.

"Shouldn't we work on cleaning the kitchen?" he offers.

"No, I'll take care of it later." I rest against him and apologize. "I'm so sorry about tonight. I meant for this to be a quiet evening with just the two of us. I had no idea she was coming."

"Hey, it's okay. She's great. I don't mind at all."

I suck air through my teeth and say, "Unfortunately..."

"I can't spend the night." He finishes for me.

I shake my head with a mock frown. "I'm sorry."

"That's perfectly all right. It seems like she needs some time with you anyway."

"Yeah, I got that feeling too."

"Tomorrow night?" he asks. "If she really is going to Mac's house?"

"Oh, she is. He has a beautiful guest room made up for her all the time. She rarely stays here."

Drew leans in and rests his forehead against mine. "I'm not sure how I'm going to sleep without you tonight."

"I know. I'm going to miss you too."

Then he pulls back just enough for the light to catch the glowing, golden flecks in his eyes. "Hey, I wanted to ask, this ceremony on Saturday... I have something planned, but if you need me, I can be there for you." He pauses, his expression turning thoughtful. "It sounds like it might be difficult for you."

I shake my head. As much as I appreciate the gesture, I really don't need him there. "No, but thank you. I'll be fine. It's not a big deal."

His eyes narrow. "You're sure?"

I place a gentle kiss on his lips and as I do so, my stomach does a little flip. He's so great and as much as I want to share everything with Drew, I'm not sure a ceremony honoring my late husband is the right place for him.

# CHAPTER TWENTY-EIGHT

## Emily

When I hear Rebecca climb the stairs, my stomach does a somersault. We both agreed to come in early, so we're alone in the office to do the pregnancy test. But I'm not ready. Last night I felt sure I could handle this. I felt sure I wanted this, but now, now that I'm faced with finding out for sure… I don't feel ready.

I know in my heart that I'm not ready to share this news with Drew yet… my pulse skips when this thought crosses my mind. I know I can't hide it, but I'm not prepared for the rejection if he's not interested in being a father.

"Good morning," Rebecca chants from the hall. "How are we feeling this morning?"

Another stomach dip.

"Sick."

"Oh, come on, Emily. Everything's going to be fine." I hear her office door creak open and a moment later, she's in my office with a small white paper bag.

I groan and drop my head to my desk.

"I take it this means your period still hasn't come."

I turn my head from side to side. "Bec…" It comes out like a whine. I lift my head to meet her eyes and say, "I'm petrified." Then my face falls.

"Emily, honey, listen to me. I know you're scared, but the reason you and I left that stuffy, male-dominated law firm was so that our lives wouldn't revolve around our careers. Right?" She reaches out and takes my hand. "We topped out there and were skipped over because of our gender. Right?"

She's right. I didn't want to grow old and be left with a life full of regret. I wanted to meet someone and have a family. I wanted to have the chance to travel and meet people and spend time with my loved ones. I nod at her and say, "Yes. This is just so unplanned."

"And unplanned is totally out of the box for you. I know that, but, I promise, I will be here every step of the way to support you and your baby. You are not alone. Besides that, from what I've seen, Drew is madly in love with you. I have no doubt he's going to be thrilled."

I shake my head jerkily. "No. I asked him yesterday, and he got really uncomfortable. He was so weird about it. I don't think he's ready for this either."

"You asked him directly?"

"No, I asked him if he'd ever thought about having kids."

Rebecca's shoulders bob up and down with her quiet laugh. "That was brazen."

"It was stupid. Not bold."

"Regardless, you brought it up as a hypothetical situation. You can't rely on reactions to hypothetical questions. That's not fair. Once he finds out and gets used to the idea, things will work out. You just have to give him time to adjust, just like you need time to adjust."

She grabs my hand, pulling me out of my chair. "Let's get this done so we know what we're dealing with. After we know for sure, we can deal with Drew."

Once we're in the bathroom, she lifts three boxes out of her bag. "I got several just to be safe." She holds up one. "This one takes two minutes and says clearly *pregnant* or *not pregnant*, depending on the results." She picks up another. "Ditto, with this one. It takes two minutes and has a plus sign for positive." She hands me the third box. "This one has a color indicator line and takes three minutes. Oh, and they all say they can detect pregnancy five to six days before a late period so you should be good." She takes a deep breath and then smiles. "I hope you need to pee."

I'm completely overwhelmed, staring at her with my mouth open and my eyes wide. "It's a bit overkill, don't you think?"

"We want to be sure." She turns to leave me alone, then asks, "Oh, do you want me to stay?"

"No," I mumble. "I think I can handle it."

After she's gone, I juggle to pee on the three strips, which is no easy feat. Once that's done, I set them on the sink basin, lined up in a perfect row, and rush away from the bathroom, averting my eyes.

I don't want to look.

Still adjusting my skirt, I head back to my office where Rebecca is waiting for me.

"It's done."

"And…"

"Are you kidding? I didn't look."

"Oh, Jesus Christ." She stands and runs to the bathroom. A few seconds later, she starts screaming.

I can't move. I know what that sound means and I'm frozen in place. I place my hand on my stomach and take a deep breath.

"You're having a baby!" Rebecca says from the door. "Emily, oh my God!" She shows me all three tests. They're all positive. "You're pretty freaking pregnant."

I bend over and place my head between my knees, feeling like I want to throw up.

She rests a hand on my back and rubs in small circles. "You're going to be fine, I promise."

"I don't have a choice now. I have to be."

"That's right, but I wish you were happy about it."

I sit upright and I try to force out a smile. "I'm not unhappy… just a bit shocked." My voice hints at a whine because I'm fighting with my emotions. "My fear has become a reality and now I have to face it… share the news with my family… deal with things I'm not sure I'm ready to deal with."

"What about Drew?"

"What about me?" he says from the door of my office.

My eyes meet Rebecca's, and she tucks the pregnancy tests under her arm.

"Good morning, Drew," she blurts.

He smiles. "What's up, ladies?"

"Oh," I laugh, popping out of my chair, hoping to lure his attention from Rebecca. I stand and approach him, lifting on my toes for a kiss. "Bec was wondering if you'd be here today, and here you are." As I say this, I hear one of my desk drawers open, then close, and I know Rebecca must have stashed the tests.

He nods, and his eyes are piercing as he watches me. "I'm on my way into the office, and I wanted to check on you and see how your evening was."

"Oh, right!" I turn toward Rebecca. "I forgot to tell you, my mom showed up last night, out of the blue."

Rebecca gives me that look and then grins as she says, "I told you that was going to happen."

I blurt out a nervous laugh. "That's right! Ha… yeah, you did, didn't you?"

"So, Drew got ambushed with meeting the mom without any warning?"

He laughs now too. "It was fine. We actually had a lot of fun during dinner."

Rebecca grins. "She is a remarkable lady. I think you'll get along great with her."

"Anyway," I say, "I forgot to mention I had an early meeting this morning, but we're all finished. Thanks for checking on me though."

"If you're all finished up," he glances at his watch, "do you have time for breakfast?"

"Oh, sorry, I can't today. I usually have brunch with Mac on Fridays but I've had to cancel that as well. I'm just too busy. Raincheck?"

He looks disappointed but then says, "Maybe dinner tonight."

Rebecca laughs. "I love how you say that like the two of you haven't had dinner together the last two nights."

I flash her a fake dirty look. "We have three weeks to make up for."

Drew winks at her. "I didn't want to be presumptuous."

"All right, all right," Rebecca replies. "I'll leave you two alone to plan your evening." She squeezes Drew's shoulder on the way out. "See you at our meeting on Tuesday, Drew."

"You can join us, you know."

I hear her laughing on the way to her office. "Probably not a good night for a tagalong, but thank you for the invite."

When she's gone, he says, "I really don't mind if she joins us for dinner." Then he tugs me closer with a little more force than I was expecting. "I missed you last night."

I'm flush against him, and I like it. His warmth is comforting, and his affection welcomed, especially knowing what I know.

"So… dinner?" he asks. "I have something I need to talk to you about."

"Perfect, I have something too…"

His eyebrows draw in. "Everything okay? I got the impression you two were scheming when I came in."

"If we were, I certainly couldn't tell you about it, could I?"

He laughs, dropping his head forward. "Very true." He nuzzles my neck. "I need a drink after the day I've had. Do you have a problem with the Pub House for dinner tonight?"

"Drew, it's only the morning. What do you mean by the 'day you've had'?"

"Okay, correction. The day I'm *going* to have."

I love it there but I don't exactly want to tell him I'm pregnant at a loud pub.

"Hum, can we go somewhere with less noise and atmosphere. How about The Dinner Club?"

"Sounds great, see you there. How about seven?"

He takes my elbow and draws me into a deep kiss. As he sinks into me, I revel in how good it feels. In his arms, I feel like nothing could go wrong. I want this and when he holds me, I have zero doubts about us. But I also know that's naive thinking. I'm carrying a baby and that's no small matter. It's a child, *our* child. I close my eyes as that thought sinks in.

We made a baby together and knowing Drew is now a part of me causes my heart to bloom with possibilities.

I love him, I realize, and feeling this sudden rush of emotion is almost overwhelming. When his hands slide to the back of my neck, I mumble, "Drew." Because I know him and what he's thinking. "Please don't take the pins out of my hair."

"How about after dinner?" he murmurs.

"How about I wear it down for dinner?" I wink and watch the grin spread across his face. It reminds me of the first time I laid eyes on that dimpled smile and my heart does a little flutter.

"I can't wait," he says as he steps away from me. "I'll see you at seven."

\*

When I arrive, my hair is down, and I'm wearing the red dress Drew bought me in Maui, hoping it's a good omen. I still haven't had time to unpack completely, but I did make sure to have this dress cleaned. Remembering the state of my house is embarrassing.

I spent my first few weeks home working sixteen-hour days and spent the last week between the sheets with Drew.

I'm going to be a mom and that means I have to stop the nonsense. I look up to the sky and make a promise to get my act together. I promise to stop dwelling on the past and over things I can't change. I promise to take this life more seriously and at the same time, I promise to have a little fun once in a while. Just please let this evening go well.

As I enter The Dinner Club, I see Drew sitting at the bar. I walk over and place a hand on his back as I lean in to say hello. He jumps at first, but then hauls me in for a kiss. Awkwardly, I fall into the stool next to him as he does and I can taste beer on him.

"Already started, huh?" I ask as he withdraws from our kiss. His face is flushed and I know for sure he's already two or three beers in.

"Emily, Emily, I'm so glad you're here," he says in a hushed tone. "Sorry, I really needed a drink, but you have time to catch up." He looks me up and down. "Wow, you look amazing." His grins spreads. "Aw, you're wearing my favorite dress and red is perfect for you."

"Thank you." I glance over at the hostess, and she gestures to a table for us. "Come on, we have a table."

He grabs his beer and slides out of the barstool. Our hands are locked, and as we're walking, he's tugging on my hand as if I'm walking too fast. I turn to look at him, and I can see he's having a bit of trouble. Is he already drunk?

Once we're seated and have menus, I look up at him. "So, you're already drinking?"

He holds up a finger. "What's happened is... I haven't had enough drinks."

"Is that right?" I can't help but feel irritated because I cannot tell him I'm pregnant if he's already had too much to drink.

"Emily, sweetness, have a drink. Relax."

My eyes drop to the table. "No, I'm not drinking today, but that's good, I guess. I can drive you home."

"Oh, right, I um…" he points to his right. "I walked here. My truck is at the office."

I feel like there's something I'm missing. This isn't like him—at least, not what I've seen from him so far. But then, I guess in reality I don't know him well. "Drew, I don't understand, did something happen today?"

"Um, yeah. We're having a talk, and I'm afraid of it, so I had a beer… or three." He reaches for my hand. "You're so awesome. Do you know that?" He tilts forward so that we're closer. "You're just the most incredible person. Really."

"Thank you… I think."

"You think?" He has a weird grin on his face. I can see he's trying not to smile, but can't help himself. "I'm sorry, babe, but I may have had some scotch too."

"How long have you been here?"

"Couple hours, I think."

As amusing as he is when he's drunk, I'm disappointed, and more than a little worried. What on earth can be so bad that he had to drink away his nerves? I've never seen him nervous, he's always so cool and collected. "What is it that you need to tell me that you're so afraid of?"

"Well, Emily, there's a lot. Probably too much for tonight. I have to tell you one important truth." He holds up his finger as if to stop me from interrupting. "This morning, minutes after leaving your office, I realized, not quite so abruptly, that I love you." He lifts a brow. "Like I said, it wasn't an abrupt realization, I sort of felt it coming… well, in Maui, if I'm honest. But see, today, I realized it's probably going to do some serious damage… one way or another."

I hold my breath. Emotions are welling in me, emotions weighing me down. I came in here ready to share my feelings with him… but now I feel off-balance. *He loves me.* Can I believe a man who says this after so many drinks? I inhale deeply, then clear the lump in my throat. "That's why you're drinking? Because you love me or because you're afraid to tell me you love me?"

His eyes grow soft and watery, and mine do too. "I'm not sure I can manage it. It's going to hurt, and I'm not strong enough to…"

I squeeze his hand. "Drew, babe, why does it have to hurt? Love shouldn't hurt."

He tugs free of my grip. "Love shouldn't hurt… but it does, Emily. You know that. You know very well."

A nagging fear creeps into my heart at the pained expression on his face. What the hell is he trying to say?

"Why don't we go home and talk?" I ask.

He bites his lip. "I think that's a good idea."

# CHAPTER TWENTY-NINE

## Drew

I feel such a dick, but it's too late now to make better choices. My nerves got the better of me, and now my mouth has run amuck, and it's doing damage. I can see the hesitation in her eyes. I can see the questions.

After stumbling through her front door, I fight to right myself and head into her kitchen. "Do you mind if I have some of your scotch?"

"I don't mind, but I thought we were talking."

"Yes, we're talking." *That's why I need a drink.* "Liquid courage."

"You don't need that with me, babe. Just be honest."

"I'm sorry." I reach out and grab her. "I really don't want to lose you. God dammit."

She strokes my hair back away from my face. "You're not going to lose me. Why would you even think that?"

"Do you promise?" I hold her tightly, afraid she'll try to get away. "If you promise, I'll be happy. If you promise, this crazy, unbearable fear might go away."

"Can we talk about what you said at the restaurant?"

I hold up my hand and say, "First, let me make us a drink." I release her and head into the kitchen. After scouring her liquor cabinet, I grab the bottle of Jameson and take out two glasses. She comes in behind me and pours a glass of water. When I hand her the drink, she says, "No, thank you. I really don't want a drink."

"I'm sorry." I look down at the drinks fisted in my hands and say, "I guess I'll have to drink them both."

We walk back into the living room and I sit down on the couch. After a few sips, I look up at her. "You okay?"

"Fine, but I'm worried about what you said before."

I squint at her because, to be honest, I don't really remember what I said that could have worried her. "Can you remind me which part you're talking about? Oh, and by the way, you're fucking hot in this red dress." I reach out and pinch the fabric between my fingers. The memory of sitting on the beach with her, watching the sunset, comes to mind.

"Thank you," she hands me the glass of water. "I think it's probably a good idea for you to hydrate." Then she sits sideways on the couch to face me. "I want to talk about when you said you love me."

"Oh, that… yeah. It's true, but you already knew that, right?" I lean forward, and we're nearly nose to nose. I can smell her perfect peaches-and-cream skin from here. I run my nose along her cheek, taking her in, getting a hint of what I now recognize as her expensive face cream… and coconut shampoo… just like in Maui.

This connection we have is strong, fierce even. It's a grasp I can't tug free of—don't want to be free of. It's a magnetic field, luring me closer until my lips touch hers. I kiss her gently, then say, "I mean, you're probably not in love with me, but I still can't help the way I feel, even if it means I have to lose you."

"I hate that you think that. Why would you lose me?"

"You need more. You need better." I shake my head because that's not what I wanted to say. I can't think clearly, but I'm trying. "That's not what I meant."

"Drew, you're all I need, and you're all I want."

"Exactly. See, that's exactly it. I'm all you want. Me. Alone." I point to my chest as I say this, but I can't finish. If I can put off telling her for one more day, if I can have her one more time, maybe then I can accept losing her, maybe I'll be a little more ready. "One day, you're going to want more, and you deserve a full life. You deserve someone who can give you that. I'm just going to fuck it up."

"Drew, you're not making any sense."

I rub my hand over my face. "I know. I'm sorry."

"Whatever you're doing, stop. I'm not sure why you're trying to be so self-destructive, but I want you to stop." She kneels up and leans against me, her hands framing my face. "Drew, I love you, too, but more than that, I need you—so get your shit together, okay?"

This sends me reeling. "I c-could be wrong… I mean, I've been wrong before." I stutter this, fighting with my welling emotions.

"If you think I don't love you, you are wrong. Now shut up and kiss me."

*She loves me.* Fuck. That's such a relief. "Will you say it again?" I ask, and I know my voice sounds small, but I can't help it.

"I love you, Drew."

I tug her closer, taking her mouth with mine. Her hair is already down, making it easy for me to tangle my fingers in it. She tilts back and says, "The next time you want to question my feelings, talk to me, okay?"

I slide my hands up her dress and say, "Your turn to shut up and kiss me."

She straddles me and fuck, she feels good. She slides down my body until she's on her knees, her hands on my belt. It takes her seconds to get my pants unfastened before my cock springs forward, standing at attention.

She bows forward, her mouth open, and her eyes on me. Christ, it's the sexiest thing I've ever seen. Her caramel hair is wild around her head, her bright blue eyes staring up at me like she's about to devour me, and her soft hand on the base of my cock. Dreams do come true.

As soon as her hot, red lips surround me, my body comes alive, every cell singing with pleasure. She drags sounds from me I didn't know I could make and my fingers get lost in her waves and waves of silky hair, giving me something to hold onto while I struggle to maintain my composure.

It's been so long since a woman has made me feel so wanted, so out of control. Being alone to take care of two kids forces me to always, *always*, be in control. My Maui trips being the exception, I'm never given the opportunity to just lose my shit. Drink until I can't stand up. Say shit I shouldn't say. I'm never allowed to be irresponsible. It's never okay to just relax and say fuck it. If I can just have that tonight. Just say fuck it, and have this night with her before weighing down the beauty of this relationship with too much real life, I promise, I swear to God, I'll tell her everything tomorrow. Please just give me a few more hours of not giving a shit about anything else but enjoying this woman.

She takes me deep, her red lips stretched around my cock. The expression on her face makes me believe it's all she wants in life and I'm watching her eyes as they watch mine, as my hips jerk forward.

"Oh, God, baby!"

I grip her hair and it's all I can do to let her control the pace. When heat shoots up my center, I have to stop her.

"Emily, Christ, come here," I groan. "Come here, please."

She stands up and licks her lips as she slips out of her panties under her dress. She's the sexiest thing I've ever laid eyes on, without a doubt. After the lacy swathe of red fabric drops between her legs, she straddles my lap again, her hands on my shoulders and her amazing breasts at eye level. I reach behind her and tug at the zipper until the dress is loose enough for her to pull it over her head.

Once it's gone, she leans forward, and I tug her nipple until it fills my mouth. She tastes sweet, like honey, and that drives me crazy. I place my hands on her hips and push her down, sliding her over my straining cock, and it's the most incredible feeling. She's hot and tight and ready for me. I lift her by the hips and then push her down again.

"I can't wait, baby. I need you now," I mumble around the mouthful of her breast. I grip her nipple between my teeth and tug as it slides out of my mouth. She leans down, locking her lips with mine as she starts moving up and down on top of me.

It's taking every ounce of strength I have to open my eyes, but I want to see her. I want to see the glow of her beautiful skin and the look on her face as she rides me. I want to watch her red mouth circle into an O as she gets closer to losing control. I move my hands up her body and can feel the contrast of her soft and supple skin against my rough hands. She's such a work of art, and tonight, I get to call her mine. I palm her breasts and when I do, I watch as her eyes flutter closed.

"Can you come with me, baby?" I ask, praying she's caught up with me. "I can't wait, I need you now."

I slide my hands around her back and hook them over her shoulders, pulling her down harder. She's lifting against me, allowing me to drag her back down.

"Fucking harder, baby, I want to feel it all, okay? Fuck me harder."

"Oh, God, Drew," she cries, and with each thrust, her breasts bounce up and down, and it's so fucking hot. I grip her shoulders harder and bring her down over and over, not letting her stop. I love the sound of her cries, the sweet little noises contrasting with my stronger grunts. It's erotic as hell and drives me even higher. Then her eyes squeeze shut and her back arches. I'm holding her upright, but I'm not sure how. Every muscle in my body flexes and pulses as I watch her come with a long, salacious moan.

When we're both spent, she falls against me, her head draped over my shoulder, and we're both fighting for breath. Her hair has fallen over my face, and I have to close my eyes as I wrap my arms around her.

"Emily… I fucking love you."

\*

When I wake up, a bright strip of light is shining across the room. My head is pounding, and for a moment, I don't remember where I am. My eyes focus on the dresser, then the perfume bottles on top of the dresser, then on the half-unpacked suitcase across the room, and that's when I know where I am… but that's about all I remember. I gently roll over, and Emily's back is to me. She has handprints marring her perfect alabaster skin, evidence of what we got up to. I sit up quickly, slanting closer to get a better look.

Without realizing it, I rub my hands gently over her skin, making her stir. I jerk back instinctively. Dammit. I didn't mean to wake her up. She stretches and rolls slightly, until one bright blue eye focuses on me.

"I'm sorry." I lean forward and let my lips land on her shoulders. "I didn't mean to wake you."

She turns the rest of the way and nuzzles into my chest. I trace a hand up and down her back, my eyes trying again to focus on the dark marks along her shoulders. "I'm so sorry, Emily." I pull her closer and say, "I'm an asshole. I'm so sorry if I hurt you last night."

Her head pops up, and with a sleepy voice, she murmurs, "What are you talking about?"

"I was too rough. You have bruises…" I brush the hair away so I can see her face. "I'm sorry."

She snorts in laughter. "You didn't hurt me last night. Don't be dumb."

I gently stroke the marks and then down her arms. "This doesn't hurt?"

"No, of course not. And if you remember correctly, I was the aggressor, not you."

I think about that, but I have trouble believing it. My mind is muddy, and I don't remember everything. I try to go over the evening, from leaving the restaurant to stumbling our way to bed. Slowly, I focus on each step, and as I do, my dick grows hard under the blankets. Emily must feel it because she travels closer toward me.

I remember her on her knees and her sultry red lips… I remember the cherry-colored dress coming off, and I grin. After losing the dress, Emily… *Oh, fuck!*

I freeze, my body turning to ice when I realize what I've done. The blood in my veins ceases to flow, and I can't believe I was so stupid and irresponsible.

"What the fuck have I done?" I blurt before I can stop myself.

"Drew…" Emily gives me a slight squeeze. "I told you, I'm not hurt."

I reach back and remove her hands from around me, inching away to sit up on the edge of the bed. I drop my head in my hands and groan. "Fucking hell, dammit. I fucked up—*we* fucked up, Emily."

"What on earth are you talking about?"

"Condom," I grunt, standing and grabbing my clothes from the floor. "I can't believe we forgot a condom. How did that happen?" Christ, that's what I get for drinking so much. "Shit!"

"What's wrong?" she asks, the color draining from her face.

I lean over Emily and rest my hand on her cheek. "Do you think you could've gotten pregnant last night?"

She pushes my hand away and sits up, clutching the blankets to her chest. "No, I don't think I could have gotten pregnant *last night*."

I close my eyes for a second. "Thank God." Then I glance at my phone and remember where I'm supposed to be this morning. "Crap. It's Saturday…" I pull on my underwear and jeans. I only have about twenty minutes to get to my mom's. With my shirt in my hands, I lean over the bed again and plant a kiss on her lips. Then I mumble, "I know we need to talk still, but I gotta go, I'm really sorry. I'm supposed to meet my mom for breakfast, and I'm late. We'll talk later. I love you."

Emily scoots farther into the bed and burrows under the blankets.

"I'll call you later," I say, as I rush out of there.

I walk the six blocks to my house and then, as I'm unlocking my front door, I call Celia.

She answers in a tone much too chipper for this early on a Saturday for someone as hungover as me. "Celia, are you heading to my mom's for breakfast? Can you pick me up on the way?"

"Of course. I was just getting ready to leave, I'll be there in about ten minutes."

"Great! I need a ride to my office—my truck is parked there. I'll leave the door open, just come on in when you get here."

"Okay, see you in a few."

Her sing-song voice echoes as I hit the end call button, strip my clothes off, and jump in the shower. I have ten minutes to get my head together and get back into Dad mode before the idiot who took over my body gets me in more trouble.

# CHAPTER THIRTY

## Emily

I can't move. I'm so hurt and so disappointed, I've turned to stone. I hear the front door close, and all I can think about is the fact that Drew's so anxious to get away that he's quite literally running away from me. The thought of not wearing a condom and knowing it could mean I get pregnant is *that* repulsive to him.

This truth breaks my heart.

I melt into the bed as I dissolve into tears.

\*

I spent the rest of my morning throwing up. Morning sickness? Maybe. Heartache? Another maybe. Either way, I'm now dressed in black and ready to give my speech. A speech to immortalize a man who deserves every accolade they can give him. A man who gave his life for the lives of others. I glance down at a photo of Tucker and smile. I need to focus on him today, not on everything else. I know this, but it still isn't easy to avoid thoughts of Drew.

I hear a knock at the front door and rush to get it. I can hear Kelley and Mac chatting as I open the door and once they're inside, Mac's first to give me a big hug. I need it, too. I embrace him and linger, so glad of his familiarity and affection. When he releases me he says, "Why do you look so tired?"

"Probably because I *am* tired."

"I imagine this isn't going to be easy."

"It's been four years. I can handle it." I turn to peek outside. "Where's Mom?"

"Oh, she has to leave as soon as the ceremony is over so she's driving herself."

I hear a chuckle from Kelley. "Actually, she was going to follow us over, but Mac was freaking out because she was making us late."

"Jeez, Mac, you're so neurotic sometimes." As I say this, I reach out and hug Kelley. "I'm so glad to see you."

"We'll have to plan a girls' night soon, it's been ages," she mutters into my shoulder as I hug her.

I hear the tapping of heels approaching the open front door and then hear Rebecca say, "Girls' night, count me in." She has Eddie in tow, and they all crowd into my living room.

"I'm sorry for the mess," I say. "It's been a busy week." I can see my brother glancing around with a raised eyebrow, and I know he's going to see everything I'm trying to hide from them.

I meet his eyes and say, "You guys ready to head out?"

Mac nods. "Ride with us."

*Yep, saw that coming a mile away.* I agree and grab my purse. "Let's go."

Once we're in the car, I'm thankful we're not going far and so I won't have to be trapped with my observant brother for very long.

"What's going on?" he asks, looking over at me from the driver's seat.

"I'm fine, Mac. You don't need to worry."

"Bullshit."

I glance into the backseat, hoping for a little help from Kelley, but she just shrugs.

"I had a feeling something was up with you when you canceled on brunch yesterday, but I let it slide. Now I can't ignore it." He reaches over and turns the radio off. "Tell me what the hell is going on with you."

"You knew something was up with me because I told you something was up. I told you about Drew and running into him this week."

He jabs a finger in my direction. "Um, no, there's something else."

I sigh and roll my eyes. "Mac, everything is fine. Can we just not do this right now?"

"Emily, we're not getting out of this car until you tell me what's wrong with you." He makes the final turn then veers into the school parking lot. They've decorated it like a party… I can see balloon arches in the school's colors: blue and white with a little green mixed in. On the side of the school gymnasium is a mural of the school's new mascot: The Dolphins.

I slap a hand on my thigh. "Come on, seriously. Are they really using a dolphin? This has to be a joke, right?"

"What the fuck is wrong with people?" he asks. "Didn't they consult you on this?"

"Yes, about the name change but I didn't know anything about the mascot."

I hear Kelley in the backseat gasp. "That's so inappropriate."

"Yes," Mac grinds out. "*Very* inappropriate."

I take a deep breath and place my hand on his arm. "It's okay. Just… let it be." I meet his eyes and the apologetic expression he gives me makes me smile. He finally grins too, and we both start outright laughing.

"Assholes," he mumbles, still fighting the humor. "It shouldn't be funny."

I glance back at Kelley, and she looks mortified. I dab at my eyes and take a breath.

"It's okay," I sigh, as I fight my laughter. "Tucker would have loved the irony."

Mac grunts and his head bobs up and down in agreement. "He's having a great laugh over this, I promise. The sick bastard."

This makes me laugh harder, and I glance out at Rebecca and Eddie as they're standing outside the car, watching us with strange expressions.

"Okay, let's get this over with."

Mac grabs my hand before I can open the door. "I'm not letting you off the hook so easily. When this is over, you're telling me everything."

"Fine. Let's just get through this, okay?"

When I get out of the car, Eddie says, "Did we miss the joke?"

I nod, still fighting with the giggles. "Yeah, but I'll tell you about it later."

I glance around but don't see my mom.

"Where's Mom?"

Mac rolls his eyes and throws his hands up. "She's freaking late, of course. That's why we left her behind."

I pat his shoulder to calm him. "It's okay. I'm sure she'll be here before the speeches start." Taking his arm, I let him lead me into the crowd, under the ridiculous balloon arch, as we approach the school district superintendent. When she sees me, she reaches for my hand.

"Mrs. Tucker, we're so happy to see you. Thank you so much for coming."

I smile, still trying not to giggle. "No, thank you so much for this honor. Tucker would have been pleased. We appreciate that he was even nominated."

"Oh, my gosh! He won the vote by a landslide. He was a very popular teacher in Sacramento. Many of his former students offered to speak today. We had trouble narrowing it down."

"Wow, that's wonderful." I turn and introduce my family and friends then she shows us where we'll be sitting.

"But I hope you'll look around and see the renovations. We've got game booths for the kids and various district organizations exhibiting today." She waves around. "Lots of people came for the celebration, as you can see."

I nod and grin. "Yes, thank you, we'll look around."

When she leaves us alone, Rebecca tugs on my arms. "The fucking Dolphins?"

I start laughing again and face her. "Yes, that's what we said."

"They're truly clueless, aren't they?"

I'm about to agree with her when I see her eyes narrow over my shoulder.

"What is it?" I ask. I start to turn, but she stops me. "What are you looking at?"

"Em, Drew's here… and he's not alone." Her eyes are stony and her expression stiff. I feel my face heat into a blush.

Across the expanse of people, I see Drew squatting next to a small, redheaded little girl. He's smiling and talking to her, then she bounces on her toes, nodding expectantly. The crowd parts some more and I see a little boy too. Then a young woman.

The heat in my face drains instantly, and I clutch Rebecca's hand on my arm. "What the hell?" I breathe. "That looks an awful lot like a wife and kids, doesn't it?" How could he have lied to me? How could he have betrayed me?

"Yes… I'm afraid it does," she mumbles.

Drew points to the playground and then both kids rush away. He straightens back up to his full height and addresses the young woman, before pointing to the school building. She nods and gestures, then walks away.

Just like this morning, I'm concrete. I cannot move. All I can do is stand there and watch him. He walks over to the information counter and picks up a brochure. As he takes it, Rebecca hands me one exactly like it. I glance down and see the front: it's a photo of the new sign with Tucker's name on it, along with his photo.

My heart squeezes as I look at it. He's in a wetsuit, and he's just come onto shore, his board under his arm. He was so beautiful, and I have to lay a hand on my chest because I remember the day this photo was taken. The school board asked me for pictures of him so I knew I'd be seeing his face while I was here, but it still takes my breath away. I'm instantly fighting tears, but not just for my lost husband.

I open the flap and read a list of events, including my scheduled speech. Then I flip to the back and read the story of how my husband died.

*On a warm October day, four years ago, Charles Tucker, a Sacramento School District High School Teacher, lost his life in the act of saving two California students off the Central Coast. He was on the shore at Pleasure Point, a popular surfing spot in Santa Cruz, when he recognized two young boogie boarders being pulled out to sea by a rip current. They'd both lost their boards and were struggling to stay above water. Immediately sensing the danger, Mr. Tucker paddled out to bring them in. Both boys survived, thanks to him, but tragically, the heroic act cost Mr. Tucker his life.*

*After a year of planning and voting, the School District has officially renamed Grove Elementary School in his honor. Today, Grove Elementary will be christened Charles Tucker Elementary School.*

*Our District is proud to commemorate the life of this brave young teacher who was taken from us much too soon.*

I glance up from the brochure to see Drew reading the very same words. Then he lifts his face and searches the crowd. It only takes him seconds to meet my eyes, and I see the sorrow and regret in his features. I shake free of Rebecca's grip and walk toward him. When she falls in line behind me, I'm so thankful. I have no idea what I'm going to say to him, but I know I can't get up on that stage and give my speech without purging some of this anger first. With every step, I'm thinking, *How could he? How could he? How could he?*

Drew looks like a deer in my headlights, but he also looks resigned. When I reach him, I want to slap the expression right off his face, but I haven't forgotten why I'm here and I will not disgrace myself or the memory of my husband over this man.

"Please tell me that woman is not your wife." Thankfully, my words come out in a whisper. It's taking every ounce of strength I have not to scream at him.

He holds up his hands as if to stop me from freaking out. As if I need *him* to help me maintain my self-respect. "Emily, I'm not married. I didn't lie about that."

"Drew, are these children yours? Please tell me they're your niece and nephew. Please." I glance over at them, one at a time, and I know in my heart they're his. Then it occurs to me... his two roommates, Kyle and Hannah. I look back at him and as I'm staring into his regretful expression, the redheaded little girl runs up and grips his leg.

"Daddy, see, I told you, your friend would be here too." She looks up at me with bright, sea-blue eyes and dimples that match Drew's exactly.

Drew's hand lands on her head, and he nods down at her. "Yeah, she is, honey. Can you say hello?"

She glances from him back to me. "Hello..." Then her eyes grow big, and she looks back at Drew.

Drew mouths the words, "Ms. Thomas."

She grins and corrects herself. "Hello, Ms. Thomas."

My heart is heavy. I don't want to lose my shit here in front of this little girl. She's certainly the sweetest thing I've ever laid eyes on. It's a good thing for Drew too because if it weren't for her, I would have already walked away. How can I now? I'm staring at the girl who's destined to be my child's big sister.

Forcing myself to be calm, I squat down so that I'm at her level. "You must be Hannah." My voice doesn't sound as sure as I want it to, but she doesn't seem to care.

She nods, and I can see a sudden shyness now that she has my full attention. "How did you know?"

I glance up at Drew and say, "Lucky guess."

She points behind her. "That's my brother… over there. He's Kyle, and um… um, he's eight."

I look over to where she's pointing. "How do you know who I am?"

"Oh, my daddy! My daddy has your picture on our fireplace." She points her finger at me. "You're with a helipopter."

"Helicopter," Drew and I both mutter at the same time, correcting her.

Before I can say more, I hear a crackle over the speakers and then the Superintendent's voice. "I want to thank everyone for coming today."

"Emily, your mom just arrived," Rebecca mumbles.

I reach my hand out to shake Hannah's, trying to regain some composure. "It was lovely meeting you, Hannah."

She stands erect and takes my hand in an exaggerated shake. "Thank you," she says, with a big, dimpled grin.

I lift to my full height and give Drew a death stare before turning away from him and walking to my seat in the front row. Mac, Kelley and Eddie are chatting with my mom, who looks a little harried.

I'm so thankful Rebecca is the only one who really knows what's happening. She's staying close, and after I've greeted my mother and taken my seat, I turn my head so she can see my eyes.

"I'm okay, I promise."

She gives me a good long look and her mouth splits into a smile. "I know you are because you're fucking fabulous." Then she reaches in and gives me a tight hug.

I listen as several speakers talk about how Charles Tucker exemplified the values of the school district. They're not wrong. Tucker was the very best kind of person. He wasn't just a hero to those kids that day on the beach, he was also my hero. I'm thankful I'm not the only one who recognizes how wonderful he was.

When they introduce me, I stand and slowly climb the three stairs on the riser. I approach the microphone and smile. Smiling isn't easy, but when I think about how special he was to these people as well as me, I have to.

"Most of you knew my husband as Mr. Tucker or just Tucker. Unconventional to his core, he never liked the formality that came with being a teacher. He wanted to be friends with his students and most of the time he was. And though he was friends with his students, he still garnered a great deal of respect from them." I grasp the podium for support and glance around before continuing. "This love, friendship, and respect are what lead us to today. Honestly, I'm not sure what Tucker would think about having a school named after him.

"Tucker was always about living, and when he was here with us, he lived every day fully. He wouldn't want us to dwell on his passing. He wouldn't want to be remembered for how he died or what led to his death. He'd want to be known for how he lived, and I think this tribute, although brought about by his death, this tribute is a testament to how he lived. He was loved. Not just by his family and me, but by you." As I say this, I gesture to the group of Tucker's former students. The same students who are now finishing up their college careers, the same group of students who still occasionally check up on me and still send Christmas cards, and who all wept at his funeral. "I want to thank you, his students, his fellow teachers, the school board, and the City for this honor and for wanting to remember him for the great man he was. While he might not have understood why we're dwelling, I understand, and it means the world to our family and me."

# CHAPTER THIRTY-ONE

## Drew

I stand off to the side for Emily's speech, and as I watch her, I'm struck by how strong she is. But I'm also incredibly embarrassed… so ashamed of myself I can barely breathe. How could I have kept up with this lie when I knew how it would end? I see now what I've missed over the last few days. I see my glaring blunder. Emily's not the kind of person to judge me for being a single dad, she's the type of person to judge me for *lying* about being a single dad. I'm so stupid. How could I not be upfront and honest about who I am—about who they are?

I'm disgusted with myself and with what I've done. Those kids are everything to me and I'm proud to be their dad, I'm proud of my family. Lying about them isn't something I do. I'd never… so why did I? I've got to be completely out of my own head to do something so crazy.

Losing Emily is what I get. This is karma, and I deserve for her never to speak to me again. I frown and lower my eyes to the ground. If she ever lets me see her again after today, it'll be a fucking miracle. Heart sinking, I glance over to make sure Kyle and Hannah are still where they're supposed to be playing.

A couple of Hannah's friends are here and I'm glad, for her sake. Kyle's playing basketball with a couple of other boys, and he seems pretty content too. I'm the only one miserable. As any liar of my caliber should be.

I had every intention of telling Emily about the kids last night. I just completely lost my nerve. You'd think even after all the drinks, I would have slipped and told her. But no, I remain a liar and horrible person for keeping my kids a secret.

The last speaker is finishing up, and as he does so, I see the crowd grow restless. A moment later, it's over, and people are standing. Emily hugs her family and friends in turn, and she's smiling, but even from here, I can tell it's not a genuine one. She's pretending, and that breaks my heart. I hear Celia's voice as she approaches. I turn to face her and say, "I need to go talk to a friend, can you keep an eye on the kids for me?"

"Oh, sure. Go ahead."

Heart hammering, I walk toward the crowd of people around Emily, and as I get closer, they grow quiet. I'm not sure who knows what about me, but I don't care. I need to speak to her. I can't leave without having this conversation with her.

"Emily," I say to her back.

She stiffens and slowly turns to face me and at the same time, her mom greets me with a welcoming smile. "Drew, it's so good to see you here."

"Marilyn, it's great to see you again as well."

She grips Emily's arm. "Em, honey, I have to get going before the traffic gets too bad. I love you." She leans in and gives her a hug and it's obvious that Emily lingers a little. When Marilyn pulls away, she narrows her eyes at her daughter. "Do you need me to stay?"

"No, Mom, I'm fine. Really." Emily gives her another quick hug. "I know you have a meeting this afternoon. Don't be late on my account."

Marilyn hugs a couple more people and says another quick goodbye before she heads toward the parking lot. Once she's out of sight, the entire group turns toward me and now I feel like I'm standing under a glaring spotlight. It's what I deserve, though. I face Emily directly and say, "May I have a word with you, please?"

Her eyes drop to the ground, but then she nods. Before walking away though, she turns and introduces me to everyone with her. This strikes me as odd. I guess mostly because I feel like she's never going to want to see me again... so why introduce me?

"Drew, this is my brother, Mac, and his wife, Kelley." She gestures toward me. "Mac, Kelley, this is Drew Whitney."

Mac reaches a hand out and shakes mine. "Good to meet you, Drew. We've heard a lot about you."

I hear Rebecca snort quietly next to me, then she mumbles, "But not everything."

I throw her a look, praying I'm the only one who heard it. Then I glance back at Mac. "Nice meeting you too, Mac, and Kelley." I shake Kelley's hand and say, "Mac, thank you for forcing Emily into a vacation."

They all laugh, and Mac replies, "She was overdue, and it looks like spending some time on the beach did her some good."

"You look familiar. Have we met before?" I ask Mac now that I've gotten a good look at him. I'm sure I've seen him before but I can't place it.

Kelley snorts out a laugh. "Probably from the buses."

Mac laughs quietly. "I'm on the KQCC morning show, *Mimi and Mac in the Morning*. We have a few ads on the city buses."

I narrow my eyes. "Oh, okay, yeah, I have seen those, but I catch a little of your show in the mornings sometimes too."

"Okay, well, guys," Emily interrupts. "If you don't mind, I need a few minutes with Drew, then we can get out of here."

We walk about twenty feet away from the crowd, then I twist around to face her. Her arms cross over her chest instinctively, but she doesn't speak.

"I'm so sorry. I should have told you... in fact, I tried several times."

"You're right. You should have told me—and I recognize that you tried to tell me something and I stopped you. But you've had more opportunities, Drew. Last night, for example, when you decided to get shitfaced instead of talking to me."

I groan at the reminder. "I know, you're right. I was so anxious about telling you, I had a few drinks and that led to way too many drinks until I completely lost my nerve. Honestly, I was scared to tell you, scared you wouldn't want me anymore."

"Wouldn't want you?" A pained look crosses her face. "So, you just decided to lie? When exactly *were* you going to tell me?" She shifts her weight. "How long were you planning to hide your kids from me?"

"Believe it or not, I didn't decide to lie. This wasn't a conscious choice. It just got away from me, but I was going to tell you tonight."

"Really? You were going to tell me tonight—or was it your plan to disappear on the weekends you have custody, then reappear after sending them back to their mother's on Monday?"

"What? No!" I shake my head, and I'm hurt that she believes this. I'm hurt that she hasn't even tried to give me the benefit of the doubt. "Is that really what you think of me, Emily?" I step closer to her, unable to contain my anger. "With everything that *has* been said between us, you choose to believe the absolute worst about me without even hearing everything?"

She throws her hand out and replies, "What do you get? Huh? Every other weekend?" She points at me. "I had a feeling when you made a crack about me being a lawyer that you were a bitter divorcé, and I guess I was right."

"You're being completely unfair, Emily." I loom in, getting even closer. "You know what I didn't lie about? I didn't lie when I said I love you. Did it occur to you that maybe I was afraid to tell you because I didn't want to lose you?"

"You love me?" She rests a hand on her chest, and I can see she's choked up, but she takes a deep breath and says, "Am I really supposed to believe that? Because I can't think of a better way for you to express just how unimportant I am to you than for you to keep your kids a secret." She drops her hands to her sides. "I'm such a fool." Then she walks away.

All I can do is watch her go.

I close my eyes and breathe. Deep breath after deep breath. She was right last night when she said I was self-destructive. All this damage was done by me and my lies. Me and my fears. I realize that now.

When I hear the kids approaching with Celia, I take yet another deep breath and open my eyes. "Are you guys ready to go home?"

"Do we have to?" Kyle whines. "I wanted to play ball, Dad."

I ruffle up his hair. "Funny coming from you since you didn't even want to come today."

"I can stay with them if you need to take off, Mr. Whitney."

"Yeah, Daddy, can we stay with Celia?" Hannah chimes in.

I look at them both and say, "Thank you, Celia, but I'll stay. It's supposed to be your day off. Go ahead and enjoy the weekend."

"All right. Thank you." She waves to the kids. "I'll see you guys on Monday morning. Have a good weekend."

"Bye, Celia."

I follow the kids over to the playground, and as I do, I see Emily and her family drive by. Well, now they can go have lunch and discuss what an awful, bitter person I am because of my divorce. The thought alone rips my heart in two. I take my phone out and send her a text.

Me: *You couldn't be more wrong about me. Hear me out and let me explain.*

After a few minutes of no response, I try again.

Me: *Please meet me tonight so we can talk.*

A moment later, I receive a reply.

Emily: *No, sorry, I'm not available tonight.*

Almost word for word what she said to Grant when he invited her out to lunch last Wednesday. I guess that's her way of telling me I won't be seeing her again.

# CHAPTER THIRTY-TWO

## Emily

I'm not up for a crowd. The original plan was for us all to meet for lunch after the ceremony, but I just can't. The thought of casual conversation makes me want to drive a spike through my eye. I can't pretend I'm not heartbroken and I refuse to try, especially in front of my family.

After canceling lunch, I manage to convince Eddie to go home and now I'm left with Rebecca, my brother, and Kelley. Mac knows there's more going on than meets the eye, and he's not letting it go. He stops and grabs salads to go for us and then drives to my house. I wish he wouldn't. I just want to be left alone. I know he's going to question me to no end until I tell him everything and I'm not up for the bombardment of questions. I might as well come clean and get it over with.

After entering the house and grabbing some plates, I try to sidetrack them with questions about their wedding. They were accidentally married in Reno over a year ago, but now they're planning a real ceremony and reception to celebrate the right way.

"So, Kelley, how's the wedding planning going?"

"Oh, ah…" She seems surprised I asked. "It's going fine. Slow… We haven't done much but pick a venue."

"Then you must have a date!" I say, glad they've finally decided.

"We were planning for mid-April," she replies.

I'm doing the math in my head mentally and realize my baby is likely due in mid-April. I look over at Rebecca, and her expression says it all. I tilt my head.

"Hmmm, I'm not so sure April is a good time to get married in Sacramento. Why not consider summer dates? Like July?"

"Um, because we don't want to melt in the Sacramento heat," Mac says.

I nod, not sure how I want to say it, but say it I must. I usually tell my brother everything.

"Well, I may have trouble attending a wedding in April."

They both stop mid-way through transferring their salads from takeout containers to their plates. Kelley's eyebrows scrunch up, and Mac looks hesitant too. "Why?" he asks. "Because I can't think of a single viable excuse for you to miss our wedding, regardless of the date."

"Um, well." I sit down because I feel like my feet might give out on me soon. "I'm… ah… going to be having a baby in April. At least if my math is correct."

I glance up, and both of their faces are frozen. I feel like reaching over and lifting Mac's chin up off the table.

"I'm pregnant. I'm not exactly sure how far along, but it happened in Hawaii."

There's complete silence. I glance at Rebecca, and she gives me a supportive nod. Then I hear a chair scratching my floor, and a second later, my brother's arms are around me. He's holding me tightly, and his breathing is hitched. I hear him mumble, "You're going to be a mom, Em. That's amazing."

When he withdraws from the embrace, he's beaming with happiness, and I'm so relieved.

"You're happy to hear it?" I ask because I'm not sure I believe it. I was expecting… I'm not sure what exactly, but I wasn't expecting such a positive reaction.

"I'm thrilled. Really. How exciting," he says.

Kelley stands and hugs me too, and she looks a little shocked but happy nonetheless. "That's such great news!" After hugging me, she glances at Rebecca. "You don't look surprised."

"Nope, I'm the one who forced her to pee on a stick."

I sit back down. "I'm so relieved you guys are pleased for me. The last few days have been so crazy, and yesterday, when I took the test, I was just shocked."

"Yesterday?" Mac asks, pinning me with his eyes. "Is it safe to assume you didn't tell Mom?"

"Um, no." I shake my head and wave a finger back and forth. "I didn't tell Mom yet, but I'll call her this week, for sure. I'd just found out yesterday and I wasn't ready to share the news yet."

"What did Drew say when you told him?" Kelley asks hesitantly. "I hope that's not why you guys were so tense today."

"He doesn't know yet either." I fight the frown that wants to take over my face. "I'm not sure I'm going to tell him at all."

"What?" Mac leans forward. "Why on earth wouldn't you tell him? He's the father, right?"

I nod because I'm choked up with emotion. When I get a grip on my feelings, I say, "He's definitely the dad. He's also *already* a dad, which I didn't know until today." I rest my elbow on the table. "He has two children already. They were with him at the school today."

"And you didn't know about them?" Kelley asks.

"No. I knew he was divorced, but he didn't tell me he had kids. He said he had roommates, Hannah and Kyle, but apparently, they're his kids."

"What a son of a bitch," Mac says.

"I'm not sure how long he thought he could keep them a secret." I bob my head a little and realize maybe Drew was right. Maybe I'm not being entirely fair. "Actually, I shouldn't say that. I'm sure he wanted to tell me at some point, he just lost his nerve." I quickly open my bottle of water and take a sip. "He's tried to tell me something all week but never actually got around to it for one reason or another. Some of the time I wouldn't even let him talk—I was afraid of the secret I was hiding..."

"And," Rebecca says, "you didn't encourage open communication at first either. When you were in Hawaii, you guys decided on that stupid rule not to exchange information. Then when you two found each other, you avoided talking about anything personal. That was your choice, remember?"

"I know that, Bec, but this isn't some small thing he forgot to mention. He should have told me this week. He had time."

"I'm confused," Mac interrupts. "What rule?"

"When we met in Hawaii, we agreed not to share any personal information. We agreed not to contact each other when we got home."

Mac whistles his appreciation. "Well, well. Look at you, going for the vacation hook-up."

I point across the table at him, refusing to let him make a joke about it. "Don't you start with me, Mac. I had good reasons for agreeing to that. And it doesn't matter now. Not now that we live in the same town. Not now that we're trying to make something real happen between us—at least we were until today."

"If that's true, then surely you can forgive that, can't you?" he says. "You obviously have feelings for him. Don't let this little hiccup keep you from being with him. You're going to want your child to have a father."

"Little hiccup?" I sit straight up in my chair, defensive now. "He lied about his kids, Mac!"

"Emily," Kelley says, and I feel like they're all talking to me like I'm a rabid dog they need to keep calm. "You're in love with him, I don't think it's going to be that easy to walk away."

"I have a feeling it's not going to be up to me since he's not interested in having more children." The words almost stick in my throat as the realization hits me. I close my eyes and shake my head. "Of course he doesn't want kids because he has them already." I rest my head on my palm. *Dammit*, that explains why he freaked out this morning when he remembered we had unprotected sex. I get it. The fog is fading and his entire demeanor makes sense now. When he said the words, *one day you're going to want more*, he specifically meant having children.

"He said that?" Mac asks.

"Not in so many words, but he said it loud and clear in other ways..."

"So, you're giving up just like that?" Kelley asks. "I did the same thing last year to Mac, over a stupid misunderstanding. I nearly lost him because I was too scared and too stubborn to face him and hash it out. I wanted to believe the worst."

I feel heat in my cheeks. It's nearly impossible to forget how I almost ruined their relationship last year after drawing up annulment papers to dissolve their accidental wedding. I was trying to be helpful but when Kelley found the paperwork, she thought Mac had it done without telling her. She's being kind by saying it was a misunderstanding. It was my interference that caused the problem. I nod and fight to keep my eyes on her, even though I want to hide at the reminder.

Kelley taps her chest with her finger. "Take my advice when I say, as someone who nearly made a monumental mistake over a misunderstanding, I think you two should talk about it at least."

I'm not sure what to say to that. "You know..." I take a second to mull it over. "I think I'll wait and see." I glance between the three of them. "He's still going to do the work on our building, right, Bec?"

She shrugs. "I don't have a problem with it. I like him, and his designs are great, but can you continue to work in such close proximity to him?"

"I want him to work on the building. I trust him professionally, and I love his ideas so far too."

"Well, then, you'll have to tell him at some point, he's going to notice the protruding belly eventually," Mac says.

"Maybe I should draft up a release of parental rights and have it ready for when I can no longer hide my pregnancy. Then I'll tell him and give him an out, which he'll probably take."

"Absolutely not! Don't do that, Emily," Mac says, "Do not go all lawyer on him. Let's not forget what happened when you jumped the gun on annulment papers for me and Kelley last year. Look how that turned out."

Kelley nods along with Mac and says, "Don't immediately jump to the wrong conclusion. That will get you nowhere. Don't do anything until after you talk to him about it."

"Don't prejudge him like that, Em." Mac says, "You did the same thing to Kelley. You assumed our marriage would drag me down before you even tried to get to know her."

My face heats again and I want to jump to my own defense but I can't because they're absolutely right. I drop my head in my hands and fight not to cry.

"Emily, I hate to gang up on you, but you do tend to believe the worst in people before giving them a chance," Rebecca says.

"W-wow." I stutter. "It's amazing any of you want anything to do with me. Am I really that horrible?"

A chorus of no's ring out around the table, but I'm too horrified with myself to hear them. I glance up to meet Kelley's eyes. "I'm sorry. I never meant to…"

Kelley reaches across the table and grips my hand. "Emily, stop. This isn't us trying to make you feel bad. I know you were protecting Mac and I love you for that. And I know you're only trying to protect yourself and your child, but do you remember what you said to me last year—when you were helping me move into Mac's place?"

I shake my head, causing tears to fall from my eyes.

"You told me to live my life fearlessly. Now I'm telling you the same thing."

I lay both hands on my chest. "But it's not just myself I'm risking."

"Listen, Emily, if you need to take legal action against him later, then do it, but give the man a chance first. Please," Mac begs. "If he loves you, he'll make it right. Just give him a chance."

\*

After everyone has gone, I change out of my black dress into shorts and a t-shirt, then sink down onto my bed, exhausted. I've never been the type of person to nap. I'm an always-on-the-move type. I spend so much time on my ass at work, I like to move when I'm not working, but now, I can barely keep my eyes open. But once I'm lying down, and the house is quiet, I can't turn my brain off.

I keep thinking about what Drew said and how all my family and friends seem to think I'm judging him too harshly. Am I? Maybe I am wrong about Drew. Maybe he wouldn't mind having another child. I think about that beautiful little girl and how much I wish I could get to know her. And his son, who looks so much like his father. I remember thinking Drew would make a good dad and now I know why. Although, from experience, I don't know how great someone can be as a weekend dad, even if they are amazing. That must be hard on him and the kids.

Do I want that for my child? Would it be better to have a part-time father or no father at all? I think about my dad again and how he was never around for Mac and me. Even though he wasn't there, I still loved him, and yes, I still grieved for him. He just never had a real impact on my life, not like a real father would.

Remembering the scrapbook my mom brought me, I get out of bed and rush into the living room to find it. I lower myself onto the sofa and rest it in my lap. When I open the cover, a rush of memories accompanies the first photo. My dad's wearing a wide open-mouthed smile, displaying a row of perfectly straight teeth. His long hair is curtained over one side of his face as he tilts his head. He looks so happy.

He started touring with his band when I was five and Mac was two. I don't really remember what it was like to have both parents at home before that, but I also don't remember feeling like I was missing anything. Our mom was everything we needed and I can be that too. But then I think about the friends who did have fathers at home. Fathers who coached their soccer teams and took them to father-and-daughter dances. Fathers who were there to walk them down the aisle.

Before I can control it, I'm crying. Dammit! I don't want to do this. I'm happy—I do miss my dad, at least what little I had of him. It wasn't until college that I realized what a loser father he really was. I sit up quickly and grab my phone.

When she answers, I can't hold back my sob.

"Mom?"

"Emily, what's the matter? Has something happened?"

She sounds panicked, and that really makes me feel bad.

"No. I just wanted to call and tell you I love you."

"Honey, I love you too. What's wrong? This isn't like you."

"I know, right? I don't cry. I don't know what's wrong with me. I must be hormonal."

She laughs. "Well, you're either PMS'ing or you're pregnant."

That really makes me cry. "Mom…" I take a deep breath. "I'm pregnant."

"Oh… Emily."

"I'm sorry I didn't tell you when you were here." I wipe the tears from my face. "I know you're probably disappointed."

"Honey, there are very few things you could do to disappoint me and giving me my first grandchild isn't one of them. Honestly, between you and Mac, I wondered if it would ever happen."

This makes me chuckle through my tears. "Are you happy?"

"I want to be, but it's hard when you don't sound very happy. Tell me why you're crying."

I tell her what happened after she left the ceremony and when I get the entire story out, she sighs heavily into the phone. "Well, you need to tell the man you're carrying his child. You cannot wait, Emily. Do the right thing."

"Why is not telling him the wrong thing? He lied to me, Mom."

"Emily Anne Thomas, stop with the excuses. You know perfectly well what the right thing is and keeping his child a secret is *not* the right thing to do."

I smack my palm against my forehead. *Why did I call her?* "Mom, it's not that easy."

"Sure it is. Just tell him." She huffs out a breath, and it makes me roll my eyes. "Drew seemed downright in love with you. I don't think you're giving him enough credit."

"Mom! He lied about having children. I can't ignore that."

"No, you can't, but you can try to see things from his perspective and then try to forgive him for it. Do you have any idea how hard it is to date when you have kids? People who don't have kids call them baggage. *Baggage*, Emily. Do you know how offensive that is?" She huffs again. "Do you know how many men asked me out but then ran for the hills when they found out about you and Mac?"

I slap my hand on my knee. "Yeah, well, lying about them certainly isn't going to improve matters."

"So, what is it, Emily? You're going to ride on your high horse and end this relationship because he has kids, or are you just afraid of telling him because he might reject you?"

I sit still for a moment, thinking about that.

"Because not telling him about the baby is just as bad as him not telling you about his kids. Two wrongs, Emily."

"Mom, what if he does reject me?"

"You don't have any control over the outcome, all you can do is say what you have to say and see what happens. If he doesn't want another child, you'll deal with that. If he does, and he's excited, you'll deal with that too. But you can't live in limbo. The stress of that alone is too much for you and your baby."

As irritated as I am, I know she's right. I just… don't know how to tell him and I'm so afraid of his response.

"You're one of the bravest people I know, Emily. You're a fighter. Just look what you've already been through in your life—and you're still standing. Don't stop fighting now, and don't avoid difficult situations because of the possibility of rejection. That's not who you are. This is one of those times when you just have to pull yourself up by your bootstraps and get the job done."

"Okay, I'll do it," I agree, resolved to get it over with. If nothing else, she's right about me needing to know where he stands one way or the other. "Thanks, Mom."

"You know I'm always here for you. Now, can I tell you how excited I am to be a grandma?"

I push back the nerves that immediately attack me when she says that.

"I'm a little excited too, and a lot nervous."

"It'll all work out in the end."

She's right. It'll all work out… one way or another.

# CHAPTER THIRTY-THREE

## Drew

I'm surprised when Emily's face shows up on my caller ID, and I'm torn between fear and hope.

"Hello?"

"Drew, hi. It's Emily." Her voice is shaky, and that makes me think something's wrong.

"You okay?"

"Ah, yeah, but I want to talk... do you still want to meet tonight?"

My heart starts racing. "Of course, let me make some calls... try to get a sitter."

"Oh, I don't want to put you to any trouble." She pauses but then says, "Maybe I can come over there."

I think about that. I don't want my children to get to know her if she's not going to be around. That's a hard lesson I've already learned. "Okay, the kids go to bed at eight, you can come after that."

"Um, okay. I guess that works."

"I'll text you the address."

"Great, I'll see you a little after eight."

She disconnects the call before I can say anything else and I stare at my phone, confused. Her tone was sorrowful, but I don't get the impression she wants to meet me to apologize since I'm the one who lied. Maybe she wants to do the same thing she did with Grant and make it clear that our relationship is over. I rub at the pain in my chest... Damn, I don't want that. I don't want to lose her.

I close my eyes and send up a little prayer for her to be in a forgiving mood. Because, temper and all, I love that woman and I want her to be mine. I glance over at Hannah and Kyle, who are now sitting in front of the TV, and I know I want her to be theirs too. I want her to want them, but I know I have to accept that she might not. She might not want kids at all. I just can't let her spend time with them until I'm sure she's in it for the long haul.

My gaze goes from them to the messy house. Toys litter the living-room floor, shoes, and discarded socks are spread all over, and their little suitcases from the trip to Santa Cruz are still sitting in the entryway, by the front door.

Oh hell, I can't have Emily over here when it looks like this. She'll run for the hills—of course, she wouldn't for that reason—but I need to put my best foot forward, considering what I've done.

"Hey, guys, can you do something for me?"

They both slowly turn their eyes from the TV to me. It's as if they know I'm going to ask them to do something they don't want to do. Kids have a weird sixth sense like that. They don't speak, so I push forward with my request. "Can you help me clean up the house?" They're not talking, they're just watching me. "If we work together, we can get it done really fast."

Nothing.

I sigh. "How about we make a game out of it? Whoever picks up the most wins."

Kyle's brow lifts. "What do we win?"

The little snot. It's not like I'm asking them to paint the house. "You'll win a giant thank you from me... maybe even a hug."

"Daaaad," Hannah says.

"I think that's pretty fair since it's your toys and your mess."

They stare at me for another long moment, then Kyle says, "Okay, fine." His voice is resigned and not at all happy. He pauses the show on TV then looks around the room. "I'm still going to win."

Hannah jumps up. "Hey, wait for me."

Competitive to the core, both of them. I grin at my own quick thinking and walk around, collecting shoes to drop them into their bedrooms. As I'm heading down the hall, I can hear them both counting. This, of course, forces me to count the shoes in my hand. Should I count by pairs or individual shoes? Individual shoes, for sure. I can't let those little heathens win.

Fifteen minutes later, I look around, pleased with our work.

"I won," Kyle says.

"No, *I* did. I picked up more."

"Pah, no," he says, "You don't even know how to count."

"Hey," Hannah and I say at the same time. "Kyle, you don't need to be mean like that."

"Yeah, Kyle, I know how to count to a hundred."

"Newsflash, genius, if you can count to a hundred, you can count to two hundred."

"All right, all right, that's enough," I interrupt.

Hannah gives him a perplexed look, then looks up at me. "I picked up a lot, Daddy, I think I won."

"I think we're all winners. How about ice cream as our reward?"

Hannah smiles, and I see the little glint in her eyes. "Yeah, Daddy. I think that's a great idea."

"Me too!" Kyle says.

"Okay." I roll my eyes. "Go get your shoes on, turn the TV off, and let's go." I know as I say this, that those shoes are going to end up on the living-room floor again in an hour. But I also know I'd never want it any other way.

*

When I hear the tap at the door, I'm a little surprised. I was waiting to see headlights in the driveway, but they never came. I open the door to see Emily standing there in shorts, a t-shirt, and the flip-flops I bought her in Hawaii. I think it's the most relaxed I've ever seen her, and that includes our last day in Maui. But then I get a closer look and see the exhaustion in her eyes. I'm quickly reminded of the evening before and making love to her late into the night. I immediately shove the picture from my head... I can't stand the thought of it possibly being the last time.

"Where's your car?" I ask, mostly because I'm not sure what else to say.

"It's so nice out, I decided to walk. You weren't kidding when you said it was close."

I chuckle. "Yes, just a few blocks."

She steps inside, and I can see the tension in her shoulders. Once the door is closed, I give her a good look. "Are you okay?" I'm trying to be more reserved, but I can't help my concern. It's not something I can turn off... it's not like a light switch I can flip.

She shakes her head a little, and I sense she's fighting her emotions. Now that she's inside, she's rubbing her hands up and down her arms. It's still pretty warm outside, so the air conditioner is on. "Are you cold? We can sit outside on the back patio."

She glances around as if looking for the kids. "It's okay to go outside? They're..."

"They'll be fine. If they need me, they know where to find me." I gesture toward the back of the house but then say, "Do you want a drink? I have a beer or juice. I don't have any wine, sorry."

"Can I have some water?"

"Of course." I turn toward the kitchen with her on my heels and grab a water bottle for each of us. Then I lead her through the house to my bedroom, and out the sliding-glass door to the side patio. I don't want Jake to show up unannounced, and usually, when I'm on this side, he doesn't realize I'm outside. I gesture toward one of the chairs and hand her the water bottle. She doesn't sit. First, she walks around, as if she's examining the potted plants and the brickwork under her feet.

"It's different... being in your space, seeing where you live." She turns to face me. "I'm not sure what I was expecting, but this is a beautiful place."

"Thank you. We like it too." I gesture toward the chair, but she still doesn't sit. This makes me nervous. "Emily, are you okay?"

She shakes her head slightly. "No. I'm really not. I'm so disappointed, Drew. I thought more of you, but..."

"Maybe you should let me tell you everything before you judge."

She shakes her head again, which pisses me off.

"You know, Emily, that's so fucking unfair. You get upset with me for not telling you things, but when I try, you don't let me. You can't have it both ways."

"Drew, I came here to tell *you* something, and I think once I do, the rest isn't going to matter."

I stand back up and step closer to her. I want to see her face. "It will matter, dammit. It all matters when you love someone."

"I think you'll find I'm right... once you know."

"You know, if you don't want to see me, just say it. I get it, two kids are a lot to take on."

Her face tilts downward, and she shuffles back a little, putting more space between us. "Drew, I'm pregnant."

The words knock the breath from my lungs. Instinctively, my head shakes in denial. I step back and hold up a finger, taking a second to get my bearings. When I can finally breathe, it comes out in pants, and it feels like my heart is about to pound out of my chest.

"That's impossible. We were careful. Last night... it's too soon. You can't know already from last night."

"I think it happened in Maui. I suspect I'm almost five weeks along, but I won't know until I see my doctor."

"This cannot be happening." My words come out broken, but all I can think about is how I can't live through another pregnancy. The last moments of Kayla's life flash through my head and I have to sit back down. "This can't be true."

"I'm just… going to go." She shuffles toward the door, but I jump up and grab her.

Before she can get away, I have her in a tight embrace. I need to hold her, feel her breathing, feel her heartbeat next to mine. One hand is wrapped in her silky locks, the other is gripping the small of her back. "I'm sorry I did this to you. I'm so sorry, Emily."

She pushes me away and shakes me off. "Don't do that. Don't act like this is some horrible thing that was done to me."

"Emily…" I'm so overwhelmed, I don't know what to say. All I know is I love her, and I don't want to lose her. I need to sit down before my knees give out. "We need to talk, babe."

I can't even look up at her… I can't face her. It's too hard.

"I'll give you some time to think things over, and then we can talk."

Before I can respond, she's through the slider and heading to the front door.

"Wait, stop," I call out.

She stops in the living room but doesn't turn.

"Please don't walk. I'll take you home."

She huffs out a breath. "I'm not incapacitated. Jesus, Drew, I can walk home." She jerks the front door open and with a voice dripping with disdain, she says, "I'll be fine."

As she leaves, all I can do is watch her go, sick over what I've done.

# CHAPTER THIRTY-FOUR

## Emily

By the time I reach my house, my anger has subsided a bit. But I'm thoroughly confused by Drew's reaction, and I'm upset, disappointed, and angry that I was right about him not wanting more kids. I knew he wasn't ready to hear this type of news from me, especially after only knowing each other for a few weeks, but in my heart, I'd hoped for acceptance. I just don't understand. First, he seemed upset, but then he acted scared. He's clear in his affection, and when he says he loves me, I believe him, but then he completely freaks out when I tell him I'm pregnant... But not really in the way I was expecting.

I'm fighting tears as I struggle to get my front door unlocked. Once I'm inside, I slam it closed and lock it behind me. As I release a relieving breath, my phone starts chiming in my back pocket.

Drew: *Are you home yet?*

Drew: *Let me know you're okay.*

I reply straight away.

Me: *I'm home and fine.*

Drew: *We need to talk properly. Let's meet tomorrow.*

Me: *I need some time to think. Let's wait a few days. We can both use the time to clear our heads.*

Drew: *Don't shut me out, Emily. I'm sorry I freaked out, but there's a history you don't know about. We need to talk.*

Me: *I know we need to. I just need some time.*

As I sink down onto the couch, a lump forms in my throat. I'm so glad he's not here. I'm sure I wouldn't be able to maintain my resolve to get some space from him if he were in front of me... but then my phone rings. Drew's face pops up on my caller ID. I stare at it for a second before answering.

"Hi."

"I'm sorry for freaking out. Really. And I don't want to freak you out either."

"Thank you for apologizing, but too fucking late, Drew. Seriously, if I had any doubts about you not wanting more children, I don't any longer." When I realize I'm crying, I stop talking and take a deep breath.

"Emily, it's not that. This—my reaction—has nothing to do with wanting or not wanting more children."

"Drew, I need some space. I told you that. Please. I promise I won't shut you out, but I just need some time to adjust to the situation, and I can't think when you're close."

"Emily, I need to know that you're not going to do anything drastic."

I sit straight up and wonder what he means. Is he worried I'll run off and have an abortion without telling him? Can he really believe that of me?

"I'm not going to do anything drastic—I wouldn't. Besides that, the only real reassurance I can give you is to tell you I love you... and I do." Once the words are out, I know they're true, and I know having a baby without him isn't what I want. I can do it alone, I don't need him, but God, I want him. As hard as it is to admit, I wanted the fairytale. I wanted him to be excited over having a baby. I wanted him to grab me and lift me off my feet, spin me in a circle and smile wide, showing me his beautiful dimples.

I didn't want him to apologize for *getting me into trouble*.

I guess fairytales don't exist and that's a fact I have to accept.

I hear him sigh into the phone. "That's enough for now. I'll give you the space you need and... see you on Tuesday." He pauses for a moment. "If you need me... or anything until then, I'm here."

"Thank you."

"Wait, Emily?"

"What?" I say, quickly wiping the tears from my face.

"I just want you to know, I don't always do or say the right thing, but I do love you too."

Then he's gone.

\*

When I park behind our building, I see that Drew's truck is already there. My stomach flutters with nervous energy. I've missed him so much over the last couple of days. It reminded me of those last few days in Hawaii, only I couldn't drink my way through it this time.

Before I left for work this morning, I gave a disgusted last glance around my house. It's horrible, and I still haven't unpacked. I worked all day yesterday and most of the evening last night, but spent almost all of Sunday in bed. I picked up a book on what to expect when you're pregnant and I feel a little better now that I know it's perfectly normal to be so tired in the first trimester. Once

I reach the second trimester, I should have more energy and damn, am I looking forward to that.

I enter through the back door, and Drew is in the kitchen taking measurements. He looks over quickly when he sees me and the relaxed expression disappears from his face. This does absolutely nothing for my ego.

"Morning." He turns to face me. "I thought I'd keep busy until you got here."

"Smart thinking," I reply, but before I can say any more, I hear Eddie calling me from the other room.

"Emily, is that you?" He peeks his head in. "I have a stack of messages for you, and Mrs. Patterson has called three times."

I walk over and grab the handful of message slips. "Mrs. Patterson needs to wait her turn. I have a meeting I'm already late for."

"All right, boss. I'll put the coffee on."

"Make mine herbal tea, please."

Eddie stops and turns slowly. "Did you just ask for herbal tea?" His eyebrows are raised as he looks me up and down. "Are you ill?"

"Yes, on the tea, and no, I'm not ill. Is there something with, like… orange and clove? That sounds good to me right now." I turn from Eddie. "Drew, are you ready to meet or should we give you a few minutes?"

"I have the updated designs already hanging in the conference room," he says, gesturing toward the hall.

"Great. Give me five minutes to put my stuff down in my office, and I'll meet you there." I walk away and as I reach the top of the steps, I hear him coming up too.

"Do you want to talk personal business first, or building business?" he asks, once we're inside my office.

"Um…" I set my bags down and open the blinds to brighten the space. "Drew, Bec and I agree we want you to work on our building regardless of our personal business." I expected this to please him, but his expression doesn't change, and I really wish I knew what he was thinking. "On that note, I think maybe building business first. Is that okay?"

"I'm going to have a hard time concentrating without talking first, but I'll try."

His reserved manner is so unlike him, but I realize it's not him. He's feeding off my coldness. I try to lighten up and smile at him.

"Yes, I know, but I have a feeling it's not going to be any easier to concentrate after we talk either so it's best to just get work out of the way." I turn and face him fully, so he knows I'm trying my best to give him what he needs.

The chill radiating from both of us is achingly painful. So unlike the picture of a happy couple expecting a baby. It's hard to be in a room with him without thinking about how he and I have created life and how incredibly special that is. Or how incredibly painful it is that I finally know what I want and realize I'll have to do it alone. Over the weekend I did a lot of soul-searching. I thought a lot about being a mother, about how much my life is going to change. I'm ready for it. I've spent the last four years alone and working more hours than not. I want a family. I want this child… and I want Drew… but now *he* seems like the impossible dream.

I hear Rebecca's footsteps clicking outside my office. Then she pokes her head in. "Are we ready to talk remodel?"

I glance at Drew, eyebrows raised.

He nods. "Yep, let's do this."

We spend the next ninety minutes going over the designs for the space. It's excellent work, and we wrap up by adding more meetings to the calendar to look at flooring and furniture. Drew shows us samples of his woodwork and his ideas for the molding, new handrails on the stairs, and color samples for stripping and re-staining the woodwork. I'm so happy with it, I can barely contain my excitement.

"Okay, well, I know you guys have some stuff to deal with, so I'll get out of your way," Rebecca says.

When she's gone, Drew starts rolling up the designs and collecting the samples he brought with him. I'm nervous, and it shows in my inability to sit still.

"Do you want to meet me in my office when you're done?"

He looks up from the box he's packing. "Yeah, give me about ten minutes."

I quietly leave the room and head upstairs, so nervous my hands are shaking. I enter my office and try to breathe deeply as I pace... waiting for Drew.

# CHAPTER THIRTY-FIVE

## Drew

I'm so nervous about talking to Emily that I feel sick. I'm hoping for the best, but expecting the worst. All I can do is tell her everything and hope she understands my crazy behavior. If she'll just give me a chance. After locking up my truck, I walk slowly up the stairs, and my hesitation is starting to make me feel ridiculous. What do I have to be afraid of... *besides losing her*?

No. That's not going to happen. I won't let it.

I lift my chin and walk into her office like I own the joint. It's the best I can do. If I can't be confident, I'll have to pretend.

"Want to talk over lunch?" I ask as I enter her office.

"Hum, maybe lunch after we talk," she suggests.

I drop into the little loveseat in her office. I refuse to sit in one of the chairs facing her desk as if this is a business transaction. It isn't. This is my life we're talking about. Her life and the life of our child.

She follows my cue and walks over and sits in the chair across from me. Then she links her fingers in front of her. She seems nervous too, and this makes me feel better.

"Drew, I know this was sprung on you without warning. Truth be told, I was going to wait to tell you, but I decided to be honest about it, especially after finding out about Kyle and Hannah." She focuses her eyes on me and I think it's to gauge my reaction.

"Honestly, I knew you wouldn't want a baby, I just didn't know it was because you already had a family."

"I appreciate you telling me, I would rather know something like this right away. But Emily—"

"I realize that another child—a baby—wasn't part of your life plan, and I understand if you're upset about it, but I want you to know, I was just as surprised as you are at the news."

"Emily, most babies aren't planned."

Sadness flashes in her eyes. "Tucker always wanted children... I didn't. At least not when he was here. I wanted to wait... Then he was gone, and I realized I had waited too long, and in doing so, deprived him of something he wanted desperately. I have trouble forgiving myself for that."

"I'm sorry. I understand that must be hard for you, but don't you think he'd rather you live without regret?" I lean closer. "Emily, I heard the speech. Tucker doesn't sound like the type of guy who would want you to sit around and mourn opportunities that have long since expired."

She purses her lips and nods. "You're right. He would hate that I feel bad about this. He would hate that it took me nearly four years to find someone else to love. He would hate that I'm hesitant and too cautious, but I need to do what's right for me and now my baby."

"I agree with that too... we *both* need to do what's right for *our* baby." I hesitate, trying to get my thoughts in order before speaking. When I focus on her face again, I realize the absolute best thing I can do is be honest with her.

"I'm sorry for the way I reacted when you told me. I was completely surprised and I'm sure my reaction wasn't what you were expecting."

"What I was expecting, what I wanted, and reality are all very different things. Life doesn't always go as expected, I already know that... in fact, I've learned to expect the unexpected."

"I know that too, more than you realize."

"Drew, I'm trying to tell you that I'm not going to force you into being a father to this child. I didn't intend to get pregnant any more than you intended it to happen, but it did happen, and I'm moving forward. At first, I was upset and unsure, but now that I know for sure that I'm pregnant, I know I want this baby, and I'm actually excited about being a mother."

The lack of happiness on her face throws me off. She's telling me she's excited but she's frowning. I gesture to myself. "I don't think you really do understand my feelings on this… at least not…" I stop because I'm not sure where to begin. "Listen, I need to explain some things to you. I need you to understand."

She stands to pace the room. Her hands are shaking and when I see her link her fingers and lock her hands together, it almost scares me.

"Drew, it's simple, really. I can take care of the paperwork for you. All you'll have to do is sign a Petition for Termination of Parental Rights and then you won't have to worry about it again."

As my brain processes what she's just said, heat rises in my body. Memories of fighting with my in-laws, hours spent dealing with lawyers and in courtrooms… the anxiety I suffered while trying to prove I was worthy of my own children—all while mourning my wife—it all storms my senses and immediately puts me on the defensive.

"You have got to be fucking kidding me." It comes out louder than I intend, but I'm too angry to care. "You're fucking joking with this shit, right? Right, Emily?"

"Drew, I just want you to know that if you don't want this baby, I'm not forcing you, I'm trying to give you a clean out—without the guilt. I understand if this isn't what you want and I won't judge you for it."

I get to my feet now, completely unable to sit still. "I thought we were going to talk, yet you haven't heard a fucking word I've said.

Not one word, Emily. You don't know anything about me. Yet, you're so sure I don't want my own child—why? Because it's easier for you to believe that? Because you want to believe the worst in me without even giving me a chance." I point to her. "Maybe you're the one who needs an easy out. Why don't you give up *your* parental rights?"

Now I see the anger building in her eyes. "I wouldn't. This is my baby."

"It's my baby too!" I shout as I tread closer to her. I'm so angry I can barely stand to look at her. "Christ, what? I can walk away because I'm *just* the father. How dare you assume this is some silly inconvenience for me—like I'm incapable of being a loving parent—what, because I'm a man?"

She faces me straight on, and I have to admire her calmness because the very last thing I feel is calm. "Drew, that's not at all what this is about."

"No, it's not? Then what is it, Emily? Because I'm thoroughly confused!"

"I'm scared!" The words come out in a low shout, almost as if she didn't want to say them. Her breath catches and she says, "Is that what you want to hear? I'm fucking scared to death—everything I want is so close, yet so completely out of reach. I don't know what to do. I don't know what you want. I'm reacting to the way you acted. What else can I do with a man who lied about having children? What fucking choice do I have?"

Before I can respond, my phone rings. Of course, I can't ignore it because I *am* a father. I glare at the phone. "Hold on, it's the nanny." I take a steady breath in case it's not Celia but one of the kids. "What's up?" I answer.

"Mr. Whitney—it's Hannah. She's hurt."

My blood runs cold, and I feel a spike of fear drive through me. "What do you mean, she's hurt? Where are you?"

I stab my fingers through my hair as I listen to Celia's crying. I can barely understand her.

"I have Kyle with me, and we're on our way to the hospital. Hannah's been taken by ambulance to UC Davis Medical Center."

"Celia, what happened?" As I'm talking, I wrench my keys from my pocket and head down the stairs toward my truck. I don't hear Emily trailing behind me until I reach the truck and fumble with the keys. My hands are shaking, and I'm having a hard time holding the phone while trying to get the truck door open.

Before I realize what's happening, Emily takes the keys from me and points to the passenger seat. "I'll drive, just tell me where we're going."

"Davis Medical Center," I say as I rush to the passenger side of the truck. "Celia, you need to pull over, you shouldn't be driving while you're this upset."

"I'm here already. I just parked."

"Okay, now tell me what happened." My heart is racing, and it's all I can do to keep from dropping to my knees and begging God to protect my sweet baby girl.

"We were walking home from the park, and a car jumped the curb and… and…"

That spike of fear jabs again and I'm almost doubled over with the pain. "She was hit by a car?"

"Yes, sir," Celia cries. "I'm so sorry. I… I couldn't do anything, Mr. Whitney. It happened so fast."

"Celia, I need you to calm down, so you don't freak Kyle out. Okay? Can you do that?"

"Yes… but he's pretty scared."

"Let me talk to him." I hear a muffle as she passes the phone.

"Daaaad—is Hannah gonna die?"

This immediately chokes me up. I place my hand over my mouth and hold my breath until it passes. I can't let him hear me lose it. "Kyle, no." It's all I can get out, and I'm struggling to find the right words. It's so hard for a kid who's lost his mother. "Listen, buddy, I need you to do me a favor, okay? I have a job for you, okay?" I need to keep him busy, stop him from thinking about the worst possible outcome.

"Okay, Daddy."

"I need you to use Celia's phone and call Nanna." Dammit, that's going to freak her out too. "Kyle, I need you to be strong, so you don't scare her, okay? Call Nanna and tell her to meet us at the hospital but you have to be calm, so she doesn't get too scared. Can you do that for me?"

"Yeah, Dad, I can do that." I hear his intense focus and the need to be useful and I know he's going to be all right.

"Thank you, son. I'll see you in a few minutes."

I disconnect the call and hit the speed dial to call my sister. "Jennie!"

"I just heard, one of the moms at the park called me. Is she okay?"

"I don't know. I'm not there yet, and Celia was too upset to tell me what happened." I grit my teeth to keep from breaking down again. "What have you heard?"

"I don't know how much is true, but it sounds like the driver suffered a seizure and lost control of the car."

"Do you know—what are her injuries?" My voice cracks when I say this and I can hear her break down too.

"I don't know, honey, but I'm on my way. I'll be there in a few minutes, okay?"

"Okay, we're pulling into the parking lot now. I'll see you when you get here."

Once the truck is parked, I look over at Emily, and it's the strangest thing. I knew she was here, that she was driving, but I'm still surprised to see her sitting there, behind the wheel of my truck. She's white as a ghost, and I can see tear streaks down her cheeks.

"Thank you for driving me."

"Drew, do you know what happened?" Her voice stutters. "Is she going to be okay?" Her hands are shaking as she wipes the tears from her face.

"I only know she was brought here by ambulance." I pop the door handle and jump out. As I'm rushing toward the large, glass double doors, Emily catches up and grabs my hand. She squeezes, and I appreciate that she's here.

When the doors swish open, I see Kyle standing there with Celia. He runs up to me, and I catch him in a hug and lift him off his feet. As he cries on my shoulder, all I can do is hold him. I carry him to the check-in counter and say, "My name is Drew Whitney. My daughter, six-year-old. Her name is Hannah Whitney. She was brought in an ambulance."

As I finish speaking, Jennie walks in. She reaches over and takes Kyle from me, and that causes a new flutter of crying from him.

"Mr. Whitney, they're checking her out now. Please have a seat, and we'll be with you in a moment."

"Have a seat? I can't have a seat. Where's my little girl?" As I lean over the counter, I feel both Jennie and Emily grab my shirt and pull me back.

"That's not going to get you what you need, Drew," Jennie says wryly, "You need to calm down."

"Don't tell me to calm down."

She points to Kyle in her arms. "If you act like this, they'll call security and throw you out of here. Please, stop. Hannah needs us all to be calm."

"All right. I got it. I'm calm."

"Here, take Kyle, and I'll try to get some information from them."

She puts Kyle down, and he clutches my waist.

God help me if something happens to that little girl.

# CHAPTER THIRTY-SIX

## Emily

I'm completely shell-shocked, and that makes me wonder how Drew can be so strong. I watch him as he talks calmly to his son, who's hysterical. The young woman with Kyle is the same person that I saw Drew with at the school on Saturday and now I realize she's the nanny. The poor thing is equally upset and I want to comfort her, but I'm honestly not sure how.

I'm assuming this Jennie person is their mother. Between the way Kyle clung to her and the way she and Drew spoke to each other, it's easy to see they're divorced. I watch her as she speaks calmly to the person behind the counter. I can't hear what she's saying, but she's definitely determined.

After a pretty intense conversation, she brushes her hand at the medical assistant and walks away. She stops in front of me and stares, then she asks, "Do I know you?"

"Oh, um, no, not yet." I reach out my hand to shake hers. "I'm Emily Thomas, a friend of Drew's. You must be Hannah and Kyle's mom?"

She draws back and narrows her eyes at me. "Did you just ask if I was their mother?"

"I'm sorry." I pull my hand back a fraction of an inch. "Are you not?"

"Oh, Jesus Christ, Drew." She grumbles with an eye-roll. Then she shakes my hand. "I'm not their mother. Are you the same Emily that Drew met in Maui?"

"Yes, that's right."

"Drew hasn't told you about their mom?"

"Ah, no, not yet. I mean, I know they're not together, but we haven't talked in depth about her."

"Emily…" She takes a deep breath. "Their mother is dead. Drew's a widower."

Now I draw back and my head starts spinning.

"Are you okay?"

"No… I need…" I should sit down. I glide over to the nearest chair and gently lower myself into it. It's all I can do to keep from putting my head between my knees.

She sits next to me. "Drew seriously didn't tell you about his wife?"

"Ah, no." But things are starting to click into place now. "If you're not his ex-wife, who are you?"

"I'm his sister." Just as she says this, the double doors swish open, and a woman walks in, looking frantic.

Jennie stands and waves. "Mom, we're over here."

The woman rushes over, and I can see how upset she is. I glance up and instantly see a shadow of Drew in her features.

Drew approaches and lays his hand on his mom's shoulder. "They haven't told us anything yet." Then she reaches in to hug him, his long arms encircling around her, dwarfing her small body.

She clings to him for a long moment. "What the hell happened, do we know anything?"

Jennie replies, "A car jumped the curb near the park and hit Hannah. We don't even know what her injuries are."

Drew's mom glances around, then her hand lands on her chest in relief when she eyes Kyle. "Oh, honey. Come see Nanna."

Kyle rushes to her and wraps his arms around her waist, clinging to her. Seeing them all together chokes me up. If I'm this worried, how hard is this on all of them? I lift my eyes to Drew's and see the fear in their golden-brown depths.

I'm such an asshole. I hate myself right now, especially when I see the worry on his face. I'm about to tell him how sorry I am when a nurse calls out his name.

"Mr. Whitney, you can come back now."

Drew rushes through the security door and follows the nurse. As he goes, I send up a little prayer to look after him and Hannah.

"Someone needs to get Kyle out of here. Do you want me to go so you can stay?" Jennie asks her mom.

"No, Nanna, I want to stay with Daddy. I need to be here."

Jennie sits down, so she's at Kyle's eye level. "Honey, we know you want to be here for your dad and Hannah, but if you're here, Dad's going to be worried about you and right now, he needs to focus on your sister, okay?"

"Kyle," Drew's mom says, "Come home with Nanna, please. I really don't want to be alone. Can you keep me company?"

He nods and cuddles Jennie. "Will you hug Hannah for me when you see her?"

"Yes, I'll do that."

When Drew's mom takes his hand, they turn, but she stops abruptly. "Celia, honey, you come too. You don't need to stay, and I can't let you drive when you're this upset. I'll take you home."

Celia, who's been standing out of the way, but crying the entire time, finally looks up and nods at her. Just like any good grandmother would, Drew's mom puts an arm around her too and leads her out.

I'm in awe. The woman must be worried sick about her granddaughter and her son, yet she's the pillar of strength for everyone else.

When she's gone, Jennie sits in the chair next to mine and rests her head in her hands. "I can't believe this is happening. That poor baby."

"I wish I could do something. I feel so helpless right now," I mutter. "Is there someone I can call? Another family member who should know?"

"No, not really. My mom will make the necessary calls when she gets home. Drew has to call his in-laws in Los Angeles. I would do it, but I want to check with him first. God knows what they'll do when they find out. Last time one of these kids got hurt, they filed another custody suit against Drew."

Now I want to throw up. "Another?"

"Yep. The first time was just after Kayla died. They didn't even give him time to grieve before hitting him with a custody suit."

"They tried to sue him for custody? Why?"

She blows out a long breath. "Lots of reasons, but none of them valid. As a single parent, they didn't think Drew could care for the kids properly. And they wanted them—it's not so much that they didn't want Drew to have the kids, it's that they just wanted to keep them. We're far away and they don't like that they can't keep an eye on things. So, whenever anything like this happens, they use it against him."

"Oh my gosh. Poor Drew." I stand up in agitation. "It's not like he could have stopped this from happening. He wasn't even there."

"Conveniently, that's one of their arguments. He works too much to be an effective parent."

"That's ridiculous! If they're in Los Angeles, they can't possibly know how much he works anyway."

"I completely agree, it's ridiculous, but I still need his go-ahead before I call them. I don't want them to bombard him with calls. Besides, I don't have anything to report until we know what her injuries are."

I sit back down. "I can't imagine what kind of damage a car can do to such a small girl."

"Emily, have you met them? Hannah and Kyle?"

"No, not exactly. I ran into Drew at the school renaming ceremony on Saturday, and the kids were with him. I met Hannah, but Kyle was playing ball."

"I take it Drew didn't know you'd be there."

"No, it was an accidental meeting… but why do you say that?"

"Drew doesn't usually let the women he dates meet the kids until he's sure they're going to stick around." Her eyes lock on mine. "He doesn't want them to get attached just to have them heartbroken when she leaves… because that's what they do. They leave."

Her point is clear and hard to ignore. I'm not sure what to say, but I feel a little heat creep into my cheeks. "Jennie, I don't want to hurt anyone, especially Drew's kids, but I didn't even know they existed until I saw them on Saturday."

"No kidding?" She presses her lips together and says, "Poor sucker."

"I'm sorry, but aren't *I* the sucker here?"

She stares into space as if deep in thought. "No, Drew is." She shrugs. "He must be in love with you."

I'm totally confused now. Usually, I'm pretty good at keeping up with people, but Jennie has me puzzled. "You think he lied to me because he's in love with me?"

"Well, I can't say for sure, but Drew isn't a liar by nature. He's got this code, you know. I think because he's raising these kids on his own, he tries really hard to live by example. He's honest and usually pretty frank. When dating, he makes a point of telling women about his kids before there's a second date. He likes to be upfront about it. I mean, why waste time? If they're going to be spooked by the dad thing, he wants to know before he invests in the relationship. Of course, whenever he tells women about being a single dad with two kids, they don't usually walk away, they run… and they run fast."

My heart sinks. Of course. God, I'm so stupid. I drop my eyes and think over the last week and how I've behaved. Those horrible words I said to him at the school yard. Accusing him of being a weekend father who didn't care. A lawyer-hating divorcé. He's right, I didn't even listen to him when he tried to talk to me about it.

I nod at her, and I have to agree because I've seen this code— I've seen how honorable he is—up close. "Do you know, the first time I met Drew, I got sloppy drunk."

"That's a great way to make a first impression."

"It's true. I got really drunk, and Drew had to help me back to my room. The man put me to bed and left hangover provisions on the bedside table before locking me in my room—fully dressed and untouched."

Jennie laughs at this. "Yep, that's my brother. A Boy Scout to his core."

The laughter dies from my voice, and I reply, "Most men wouldn't have been so kind."

Jennie gives me a good long look and asks, "So, Emily, what did you do when you found out about the kids? I'm hoping, since you're here, that you didn't break up with him."

"Not exactly. But I was hurt and angry that he lied. I said some pretty nasty things to him… all things I sincerely regret now."

"Well, if he really does love you, it won't matter in the end."

"I hope you're right because he's stuck with me now…"

"Why? You guys didn't get married in secret or anything like that, did you?"

I drop my head and mumble, "I'm pregnant with his baby." I'm not sure why it's so hard to say, but it is. I guess because of the shame I feel about suggesting he give up his parental rights today.

Jennie's quiet for a long time and when I look back up at her, she has a single fat tear running down her face. "Poor Drew. He must have freaked pretty hard when you told him."

"He didn't take it well at all."

"Oh, God." She lifts a hand and wipes away the silent tear, and once again, I am puzzled by her reaction. After a moment of quiet between us, she says, "When did he find out? Fuck. No wonder he's been acting so weird. I wish he'd told me."

I want to think she's overreacting but when I think about how Drew behaved when I told him, I realize maybe being a single parent with two little ones would make it hard to accept the idea of a third child. "I told him Saturday night, and he made it pretty clear he didn't want another kid."

"Oh God, Emily. You don't get it, do you?" She reaches down and grabs a pack of tissues from her purse. "Of course you don't, because Drew hasn't told you anything."

"I'm sorry, but I don't understand. What don't I *get*?"

"Of course Drew's freaking out about this. His wife died giving birth to Hannah."

# CHAPTER THIRTY-SEVEN

## Drew

When I step into the curtained room, Hannah is lying with her eyes closed, her small body dwarfed by the huge hospital bed. Her clothes are gone and she's dressed in a child-sized hospital gown with little tigers on it. It takes everything I have to hold in my gasp when I see the bruising. Every inch of exposed skin is spotted in black and blue from her ankles to her shoulders. "Oh, my God…" Just as I'm about to reach out to her, I hear someone say my name.

I turn quickly, startled. I was so focused on Hannah, I didn't realize I wasn't in the room alone.

"Mr. Whitney, good afternoon. I'm Dr. Rossi."

I reach out to shake his hand and as I do, I realize my movements are jerky. After greeting him, I immediately turn back to Hannah. Her arm is in a splint, but besides that and the bruising, it looks like she could just be sleeping.

"…broken arm," I hear, then: "We're going to do some tests to be sure we didn't miss anything. She has a grade 2 concussion so we're also going to check for any blood on the brain."

I quickly turn back to him and I know my expression is pure fear since that's exactly how I'm feeling. He holds out a calming hand.

"It's just a precaution. I don't think there's any bleeding but I want to be sure."

I clear my throat and say, "A broken arm and a concussion. You're checking for any internal bleeding, but you don't think there is any, after examining her, is that what I heard?"

He nods and one side of his mouth tilts up. "That's exactly right. I know she looks bad, and she's going to be in pain when she wakes and the meds wear off, but I think she'll make a full recovery."

The tension I've been holding onto releases slightly and I feel the weight of my body bringing me down. I lower myself into a chair and drop my head into my hands. After several deep breaths, I send up a little prayer of thanks.

I don't know what I would have done if I'd lost her. When I look up to thank the doctor, he's gone. I stand over Hannah's bed and lean in. Then I rest a kiss on her forehead and squeeze my eyes closed, fighting with my emotions. It's no use though. My tears come hard and hot. I instantly think of her mother and how much I need her right now. How much Hannah needs her and God, how much I hate that she's not here.

*She's going to be okay.* I repeat these words to myself several times until I can breathe evenly, until my heart rate feels normal, and some of the fear has faded. I rest my hand on Hannah's chest. I want to feel her little heart beating. It's strong and her chest rises with her breathing. I lift my hand away and reach down to pull the blanket up over her. Just as I get her tucked in, they come in to take her for testing. I watch them gently move her to a gurney and push her out of the room. With a heavy heart and a strong sense of helplessness I follow them to radiology.

\*

Three hours later, I enter the waiting room to find Jennie and Emily sitting side by side in complete silence. Jennie looks like she's been crying, and Emily looks pale and a little lost.

When they look up at me simultaneously, Jennie jumps to her feet. "Dammit, Drew, what the hell is going on? How's Hannah?"

"I'm so sorry. My phone doesn't have service. She's going to be fine. She has a broken arm and a concussion."

Her hands jump to her mouth, and her eyes instantly tear up. "Oh, God. Our poor baby. Is she in a lot of pain?"

"They've drugged her up. She's not feeling anything right now." I shake my head as the image of her broken little body in the big white hospital bed comes to mind. It takes me a moment to get a grip on myself, but when I'm sure I can get the words out, I say, "She looks much worse than that, though. She's covered in bruises. They think she was thrown when the car hit her. It's a grade 2 concussion, and luckily, there's no internal bleeding. They want to keep her overnight for observation and they need to reset her arm before casting it."

"Reset her arm? Holy fuck." She grips my hand, her eyes locked on mine. "I'm sorry," she mutters. "I know it's hard to see our kids hurt, but she's a strong little girl, she's going to be fine."

I nod because I know she's right. It could have been so much worse.

"She's her mom. Strong, stubborn, and sweet as sugar all the time."

"It's hard not to think about Kayla when things like this happen, isn't it?"

"It's very hard, but I can't imagine a better guardian angel for my kids. I have to believe she's up there watching out."

"She is, Drew. You can count on it."

I look around again and my eyes land on Emily, still sitting where she was when I came out. Her eyes are locked on the ground and she looks exhausted. I take a few steps closer to her and say, "Emily, you didn't have to stay."

She clears her throat and nods, her eyes finally lifting to mine. "Of course I did. I couldn't leave… not without making sure you and Hannah were okay."

"I'm sorry you had to drive me, but we're fine." I pull my phone out of my pocket and say, "I'll get you an Uber so you can go home."

"Drew…" Jennie says, her eyes narrowing at me.

"I can't leave to take her home, Jennie. I'm not leaving Hannah."

Emily holds her hand out to stop me as she stands. "It's okay. Mac will pick me up. I… I don't want to be in the way. I just wanted to make sure you were both okay before I left." She reaches into her purse and pulls out my keys. Handing them to me, she turns toward the glass doors.

"Emily," Jennie says, stopping her before she can get away. "Thank you so much for sitting with me for so long. I'd have gone stir-crazy waiting by myself."

"No, thank you for letting me stay. I would have been at home bouncing off the walls, waiting for news." Her eyes shift to me then she says, "I'm glad Hannah's going to be okay. Let me know if you need anything. Anything at all."

I watch her leave, torn between my anger and my need for comfort. Because it's true, I need her here with me. I need the support and comfort more than I want to admit, but I just can't trust her after today.

Once the glass doors close behind her, I turn back toward Jennie. "Where is everyone? Who has Kyle?"

"Mom has Kyle and she also took Celia home."

I lift my palm to my forehead. "Oh, crap, Celia. I didn't even talk to her when I came in. Was she all right?"

"She'll be okay, but it wouldn't hurt to call and check on her later. I'm sure she feels a sense of responsibility since Hannah was in her care."

"That could have happened to any of us. It's amazing she and Kyle weren't hit as well."

"I know, that was my thought too." She lays a hand on her chest and says, "One of the moms at the park recognized Hannah and called to let me know what had happened. I thought the worst—it really scared me."

"Is that how you knew before I did?"

"Yeah." Jennie goes quiet, but her piercing blue eyes pin me down. I know she's irritated with me about Emily, but she doesn't understand what's happening. "Why did you treat Emily the way you did? What the hell is wrong with you? She was worried sick about you and Hannah and you just brushed her off like she was in the way here."

I press my lips together and nod. "Yeah, well, there's more to the story than you realize."

She crosses her arms over her chest. "Just like there was more to the story than *she knew*, Drew?" She smacks my arm. "How could you not have told her about Kayla?"

"Christ, Jennie! Did you talk to her about that?"

She lifts then drops her hand on her leg. "Well, duh, asshole! I had no choice when she asked if I was Hannah and Kyle's mom."

"Shit, Jennie, I can't believe you told her." I walk in a circle in an attempt to calm my aggravation. "Now I don't know what the hell I'm going to do about her."

"Do you ever know what to do?"

I turn toward her, confused by this question.

"Seriously. Do you think about *everything* before you decide? Just follow your heart."

"I don't have the luxury of following my heart."

"What about when you met Kayla?"

"That was different, and you know it. I didn't have two kids to think about. I was young with nothing to lose. I could jump without thinking then."

"Yet, it still worked out."

"Emily isn't the same as Kayla. She's more thoughtful, more cautious."

"Exactly my point, Drew. When you met Kayla, neither of you were thoughtful or cautious, but you certainly are now. Kayla and her carefree ways were perfect for you. At the time you needed that in your life. Maybe Emily is perfect for you now—when you need it."

"She's pushing me away, she doesn't trust me. I've fucked up too much already. I can't turn back the clock and fix what I've done."

"You should have told her, Drew."

"I tried on several occasions, but it was never the right time."

"When is it ever the right time to say *my wife died giving birth to my daughter*?" she huffs. "You can't control how people are going to react so stop trying. Just get the damn words out and let the chips fall."

"It doesn't matter. She doesn't want this life. Look around you, Jenn, she ran out of here the first chance she got."

"Now you're an asshole. She only left because you made it clear you didn't want her here. You practically threw her out."

"I did not! She clearly didn't want to be here; she only stuck around because she felt obligated." I try to wave her away and say, "You don't know what's going on so you can't judge."

"You mean about her pregnancy?" She gives me an exaggerated nod. "Yeah, I know about the baby. She's much more forthcoming than you are."

"Emily told you she was pregnant?"

"Yep, but why didn't you? I know you have to be freaking out about it."

"Did she also tell you that she asked me to give up my parental rights?"

This makes Jennie pause. She stares at me like she doesn't believe it. "You mean she doesn't fully trust the guy who lied about his kids? Surprise, surprise."

"That was an accident," I reply before she can say anything else.

"Drew, all I'm trying to say is, don't be so quick to give up on her and this relationship. Give it some time. Maybe there's a reason she doesn't fully trust you. Maybe she has her own fears, just like you. Maybe you don't know everything—just like she didn't know everything. Accident or not, you are the guy who lied to her about having kids. That alone would make any woman hesitant."

My phone chimes in my pocket. I pull it free and read a text from Emily.

Emily: *I just made it home. Please keep me posted and let me know how Hannah's doing.*

Drew: *Thank you. I appreciated you staying before, but you didn't have to. I know you're probably exhausted.*

Emily: *Yes, exhausted but very worried too. Please remember that I'm here if you need anything at all. I want to be here for you.*

I reply saying thank you, but that we're fine, and I'm wondering if she really means that. I hate that I'm questioning her, but after today, I feel like I have to. I want to rant and scream at her. Just thinking about her being so quick to assume I would want to give up my kid pisses me off beyond belief. She was so quick to believe the worst in me. Have I behaved so badly that her expectations of me are rock bottom? I've tried to do the right thing. Yes, I waited to tell her about the kids, that was a mistake, but it doesn't define who I am. I'm going to have a damn hard time forgetting that she was trying to get me to give up my child.

# CHAPTER THIRTY-EIGHT

## Emily

I stare at my phone with a frown. It hurts that he doesn't need me, but it doesn't surprise me... not after what I did. If I could just talk to him... apologize. He's got to know that I didn't want him to give up his parental rights. He must understand that I was just trying to do the right thing by offering him an out—and now I see how stupid I was to even consider asking him to do that. I really am horrible. Bec, Mac, and Kelley tried to tell me on Saturday... I wish I'd listened.

In the end, none of it matters compared to what's happening with Hannah. He has much too much to worry about now without me adding to his stress. I need to let it rest for a while.

When I saw Drew's reaction to Celia's phone call, I knew it was bad. He could barely hold the keys, much less drive. The worry on his face will haunt me forever. The reminder of what parents go through with their kids is enough to scare away even the strongest person.

If I'm honest with myself, I have to admit I'm scared to death. After everything, I'm not sure I'm the person Drew needs in his life. Maybe I'm not worthy of having a relationship with his kids. He's right to be cautious of women... maybe he's right to be cautious of me. It must be incredibly hard to grow attached to people just to have them reject you because you're a dad.

I think about what my mom said about being a single parent, and I understand. But I also understand the other side of it. Taking on a family is daunting. Downright scary…

I have always considered myself a good and caring person, but I'm even questioning if I'm up for the task. I'm no superhuman. I'm not a mom. I wasn't even a good wife. Admitting this brings tears to my eyes, but it's true. I neglected my husband for a career. Every day I spent in the office instead of with Tucker, he reminded me that I just floated through the marriage doing the bare minimum. Now that he's gone, I know to an extent that he was right. My career was important to me, it still is, but if I had a second chance, I'd find a way to juggle better. Tucker deserved better and so does Drew—so do Hannah and Kyle.

I stare around my lonely house, thinking that this is what I deserve. I should be alone. Who am I to think that I can be a mom… to think that I can be a wife? I had it and let it go. Tucker is gone because of me. Because I chose a new client over a day out with my guy. Again.

Maybe if I had gone with him that day, if I'd spent that day with him at the beach, instead of going to work, maybe things would have been different. Maybe he wouldn't have gone into the water. Maybe he wouldn't have tried being the hero. Maybe he'd still be here…

I remember the first few weeks after losing him and how angry I was. Yes, he was a hero, but what about me? What about our life together? I know now that I was projecting. I was actually angry with myself for not being there with him. He died on the shore… and I wasn't there. It's taken me a long time to come to terms with that.

I walk down the hall to my bedroom and stand at the foot of my bed. I haven't slept here since Friday night. I can't bear to smell Drew on my sheets. I can't do it. My eyes travel around the room at the mess. What does he even see in me? I'm pathetic.

I grip the base of the sheet and rip it from the mattress, stripping the bed. I pile the linens and kick them into the hall. Then I gather the laundry lying around the basket and shove it in. I grab my shoes and line them in the closet. A couple of pairs are missing. I look around the floor and my eyes land on the suitcase I haven't unpacked yet.

I walk over, tug the shoes free, and return them to the closet. Maybe if I can get this house back in order, my mind and body will feel better. I put fresh sheets on the bed and throw the rest of the linens in the washer. Then I stand and stare at the suitcase. I need to do it. The reminders of Drew are going to hurt but I need to get my shit together, and I can't do it without facing this task.

I lift the flap and gather the laundry. I take out the few souvenirs I bought and place them on the dresser. Then I check all the pockets and tug the zipper. That's when I find an envelope.

I take it out and read the script, heart thudding.

*When you've decided you can no longer live without me, open this. Love, Drew*

I stare at it, confused. When did he put this in here?

Lowering myself to the bed, I rip the flap open and pull out a greeting card with a Hawaiian sunset on it. The front of it reads *I miss you.* My jaw drops. Did Drew sneak this in before leaving Maui?

"That sneaky bastard," I murmur with a smile.

I open the card, and I'm greeted with a full page of writing.

*Dearest Emily,*

*Let me start with an apology. I tried to respect your wishes, but I'm afraid I'm a weak man. I knew right away that I wouldn't be happy without you in my life. I fought hard against it, but my heart wanted you.*

*I realize as I write this that I have our one little rule to blame for not only losing you but for loving you. I know it sounds odd, but without that stupid rule, there's a possibility I'd have you in my life right now. But, without that rule, without our inability to talk about real life, work, friends, lovers, kids, whatever happened outside of Maui, I might not have had the opportunity to know the real you. I'd only know the woman who hid behind her tight bun, business suits, and grief.*

*That's not who you are.*

*I know, without a doubt, that if I'd learned about where you live and what you do for a living before experiencing you, I would have missed out on the really important stuff. So, I am painfully grateful for losing you because, without the loss, I would have missed you.*

*You're vibrant, fun, and easy to love. You're funny and smart, and you have an openness I believe most people don't get to experience because you hide behind that take-no-shit façade. You expect the worst from people, I see that too. Breaking our one rule with this letter may prove your worst expectations about me to be correct, but I don't care because I am breaking the rule – I have to.*

*Enclosed is my address and all my contact information. PLEASE USE IT because I miss you and I don't want to live without you.*

*Yours truly,*
*Drew Whitney*

With blurry, tear-filled eyes, I flip the card over to find his address and phone number. I read it again and feel the heaviness of his words.

*He sees me.*

This isn't a new revelation. I've known this almost since the moment I met him. Drew sees me. Something nobody else has ever done. Grant looked through me from the beginning. Tucker looked past me to what he wanted me to be… to what he wanted *us* to be. Yes, I neglected him for my career, but he also never understood how important that career was to me. I think about all the time I've spent with Drew. The things he observed that always surprised me: knowing I needed to let loose and relax my first night in Hawaii; knowing I needed to spend time at the beach and work past my hesitation about getting in the water; recognizing my grief even before he knew about Tucker; even guessing my profession just from a conversation… and then I used it against him.

How could I be so judgmental and short-sighted, cruel and accusing? I never once tried to give him the benefit of the doubt… at least not to his face. "Oh Drew, I'm so sorry," I say aloud to the empty room.

I hold the card to my chest, and I know in my heart, I'd forgive him anything right now. Hopefully, he still feels the same about me. Somehow, I'll find a way to make this up to him. Somehow, I need to be worthy of him… and his family. But first, I need to get my life in order. I need to stop the nonsense, stop feeling sorry for myself. What's to pity when a man like Drew loves me… for me?

# CHAPTER THIRTY-NINE

## Drew

"Why can't I go to school, Daddy?" Hannah whines as I lay her on the couch. The child has been counting the days until school starts, and now that it's here, she can't go. It's heartbreaking.

"Honey, you can't possibly feel like being at school today. Doesn't your head and your arm hurt?"

"But, Daddy, it's the first day. I'm supposed to be there. My friends are there and what about my new teacher?"

"They all know why you're not there, Hannah, don't worry."

She tries to sit up and winces.

"See, you're in pain. You can't go to school this week. Maybe you'll be well enough next week."

I walk back into the kitchen to grab Kyle's lunch, and as I hand it to him, he says, "Can I stay home with you guys?"

"Kyle, you can't miss the first day of school, and you know that. Can you please try to make this easier on me?"

He crams the lunch into his backpack and zips it closed with just enough force to let me know he's not happy with me.

"Don't complain to me when you have to eat a smashed sandwich for lunch. It's your own fault."

He shrugs at me and walks away. Jesus, he's not even a teenager yet.

"Hello?" I hear from the open front door.

"Come on in, Celia."

She comes in and heads straight for Hannah. "Hannah Banana! I'm so happy to see you. You scared the life out of me."

"Celia!" Hannah stretches her good arm out for a hug and the two embrace for a long time. When Celia gets to her feet, I grab her too.

"I'm so glad you were there for her. Thank you for taking care of my little one."

"I was so scared. I felt so helpless," she says when she draws back.

"You did everything right. I hope you know that."

She nods, and I sense she's a little choked up, so I change the subject. "I'll be working from home today and probably for the rest of the week to be with Hannah. I'm hoping you can still handle school drop-off and pick up for Kyle."

"Of course. I'll pick him up and help him get any homework done." She gives me a thumbs-up. "I've gotcha covered, Mr. Whitney." The girl's enthusiasm makes me want to hug her again. What would I do without her?

"Thank you, sincerely, Celia."

"No problem." She looks over at Kyle. "You ready to go?"

"I guess so."

"Hey, I saw Jared walking. We can try to catch him and see if he wants to ride with us."

"Cool. Let's go." And just like that, Kyle's out the door.

"Goodbye," I holler. "Have a good first day."

Once they're gone, I close the door and turn toward Hannah. She's lying on the couch, on her left side, sound asleep. I snort out a laugh. *Sure, she would have been fine at school today.*

I toss a blanket over her and turn the TV to a station I know she'll like when she wakes up, then I head back to my office.

As I settle in at my desk, my phone chimes.

Emily: *How's Hannah this morning?*

I rest back in my chair, staring at the screen, heart thudding rapidly in my chest. I'm not sure what to do now. Especially with how we left things… me screaming at her, for a good reason, and her admitting she was scared… also for a good reason.

Me: *Upset she can't go to school, but okay besides that. She's sleeping right now.*

Emily: *I bet she's exhausted. How are you?*

I hesitate, not sure how to answer. It's been a while since anyone has asked how I was doing. I'm not even sure how to respond. With honesty?

*I'm horrible and heartbroken that you're not here with me.*

*I'm achingly afraid for my daughter, guilty that I wasn't there to protect her.*

*I'm wondering how long it's going to take for you to drift away because you're too chicken shit to fight for me, and with me, for this love that means so much to me.*

But I choose to lie—why not when she already sees me as a liar?

Me: *Fine.*

Emily: *Liar.*

*Exactly.*

I sigh because what can I say to that? I set my phone down and try to focus on my work. Which of course is work I'm doing for her so even that doesn't take my mind off her. Then my phone chimes again.

Emily: *What if I came over there?*

Me: *Please don't. I have work to do.*

Emily: *What if I came anyway?*

Me: *Emily, it's not a good time.*

Emily: *But I think you might need me?*

Me: *I'm fine.*

Emily: *Liar.*

Me: *Don't you have to work today?*

Emily: *You're more important to me than work.*

This makes me pause. *Am I though?* Or is she just trying to make up for whatever guilt she's feeling about her husband… about not having his baby? Ugh! I want to throw my phone, but I don't.

Me: *I'm fine.*

I'm still so mad at her, I can't bring myself to say anything more.

I'm staring at my phone when the doorbell rings. *Dammit, Hannah's sleeping.* "Who the hell is that?"

I walk to the door and peer through the peephole to see Emily standing on the other side. I creep it open and step outside. "I told you I was fine."

"I wanted to see for myself." She has her hair down, and she's wearing jeans with a t-shirt. I look her up and down. "You're really not working today?"

"No. I told you, I want to be here for you."

"And I told you that I'm fine, Emily."

She holds up a covered dish. "I brought you a lasagna."

"Emily, you don't understand." I click the door closed behind me, trying to be quiet, hoping Hannah doesn't hear us. "I don't want Hannah to see you. She won't understand."

Her eyebrows raise. "Understand what? That I'm bringing food to a sick friend?"

"You know that's not what I mean."

"Then be frank, Drew. Seriously. It's time to stop dancing around this and work it out."

Before I can say anything, I hear the door creep open and see Hannah's little red head pop out from behind it. "Daddy, why are you outside?" Her eyes move to Emily. "Ms. Thomas?"

"She's just here to drop food off," I snap and instantly regret it. Hannah's face falls. "Oh, sorry."

"Actually." Emily lowers to a kneeling position. "I brought something for you, Hannah. It's in the car."

"Thank you very much," Hannah replies, in her very best effort at being polite. "Would you like to come inside?"

"Thank you," Emily says and winks up at me. "I would love to come inside."

Oh, hell. This woman is brutal. She knows exactly how to get what she wants. She hands me the lasagna and turns back to her car. "I'll be right back."

I get Hannah back inside and carry the lasagna to the kitchen. As I'm trying to fit it into the fridge, she enters the kitchen and says, "And here's a pot of spaghetti."

"When did you have time to do all of this?" I ask, taking the pot from her.

"Last night, after I thoroughly cleaned my house and unpacked my suitcase."

"Oh, so you finally got around to that, huh?"

"I did… and got a nice surprise, too."

She's grinning at me, but I'm not sure why. "Surprise?"

"I received quite a surprise among my missing shoes."

I stare at her smile for a moment, and then it occurs to me. "Oh, right… Jesus, that card." I take the spaghetti and once again fight for space in the refrigerator. "I'm sorry." I meet her eyes. "I was desperate."

"Don't apologize. I'm also learning to break the rules."

"Ms. Thomas, do you want to watch TV with me?" Hannah says from the kitchen doorway.

Emily turns toward her then back to me, mischief in her eyes. "Hannah, why don't you call me Emily, since we're friends now too."

"You little snot," I whisper to Emily. "Careful or I'll make her call you 'ma'am'."

"Haha, very funny."

"I would love to watch TV with you, but let me give you the gift I brought." She leads Hannah into the living room, and I watch, feeling a great deal of trepidation. I want to trust Emily, but it's tough to trust anyone with the heart of my little girl.

Emily helps Hannah get up on the couch in a comfortable position and hands her a gift bag. She holds the bottom while Hannah one-handedly pulls out something wrapped in tissue paper.

Once Hannah gets all the paper out of the way, she gasps. "Oh, my goodness…" She's staring with awe. "She's just like me now."

"Yes, but she's going to heal just like you, and when that happens, this little sling comes right off."

I walk closer to get a look, and my heart does a little flutter when I see the Merida doll with her fiery red hair, just like Hannah's.

"Thank you so much." Hannah leans forward for a hug but can't put her arms around Emily because one is wrapped around the new Merida doll and the other is tied tightly in a sling. "How did you know she was my favorite?"

"Another lucky guess."

"Hey, do you want to watch *Brave* with Merida and me?" Hannah asks.

Emily nods. "I would absolutely love to, if it's okay with your dad."

Hannah looks up at me, and at the same time Emily turns and gives me the same pleading expression. How can a man resist these two?

"If it keeps you on that couch, Hannah, it's fine with me."

"Daddy, will you watch with us?"

"I can't, honey. I have some work I need to get done, but maybe later." Emily's shoulders droop when I say this, but I did warn her I was working. Besides, I'm still not sure about this... and what did she mean when she said we need to stop dancing around and work this out? Work what out? How she wants to keep my child from me?

I stand there long enough to watch Emily get comfortable, as Hannah expertly operates the remote control until the movie's playing. Then I sneak back into my office and pace the room for a few minutes before I can sit down.

What the hell is she up to? I run my hands through my hair and pray to God she's serious about this. I don't need my kids walking around feeling the same shit I've felt since our fight on Tuesday. And, God dammit, we haven't even talked about Kayla. I could kill my sister for telling Emily about that before I had the chance. That's just one more thing I'm going to have to explain... assuming she's interested in listening.

I take a couple of deep breaths and sit back at my desk to get to work, forcing myself to concentrate.

Over an hour later, Emily pokes her head in, and I'm a little surprised she's still here. I thought she might have left without saying goodbye. "Drew, I hate to skip out while Hannah is sleeping, but I have a web meeting in half an hour."

"Emily, you can go. You don't have to be here." I'm not trying to be nasty to her, but I've been through this with women... too many times. The novelty of children will wear off and she'll be gone just like the others.

"Drew, if I didn't want to be here, I wouldn't be." She walks around and props herself against my desk facing me. "Listen, if you want to talk, you know where I am. I'll be home all night."

"I can't leave Hannah."

She lifts her eyebrows as if in challenge. "Gee, I guess it's a good thing I live close and can walk on over here anytime I want." She turns toward the door. "See you." Then she makes her way quietly down the hall and out the front door, and I'm left feeling very alone.

\*

"I know you don't want to leave Hannah, but I'm here with her, and she won't miss you for an hour or two. You need to get your ass over there and talk to Emily, Drew." Jennie pokes my chest. "She's having your baby, and I know that means something to you."

I close the fridge once I get the remains of Emily's lasagna put away. It was actually quite helpful not having to cook dinner tonight. "There isn't much left to say, you already told her all my secrets."

"Yes, I did, and she still showed up here today, to see you and Hannah. She wouldn't have done that if she didn't care about you. Go, Drew! Jesus, stop being so proud. The woman is having your baby. You're worse than a girl with your self-destructive behavior."

I stand there and stare at her for a few minutes, not sure what to do. Admittedly, I'm scared. I'm not sure I can take a rejection from Emily, but Jennie has a point: Emily did show up today, and she stayed at the hospital for hours waiting for news after Hannah's accident. She didn't have to do that. That means something. She brought us food... I grin at that. Lots and lots of food.

"You won't know until you talk to her. Just go, jerk. You can thank her for dinner too."

*My loving sister, everyone.*

"All right, I'll walk over there." Maybe the walk will help clear my head. I don't want to face her with anger in my heart. I love her, and Jennie's right, it'd be stupid to lose her over my own stubborn pride. Anything but that.

# CHAPTER FORTY

## Emily

When I hear a knock on the door, I'm surprised. I close my laptop, place it on the coffee table, and tiptoe over to the door, before peeking through my peephole. When I see Drew, my heart jumps in my chest.

"Hey, everything okay?" I ask as I open the door. "Is Hannah okay?"

He stares at me, his expression stony. "She missed you when she woke but other than that, she's fine." He shifts his weight and his posture is tight, not relaxed like he usually is. "My sister is with her, so I thought this would be a good time to talk, do you mind?"

"I would like that. Thank you for coming over."

"I was hurt," he blurts outs as he steps inside. "And I'm still pissed at you." He turns and crosses his arms over his chest. "I walked over here, hoping my anger would dissipate. Hoping I'd be clear-headed when I got here. Hoping I could be humble and apologize and take the blame for all of our misunderstandings—but then I realized that'd be stupid. That would be unlike me."

I don't say anything. It's only fair that I let him get it off his chest. Especially after suggesting he release his paternal rights. After that, I deserve his anger.

"I get mad. I'm not going to pretend to be some saint who doesn't lose his temper. I want you to know who I am and that includes every little facet. Everything—even the shitty stuff. You need to know I won't always take the blame for our misunderstandings—or our fights." He throws his hands out. "I'm sorry for my part. I am sorry I didn't tell you about the kids. I'm sorry I didn't tell you about Kayla. I feel terrible for what I did, but I'm *not* sorry for wanting you so badly that I made a couple of very bad decisions." He huffs out a breath and drops his hands. "I'm sorry for the way I treated you at the hospital, but dammit, I'm pissed that you think I'd give up my child so easily."

I nod, expecting more.

He stares at me, and as he does, his breathing slows a little. Then his eyes lower to the floor. "Aren't you going to say anything?"

"Yeah. I am, but I wanted to make sure you got it all out of your system before I interrupted."

"You do have a problem with interrupting me when I want to say something." He nearly shouts it and that brings heat to my face, even though I know he's right.

"Are you done now?" I ask. "Or is there another character flaw you'd like to point out before I get to speak?"

He narrows his eyes at me. "No, I think I'm done."

I lift my brows and point to myself. "I'm hurt too, Drew. You were so sure I wouldn't want to be a part of your life because of your children that you pretended they didn't exist. You never even gave me the chance."

"You assumed I wouldn't want more kids. Isn't that just as bad?"

I stand on my toes and point to his face. "It's still my turn!"

He drops his hands on his hips.

"How was I to properly judge the situation when I didn't even know what the situation was? I thought you were a bachelor with roommates. I didn't think you'd want to be tied down, especially after your reaction when I told you I was pregnant. How would I know you're a family man? How would I know you're a widower—

just like me! You couldn't even come clean about your wife after I poured my heart out to you about losing Tucker."

"Yes, Emily, my wife died. She gave me a daughter and then she was gone. Is that what you want to know?" He's no longer shouting—he's calm and that just makes him more intimidating. It makes him more powerful and it makes his words all the more agonizing. I see the hurt in his eyes... it's something I've never seen before. How he manages to hide this on a daily basis is beyond me. He exhales heavily. "You want to hear how fucking scared to death I am that you're pregnant?" His voice raises again, more anguished than angry. "How frightening it is to me that something like that could happen again... that I could lose you?"

"And that's why you acted the way you did?" I step closer to him, wanting so badly to understand but also wanting to give comfort. "You're afraid I'll die?"

"Of course! What did you think? You thought I didn't want kids?"

"That's the only reason I offered the release of paternal rights. I thought you were happy being a bachelor, but then when I found out about Kyle and Hannah, I thought you didn't want more kids."

"You asking me to give up my rights as a parent hit me hard. After Hannah was born, my in-laws thought I'd just hand over custody of my kids. When I didn't, they tried taking them. They didn't think I was capable of caring for a newborn and a toddler." He runs his hands through his hair and says, "Questioning my ability to be a parent sets me off."

"I'm sorry. I wish I'd known that."

"Emily, I love you. I want nothing more than to be with you and have a dozen children—I just don't want to do it without you." He turns and steps away, pacing in a circle, and I can see the defeated slump to his shoulders. "Kayla was perfectly healthy... her pregnancy with Hannah was completely uneventful, but then after Hannah was born, everything changed. One minute they were cutting the umbilical cord, and the next they were kicking me out of the room. Kayla was bleeding and…" He visibly wilts even further. "Then she was gone… and everything in my life changed. I won't survive something like that again."

I feel hot tears drip down my face, and I know that's not helping, but I can't stop them. His pain surrounds me and seeps through me. I know it too well and as much as I want to take it away from him, as much as I'd like to carry the burden for him, I know I can't. Just like he can't carry mine. "I'm sorry about Kayla, Drew." I close my eyes and say, "And dammit, I'm sorry for all the nasty things I said at the school on Saturday. There's no excuse for that." I tap my chest. "I know who you are. I know deeply what a great man you are and I should have known and remembered that before I said all those horrible things to you."

"Emily, I'm sorry."

I so badly want his arms around me but he's keeping his distance and I hate this. I hate having a wedge between us.

"I'd never in a million years pretend my children don't exist— not on purpose. That morning, when Hannah called, you asked about her and I was torn between lying and telling the truth. The truth went against our agreement but the lie… was a lie," he says these last three words in a whisper.

I nod and I know he's right. "I understand, Drew. I really do. I was feeling exceptionally vulnerable that morning. If you had told me the truth, I might have ended our relationship right then… and that's not what I wanted."

He runs a hand through his hair. "But then when we found each other here…"

"I know, that was my fault too," I admit. "The day before our meeting with Grant, I'd figured out that I might be pregnant. I spent the entire night scared to death over facing a pregnancy and having a child alone. But then you were there and that scared me just as much. I wasn't sure what a baby would mean for us so I asked for a day to just be with you. I wanted another peaceful day without real life screwing everything up." I close my eyes and remember that first night together and how perfect it was. How happy I was to have him there with me, but also how terrified I was of losing him.

"I'm sorry." Finally, he reaches out for me. When his arms are tight around me, I try to relax and breathe away my fears. "And then I freaked out when you told me," he groans. "I'm sorry."

"Why didn't you tell me about Kayla? Even when I told you about Tucker, you could have mentioned that we have that in common."

"No, I couldn't." He leans back a little to meet my eyes. "What was I supposed to say? *I know how you feel?* I couldn't overshadow your feelings with my own. I wouldn't dare throw out my own story to compete with yours. Especially at that moment. That wouldn't have been right."

He's right. That definitely wasn't the right time, and when he tried to tell me the first night he was here with me, I stopped him. Even when I told him I was pregnant, he tried, but I wouldn't let him. "I wish I could start all over again. From that first meeting, in the hall outside my room after locking myself out."

"I fell for you fast and hard, Emily. After one night with you, I knew I was a goner."

"I'm sorry I was so stupid in Maui. I should never have made you stick to that rule."

"None of that matters now." Before I have time to react, I'm off my feet and in his arms. His lips are over mine and his possessive kiss shoots heat through me. He pushes me against the wall and grinds against me, his erection pressing firmly between my legs. "No more holding back, Emily," he mutters to my lips. "No more stupid shit, okay?"

"Okay," I breathe. "No more secrets."

Carrying me into the bedroom, his intense eyes meet mine. "I want you, I want our baby. I want all of it." His chest pumps in his effort to breathe through his emotions. "I want all of you, and I want to share this crazy, messy, and confusing life with you—every damn day."

"I want that too, I really do," I reply breathlessly.

He places me on my feet, and our eyes stay locked as we both undress. Once our clothes are out of the way, Drew's hands wrap around me, his heat enveloping me, and I know this is where I want to be. In his arms. He slowly kisses his way down my body until he's on his knees. When his lips rest on my stomach and his hands rest on my hips, I feel a sense of calm. I run my fingers through his thick, silky hair and I set the moment to memory. Our future holds a thousand moments and a thousand memories, but none of them will share the beauty of this one.

Drew kisses his way back up then he snatches me off my feet and lays me on the bed. He's hovering above me and I know he's hesitant, I know he's worried, and with what he's been through, I can't pretend he doesn't have reason, but with the two guardian angels up there looking out for us, how could this possibly go wrong?

"It'll be okay, Drew."

We're nose to nose, our lips so close, I can feel the smile as it spreads across his face. A moment later, he's inside me and as I gasp out his name, I hear him whisper, "I know it will be… It'll be perfect."

# EPILOGUE

## Emily

### *Eight months later*

"Well, Miss Leia, what do you think of your new room?" I dance around the room with her in my arms and point to the family portrait over her changing table. "See that? There's Daddy and Hannah and your big brother Kyle, and Mommy."

Then I move toward the crib. "And the beautiful crib your daddy made for you. Isn't it gorgeous? I just know you're going to have many, many great sleeps in this room."

It's our first day home from the hospital, and I'm exhausted, but it's the most exquisite exhaustion I've ever experienced. I'm trying to treasure every moment with Drew and the kids. I moved in a few months ago and it's been an adjustment, but I really love all the activity and noise in the house. After living alone for so long, I didn't realize how much I missed having people around. I didn't think I was missing anything, but having Hannah and Kyle in my life every day has been amazing. They're great reminders of what I want in life. I want love, and family, and moments to cherish—not just work. I want it all and I have a great deal more appreciation for everything.

When I hear a noise, I tilt toward the bedroom door. "Can I come out now?"

"No," the trio of voices rings out from down the hall. And then Hannah's sing-song voice says, "Just a few more minutes."

"Okay, well, just a few more minutes. Leia, what should we do? How about a story?" I sit down in the rocker and begin. "Once upon a time, there was a sad and lonely girl. This sad and lonely girl thought she was happy. She had friends and a small family who loved her, even a pushy little brother who thought he knew everything. One day, that pushy brother forced the sad and lonely girl into spending a full week alone in paradise." Leia coos at me, her wide eyes staring up in interest. She's so seldom awake that when she is alert, I don't want to put her down. "When the sad and lonely girl checked into her hotel, things weren't going as planned, but then she met—"

Just as I start to tell Leia about her dad, I hear someone coming. I glance up to see Drew standing in the door frame. "The girl meets the guy and they fall in love while dancing in the rain," he says and then he's smiling from ear to ear. I'm reminded of just how much our little girl looks like him, only softer. I can already tell she's going to have his dimples and her patch of dark hair is the exact same shade as his.

"Can we come out now?"

He swoops in and takes the baby from me with an expert hand. I cringe a little, but when I look up at his smiling face as he looks down at our daughter, I know it's my turn to be paranoid. He was a complete wreck during my entire pregnancy, and I've been one since the moment she was born.

"She's so small, how will I ever be able to protect her from everything?"

He grins down at me. "You can't. You just have to guide them down the right path and pray they make good decisions." He reaches down for my hand. "Are you ready for your surprise?"

"I'm more than ready! I was starting to think you guys were just trying to tease me and didn't actually have a surprise."

"Of course we do. It's our first family dinner with Leia after all."

"Well, I've been waiting, get on with it."

He chuckles. "All right, follow me."

I follow him down the hall and into the dining room. It's lit with candles, and the table is set for four in our fine china. There's a roast chicken in the center of the table and a bottle of sparkling cider bubbling next to it. "Ah! Wow, this is all for me? It's so beautiful!"

Drew lays Leia down in her bassinet, which has been placed within reach of the table, then he gestures to a chair. "Please have a seat."

Hannah leans over the bassinet at her sister and whispers her name. It was Kyle and Hannah who made the final decision on her name. The four of us created a list of favorites, and Leia was on the list because it's a Hawaiian name that means "heavenly child", which we both thought fitted her and our circumstances. It also turned out to be Hannah's favorite too. I'm pretty sure Kyle agreed because it was easier than arguing with his sister. Besides that, he was counting on a baby brother instead of another sister.

"Maybe the next one will be a boy," Drew told Kyle when Leia came out a girl. *Maybe the next one?* Believe it or not, he was serious about that too. I guess he's no longer afraid of what could go wrong during childbirth. I can't wait to see what our future holds for us.

I sit in the chair they reserved for me and take another good look around the glowing room. Kyle is pouring sparkling cider carefully into four champagne glasses. Hannah is whispering in Drew's ear, and I realize it's a complete set-up. "What's happening here? Are we having dinner?"

The three of them approach with huge dimpled smiles and then Drew slowly drops to one knee and the twinkle in his eyes is contagious. They all look like they're about to burst.

"Emily." Drew looks from Kyle to Hannah and at the same time, the three of them say, "Will you marry us?" A second later,

Drew opens a ring box and flashes a sparkling diamond ring. "We all picked it out together," Kyle blurts.

"It was so hard to keep secret," Hannah says and her voice chimes like a bell through her excitement.

I meet Drew's eyes as thick, happy tears drip from mine.

"Well…" he prompts.

"I would love to marry… all of you!"

Hannah and Kyle both whoop and start dancing around the room. Drew grabs my hand and tugs me to my feet. After placing the ring on my finger, we both look down at it. I'm so surprised and happy, it's hard to talk, but I swallow around the lump in my throat and choke out the words I want to say. "I'm… wow, it's so pretty, thank you."

He ducks his head. "We decided an oval was best… it represents our family table, but we wanted to make sure it was large enough so we could add more chairs… you know, in case we continue to grow."

"Continue to grow?" I quip, now laughing. "Maybe the diamond should have been a bigger house."

"No worries, I'm working on that too."

I press against him. I wouldn't trade one minute of this for all the diamonds in the world. "As long as I have all of you, I don't need anything else."

# A LETTER FROM DANA

I want to say a huge thank you for choosing to read *Accidental Lies*. As a reader, I understand how many options we have for great stories in today's market, and that's why I'm so glad you decided to choose mine. I can't thank you enough for your support. If you enjoyed it, and want to keep up-to-date with all my latest releases, including the third installment of the *Accidental Love* series, just sign up at the following link. I promise, I won't fill your inbox, but I'll keep you updated on what's happening with my books. Your email address will never be shared, and you can unsubscribe at any time.

www.bookouture.com/dana-mason

I hope you loved reading *Accidental Lies* as much as I enjoyed writing it and if you did, I'd be very grateful if you could write a review. Just a few words and a star rating go a long way toward helping new readers discover my books for the first time, and I can't wait to hear what you think.

I love hearing from my readers and encourage you to connect with me on my Facebook page, through Twitter, Goodreads or my website.

Thanks,
Dana Mason

 danamason06

 @danamason06

 danamasonromance.com

# ACKNOWLEDGEMENTS

If it wasn't for my amazing family, I wouldn't be able to do this dream job. Thank you so much for all your understanding. Thank you for picking up the slack when I'm working on a deadline. Thank you for the rushed dinners and forgiving me when I'm not around as much as I should be.

To all of my extended family and friends, I'm sure it gets annoying when my promo posts keep popping up on your Facebook feeds, but you share them anyway. I appreciate you! Thank you for your constant support. Please keep sharing and spreading the word. I couldn't do this without you.

To the ladies who read everything I send them. Katie, Nancy T, Paige, Nancy G and Linda, thank you so much for your valuable feedback and for answering my never-ending questions. I'm forever grateful for having you ladies in my life. Lisa, thank you for reading, suggesting, and commiserating! Also, thank you for always being available when I need someone to bounce ideas around with. You're like an idea machine!

Valerie, thank you for the Hawaiian Hike! You always have such great ideas and I hope you always share them with me.

Christina Demosthenous, thanks for your hard work and for helping me clean this up. You're so patient and I need that. Thank you for seeing Emily and Drew's story through the mud.

Made in the
USA
Monee, IL